"Before I can ... employment,

...

Tho...
word...
ten ...
gove...
do y...

Why...
othe...
wou...
truth...
after...

She...
to su...
way ...
was ...
pull ...
appe...
gent...
her ...

Books by Deborah Hale

Love Inspired Historical

The Wedding Season
  "Much Ado About Nuptials"
*The Captain's Christmas Family
*The Baron's Governess Bride

*Glass Slipper Brides

DEBORAH HALE

After a decade of tracing her ancestors to their roots
in Georgian-era Britain, Golden Heart winner Deborah Hale turned to historical romance writing as a
way to blend her love of the past with her desire to
spin a good love story. Deborah lives in Nova Scotia,
Canada, between the historic British garrison town of
Halifax and the romantic Annapolis Valley of Long-
fellow's *Evangeline*. With four children (including
twins), Deborah calls writing her "sanity retention
mechanism." On good days, she likes to think it's
working.

Deborah invites you to visit her personal website at
www.deborahhale.com, or find out more about her at
www.Harlequin.com.

The Baron's Governess Bride

DEBORAH HALE

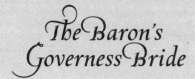
Love Inspired

Recycling programs
for this product may
not exist in your area.

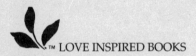 ™ LOVE INSPIRED BOOKS

ISBN-13: 978-0-373-82920-0

THE BARON'S GOVERNESS BRIDE

Copyright © 2012 by Deborah M. Hale

www.LoveInspiredBooks.com

Printed in U.S.A.

Let your adorning be the hidden person of the heart with the imperishable beauty of a gentle and quiet spirit, which in God's sight is very precious.

—1 Peter 3:4

To Elaine Logan Melanson, a wonderful mother
and stepmother and an amazing friend!
I've been waiting for just the right story
to dedicate to you, and this was it.

Chapter One

Most governesses heading off to meet with a prospective employer for the first time would have made every effort to look their best.

But Grace Ellerby did quite the opposite.

In her tiny room at Reading's George Inn, Grace retrieved a small, cracked mirror from her trunk to check that not a wisp of golden hair peeped out from under her cap. With long lappets down each side, it was the type of cap worn by older women who had entirely given up hope of finding husbands. Grace approved of the way it narrowed her face, making her features appear flatter and plainer. Its starched whiteness conspired with the drab green of her high-necked dress to drain all the color from her complexion. Once she put on the tiny spectacles to obscure her eyes, she would be prepared to meet Lord Steadwell.

From outside, the bells of a nearby church tolled the half hour. She must be on her way.

Grace tucked the mirror away and donned her dark bonnet and shawl. Then she slipped out of her room and made her way to the Old Castle Coffeehouse, where she had been directed to meet the gentleman.

The entire process was most irregular in Grace's experience. Most families seeking a governess simply inquired among their acquaintances until someone recommended a suitable candidate. When they *were* obliged to place a notice in the newspapers, the hiring would all be managed through an exchange of correspondence. Grace had never heard of a prospective governess being summoned for an interview, especially from such a long distance with funds supplied for her traveling expenses.

That irregularity had worked to her advantage, Grace reminded herself as she picked her way through the streets of Reading, her gaze modestly downcast yet alert for any potential threat. From the money Lord Steadwell sent for her journey, she'd been able to save a bit by riding on the outside of the stagecoach, eating sparingly and taking the cheapest rooms. Even if she did not secure this position, surely she would have a better chance of finding another here in the south. The funds for her return trip together with what she'd already saved should keep her for a while if she was careful.

She hoped it would not come to that.

Spying the sign for the coffeehouse, Grace rummaged in her reticule and pulled out the spectacles that were her only tangible reminder of her late father. When she peered through the thick lenses, the world swam and wobbled, forcing her to squint in an effort to focus her vision.

She breathed a fervent prayer that the interview

would go well then crossed the threshold of the coffee-house and glanced around for his lordship. The baron and his wife had put themselves to some trouble and expense to find the best possible governess for their children. He had written good letters, too—plain and direct without the superior airs Grace had expected from someone of his rank. Those things led her to hope a position with the Steadwells would be more agreeable than any of her previous ones.

No sooner had she entered than a gentleman rose from a table near the door and approached her with a respectful bow. "Have I the honor of addressing Miss Ellerby from Lancashire?"

Squinting through her father's thick spectacles, Grace could not make out his features very clearly, but she could tell he was tall and lean with dark hair. His voice had a most agreeable timbre, rich yet mellow. His courtesy certainly recommended him—addressing a humble governess as if she were a fine lady. If she had met him without her disguise, Grace might have been suspicious of his intentions. But she could have nothing of that nature to fear in her present state, especially not from a happily married man.

"I am Grace Ellerby, sir." As she curtsied, Grace reminded herself not to smile. She dared not risk anything that might make her look more attractive. "Are you Lord Steadwell, with whom I have corresponded?"

"I am, indeed," he replied. "I hope you had a tolerable journey south. I appreciate you indulging this whim of mine to meet in person before making you an offer of employment. As a countryman born and bred, I cannot reconcile myself to buying a pig in a poke when it comes to the education of my daughters."

Some women might have resented being compared to a market sow, but Grace welcomed it. There was something about his lordship's direct, down-to-earth manner that made her feel more at ease in his company than she did with most men.

Once again she fought the dangerous urge to smile. "My journey was quite satisfactory, sir. And your concern for your daughters' education does you credit."

That was something else Grace found odd about this whole situation. In her experience the gentleman of the house seldom took any interest in hiring a governess unless a young son of the family was to be among the pupils before being sent away to school.

"Charlotte, Phoebe and Sophie are all the world to me." Lord Steadwell's tone of warm affection for his daughters raised him even higher in Grace's esteem. "Let us retire to a private parlor where we may discuss my girls and your qualifications at greater length."

He led her through the main room, where a number of men sat reading newspapers and talking together in hushed tones. The rich aromas of coffee and chocolate hung in the air, making Grace's mouth water.

She followed Lord Steadwell up a set of narrow stairs to a snug parlor on the upper floor.

"Pray be seated, Miss Ellerby." He gestured toward a pair of armchairs and a small settee clustered around a low coffee table. "And tell me what manner of refreshment I may order for you. Do you prefer coffee or chocolate?"

Though the toothsome luxury of chocolate tempted her, the last thing Grace wanted was to relax and enjoy herself.

"Coffee, if you please." She replied as she sank onto

one of the chairs. The bitter, stimulating brew would help keep her wits about her.

As they waited for their beverages to arrive, Lord Steadwell told her a little about his estate. "Nethercross lies ten miles north and east of here on the bank of the Thames. It has been home to my family for more than two hundred years. The countryside is some of the finest I have ever seen—not that I am any great traveler. Why venture abroad when one has been blessed with such a beautiful home?"

"Your estate sounds like an ideal place to raise children." Grace's desire to secure the position intensified. Nethercross sounded like a wonderful place to live and work.

His lordship nodded. "As a boy, I was sorry to leave it for my schooling and very happy to return whenever the opportunity arose."

Grace could sympathize with his reluctance to go away to school, though she envied his chances to return home at holidays. Once she'd been sent away to the Pendergast School at the age of eight, she never saw the vicarage in Oxfordshire again. This was the closest she had been to her old home in nearly twenty years.

"My girls love the old place, too," his lordship continued. "Though Charlotte is only thirteen, she takes a great interest in all matters of housekeeping. Only last week she suggested we hang new wallpaper in the music room. Sophie, my youngest, is six. She likes nothing better than to explore the house from cellars to attic. Once she disappeared for hours and we were frantic until she was found napping on the window seat of a back landing."

Lord Steadwell's daughters reminded Grace of two of

her friends from school—Hannah, the capable domestic, and Evangeline, the intrepid explorer. She felt certain she would get on better with them than with some of the proud, sulky and downright malicious pupils she had taught in her previous posts.

"What about your other daughter?" Grace racked her memory for the name of the middle child, who was ten, as she recalled from his lordship's letter. "Does Phoebe love Nethercross as much as her sisters do?"

A waiter appeared just then with their coffee and a plate of muffins. Grace feigned a cough to cover the rumbling of her empty stomach.

"Ah, Phoebe." The baron greeted Grace's question with something between an indulgent chuckle and an exasperated sigh. "I fear she is more attached to the stables and the grounds than to the house. She would sleep in her pony's manger if she thought she could get away with it."

As Grace added a little cream and sugar to her coffee, she warmed even more to Lord Steadwell's middle daughter than to her sisters. She admired and rather envied Phoebe's indomitable spirit.

"Enough about me and mine." His lordship leaned back in his chair and took a sip of his coffee. "Tell me about yourself, Miss Ellerby, and why you feel you would make a suitable governess for my girls."

"Very well, sir." Grace recited a brief account of her background. "I was educated at the Pendergast School in Westmoreland and later served as a teacher there before becoming a private governess. Since then I have been employed by three families in the north, most recently the Heskeths of Burnley in Lancashire. I have a letter of recommendation from Mrs. Hesketh if you would care to read it."

She retrieved the letter from her reticule and held it out to Lord Steadwell.

His lordship unfolded the letter and quickly scanned its contents. "It is perfectly in order and says the same things most such letters do. What I wish to know, Miss Ellerby, is what sets you apart and makes you uniquely qualified for the position of governess to my girls?"

Relieved though she was that he had found Mrs. Hesketh's recommendation acceptable, Grace scarcely knew how to respond to his lordship's unorthodox question. Harsh experience had taught her that security and peace came only at the price of conformity. She had gone to great lengths to mask her uniqueness.

"I do not know what to tell you, sir." She cast her gaze down to her lap where her fingers toyed with the strings of her reticule. "I am not accustomed to recommending myself. From a young age, I was taught the importance of humility. All I can say is that I want this position very much and if I get it, I will do everything in my power to give satisfaction."

She cast a fleeting glance up over the top of her father's spectacles and saw Lord Steadwell's face clearly for the first time. He looked younger than she had expected, with strong, attractive features and dark eyes. He considered her reply with a thoughtful nod as if it was what he'd wanted to hear. But how could that be?

"You are the last of the applicants I have interviewed, Miss Ellerby, and I suspect the best suited for the position."

A sob of relief rose and caught in Grace's throat. "Thank you, sir."

"But before I can make you an offer of employment, there is one matter we must first settle to my satisfaction." Though his lordship spoke in a kindly tone, his words chilled her. "Three different positions in ten years is more than one would expect of a governess who gave satisfaction in her work. How do you account for it in your case?"

Why must he ask the one question above all others that she could not bear to answer? Grace's breathing sped and a wave of dizziness came over her. How would Lord Steadwell react if she blurted out the truth—that she had fled each of those households after receiving unwelcome advances from men?

Coming from a woman who looked as she did, he would probably think she was stark, raving mad! But she would not dare pull off her cap and spectacles to reveal her true appearance. His lordship seemed an honorable gentleman, but Grace knew all too well the effect her cursed beauty could have upon men.

Miss Ellerby seemed perfect…in appearance at least.

As Rupert Kendrick waited for her to answer his question, he could not help but approve of her looks. She was, without a doubt, one of the most thoroughly unmarriageable women he had ever beheld. Pale and plain, the poor creature did not help herself with her choice of prim, dowdy clothes. If anything, they proclaimed her total disregard for ever securing a husband.

That was precisely the sort of governess Rupert required for his daughters. It was the reason he'd taken the unorthodox step of insisting to *see* the applicants for the position before making his choice.

The girls' previous governess had abandoned them

to elope with the younger son of a neighboring family. His daughters had been much upset by her sudden disappearance, especially little Sophie.

In the wake of Mademoiselle Audet's defection, Rupert had made two vows. The first was that he would hire a governess who would remain with his daughters for as long as they needed her. The second was that he would put aside his lingering grief for his late wife and find the girls a new mother to love and care for them.

Because securing a suitable governess had seemed more urgent and easier than finding a suitable wife, he had undertaken the task with his usual determination. But after placing notices in several newspapers, reviewing all the letters of application and arranging to interview the most promising candidates, he had found them all too young and attractive for his liking. Until Miss Grace Ellerby, who was the embodiment of everything he sought.

Part of him wanted to offer her the position the moment he laid eyes on her. Miss Ellerby's interest in his children swayed him even more in her favor. But prudence would not let him go further until the question of her past positions had been answered to his satisfaction. Clearly she had not quit those other households to elope, but she had left, or been asked to leave, for some reason. To be certain Miss Ellerby would remain at Nethercross until Sophie was ready to leave the schoolroom, he must discover what that reason was.

Could she have been too strict with the children? Did she have revolutionary theories of education? Was she a secret drunkard?

That last possibility made a grin tug at Rupert's lips. But his deeply ingrained sense of caution wiped it away before it fully developed. What was taking Miss Ellerby so long to answer a simple question? Was it possible she *did* have something to hide?

"Forgive me, sir." She set her coffee cup down on the table with trembling hands. "I am feeling unwell suddenly."

Rupert might have suspected her claim was a ruse to keep from having to answer him, but one look at Miss Ellerby erased any doubt. Her face had gone even paler and her breath came fast and shallow. One hand rose to her forehead.

"I am sorry to hear it." He leaned toward her. "Is there anything I can do?"

The lady did not answer but sprang from her chair and bolted for the door.

Rupert set down his cup and rose to follow. When Miss Ellerby swayed on her feet and crumpled, as if all her bones had turned to jelly, he barely managed to catch her before she swooned to the floor.

"Forgive me, I should have realized you were unwell." He scooped her up and deposited her on the settee. Kneeling beside it, he patted her hand in an effort to wake her. "Lie quietly and I will send for an apothecary."

To his relief, her eyelids fluttered open. But when she caught sight of him hovering over her, she gave a violent start and snatched her slender hand from his grasp. "That will not be necessary, sir. I do not require pills or potions. I only felt a little faint. The journey south must have tired me more than I realized."

Her situation stirred his strong protective instincts, not to mention a qualm of guilt for perhaps having upset her with the suspicious tenor of his questions.

When she struggled to sit up, he protested. "You should not stir so soon or you may swoon again."

Miss Ellerby refused to heed him. "I will rest a moment, but I assure you I feel a good deal better already."

The quivering tightness of her voice belied that reassurance and so did her eyes. Behind the thick lenses of her spectacles, they blinked rapidly. Rupert thought he detected a film of unshed tears.

"Well, you do not look it." He picked up her coffee cup and pressed it into her hands. "Have you eaten yet today?"

As she raised the cup to her lips, she cast him a brief glance then looked away.

"I thought not," Rupert muttered.

He rose to his feet then rang for a servant, who swiftly answered his summons. While he ordered a more substantial meal, Rupert kept a concerned eye upon Miss Ellerby.

"That was not necessary," she said when the servant had departed.

Rupert returned to his seat. "I shall be the judge of that."

"Truly, I am quite recovered," Miss Ellerby insisted. "Please let us conclude this interview then I shall be on my way."

The interview—preoccupied with his concern for her, he'd almost forgotten. "I refuse to let you stir from this room until you have eaten and I am satisfied you will not fall faint on the street. I must warn you, I have a well-deserved reputation for stubbornness, so it would be unwise to defy me."

"Very well, then." She pushed up her spectacles, which had started to slide down her nose. "If you insist."

After a moment of awkward silence, Rupert decided he might as well proceed with the interview while they waited for the food to arrive. After what had just happened, he was loath to raise the matter of her employment history again for fear of upsetting her further. Besides, there was likely an innocent explanation. Putting aside his suspicion, he found one came to him readily.

"About your past positions…" He tried to keep his tone mild so as not to alarm her. "I did not mean to accuse you of anything untoward. It is just that I want the governess I engage to remain with us for a good many years, until all my children are grown. I do not think too much change is good for them."

"I agree, sir." Miss Ellerby took another sip of her coffee. "There is nothing I would like better than to have a secure position."

Hearing the edge of longing in her voice, Rupert sensed it had not been *her* choice to change positions so often. "It must be difficult when children outgrow the need for a governess and it becomes necessary to seek a new post."

Miss Ellerby gave a slow nod that suggested weariness and discouragement.

So the explanation was as simple as that? Rupert chided himself for jumping to conclusions. Poor Miss Ellerby must have had the misfortune to teach a succession of older girls who only needed a governess for two or three years. No wonder she was so eager to find a more secure position. He could imagine few fates worse than being forced to move so often from place to place with nowhere to truly call home.

"In that case," he announced, "I am satisfied. The position is yours if you want it."

"Do you mean it, sir?" Behind her thick spectacles, Miss Ellerby blinked rapidly. "Just like that?"

Just like that, indeed. Rupert was not accustomed to making decisions in such haste, but guilt, pity and necessity had conspired to force his hand. He hoped he would not regret it.

Determined not to betray any sign of uncertainty, he gave a firm nod. "Of course I mean it. Why would you ask such a thing?"

Miss Ellerby gnawed on her lower lip. "I only wondered whether you wish to consult your wife before making your decision."

For quite some time now, Rupert had believed the worst of his grief was over. Life at Nethercross carried on as it had always done…except for Annabelle's absence. But Miss Ellerby's casual mention of his late wife, as if she must still be alive, taunted him with the fear that he might never truly recover from his loss.

"I do not have a wife," he snapped then realized how that might sound. "I did once, of course, but she died four years ago."

Four years, five months and eleven days. It shocked Rupert to realize he still kept count.

"I am so sorry!" Miss Ellerby seemed torn between shrinking from his gruff outburst and reaching toward him in sympathy. "You never mentioned…that is, your letter referred to *us* and *we,* so I assumed you meant…"

Rupert shook his head. "I was talking about my daughters and me."

It was an understandable mistake, he admitted to himself, and his fault for being so reluctant to mention his widowed state. In those first terrible weeks and months after Annabelle's death, he'd had a daft fancy that if he did not speak of his loss, it would not be final. Gradually that resistance had settled into a habit.

Even now, it made him uneasy to talk about his bereavement. That uneasiness compelled him to change the subject as quickly as possible. "So you see, the decision to hire you rests with me alone and I wish to offer you the position. If you are minded to accept, we can start for Nethercross at once."

His gaze focused on Miss Ellerby as he awaited her answer. Surely she would accept. She had traveled all this way, after all, on the mere hope of getting the position. She had said herself how much she wanted it.

What could possibly be making her hesitate?

Grace stole a wary glance toward the baron as he awaited her answer. She could not possibly join his household under the circumstances... Could she?

In her past positions, she had never received unwelcome advances from the head of the household. Her trouble had been with single gentlemen visiting the family. However, there had been the occasional look or word that made her grateful the master's marriage vows kept her safe from anything more. With Lord Steadwell, she would have no such protection—only her caution and her disguise.

His lordship had already startled her with his touch when he'd picked her up and borne her off to the settee. When she'd first roused from her swoon to find him hovering over her, she had barely been able to stifle a scream. Yet she must admit his actions had been prompted by kindness and were not the least bit improper.

Lord Steadwell cleared his throat. "It occurs to me that if my aim is to find a governess who will stay, I ought to provide some incentive. I believe I mentioned in my letter a salary of twenty-five pounds per annum. I would be willing to offer a rise of one pound per year for each that you remain at Nethercross. Would that be satisfactory, Miss Ellerby?"

More than satisfactory. Grace ran through the arithmetic in her head. At that rate, if she stayed at Nethercross for ten years, she should be able to put away a modest little nest egg for her later years. Everything she'd managed to save until now had gone to keep her during those uneasy times after she'd bolted from one position until she found another.

"I did not hesitate in order to drive up the salary, sir." Much as part of her longed to accept this generous offer, another part resisted. It was all very well to daydream about staying in his lordship's employ for years and putting money away. But how could she be certain her past troubles would not repeat themselves? Could she maintain her disguise for that long with Lord Steadwell never suspecting her secret?

"Then why do you hesitate, Miss Ellerby?" Lord Steadwell's words interrupted the struggle within her. "You seemed eager to secure the position until I offered it to you. Is there some difficulty of which I am unaware?"

The fear that he might withdraw his offer tipped the balance. "Only that this all seems too good to be true, sir. I did not expect to be offered the position with so little effort and on such generous terms. I have been much more accustomed to ill fortune than good in my life. I mistrust the latter because it is unfamiliar to me. If you had questioned me for hours on end then made me wait several days to learn your decision, I might have been quicker to accept."

How perverse her feelings sounded when she tried to put them into words.

Yet Lord Steadwell listened with an air of sympathy. "Would it help if I assure you this situation will hardly be a dream come true? Though I love my daughters, I am not entirely blind to their imperfections. You will have your hands full with all three to teach. Charlotte thinks herself quite grown up with nothing more to learn. Sophie's head is so full of imagination she scarcely has room for any knowledge of the real world. And Phoebe... You will have your work cut out for you keeping her still long enough to learn anything."

It did sound like a challenge, but one Grace was eager to undertake.

"And with my wife...gone," Lord Steadwell continued, though it sounded as if the words came hard to him, "my girls will need more from a governess than book learning alone. For a while at least, they may look to you for the guidance and affection of a mother."

That possibility did not discourage Grace, either. She had long yearned for a closer bond with her young pupils. But the women she'd worked for previously had often seemed jealous of any attachment she tried to cultivate with her charges. They sought to secure their children's affection by indulging their every whim, leaving it up to her to exert discipline. If her pupils misbehaved, their mothers took *her* to task for failing in her duties.

Yet if she tried to exercise control over them, the children knew they had only to complain to their mothers to escape punishment. Such a system had made her pupils resent her and she them.

Despite the hazards of teaching in a motherless household, Grace recognized there might also be some advantages.

"Besides those difficulties," his lordship concluded, "Nethercross is rather isolated and I am not in the habit of taking my family to town for the Season. We are near enough to London that I can go there through the week when my attendance is required in the House of Lords. I fear you may find little to amuse you on your half days."

So his lordship would be away from home for a great part of the time through the spring and fall? Perhaps there was less to fear from this situation than she'd supposed. "That is no hardship for me, sir. My chief amusements are reading, writing letters and going for solitary walks in fine weather."

Lord Steadwell heaved an exaggerated sigh. "In that case, I fear Nethercross will seem like a paradise. I hope it will not discourage you further from joining my household."

His wry levity was difficult to resist. "No sir, it will not. Nor will any of your other *dire warnings*. If you are still willing to hire me, I would be pleased to accept."

Had she made the right decision? The moment the words were out of Grace's mouth, doubts returned to assail her.

The position in Lord Steadwell's household promised greater security than she had known in many years— but not without a subtle threat of danger.

Chapter Two

There was something distinctly odd about the new governess he'd hired. As they drove back to Nethercross that afternoon, Rupert stared at the woman sitting across from him, her head lolled to one side in sleep.

Somehow she looked younger and more appealing than when she was awake. Her dreadful little spectacles had slipped down her nose and her features relaxed into a less forbidding expression. Her pale complexion benefited from the faint flush of sleep. Innocent as she looked, he could not escape the feeling that Miss Ellerby was hiding something. But that was ridiculous surely. What could a woman like her have to hide?

Her air of vulnerability made his chivalrous nature want to protect her…even from his own doubts.

But he had his daughters to consider. *Their* well-being mattered far more to him than that of a woman he'd just met. Miss Ellerby had never explained why she'd moved so often from one post to another, allowing him to draw his own conclusions, which might not be correct. There was also her curious hesitation about whether she wanted to work for him. At first she'd seemed so eager, almost desperate to secure the position. But when he offered it to her, she'd been suddenly reluctant. Was it truly because she could not believe her good fortune?

Their situations were quite opposite in that respect. For most of his life, he had known nothing but good fortune until Annabelle had been taken from him without warning. Miss Ellerby's past experiences made her reluctant to trust any boon that came too easily. Had his loss made him cling too tightly to the things and people he treasured for fear they would be whisked away, too?

He chided himself for offering Miss Ellerby the position so quickly then insisting she accept when she'd hesitated. Rupert blamed it on his stubborn streak. He had come to Reading with the idea of hiring the least attractive applicant and he could not abandon that plan, even when questions arose regarding her suitability.

Rupert was so absorbed in his contemplation of Miss Ellerby that he had no idea how long they'd been driving until his carriage turned off Bath Road and headed north, skirting Ashley Hill. This road was rougher than the main one, making the carriage bump and sway. Its jolting soon woke Miss Ellerby.

Her eyes flew open and her gaze immediately collided with his. Shame slithered through him, as if he'd been caught doing something improper. She gasped and her hand jerked up to push her spectacles back in place.

"Do not be alarmed, Miss Ellerby." He shifted in his seat, drawing back his outstretched legs. "You fell asleep and woke when we took the turn-off. The longest part of our journey is behind us now. A few more miles will bring us to Nethercross."

She peered out the carriage window. Rupert wondered if it was only to avoid looking at him. "This is lovely countryside. No wonder you are reluctant to leave it."

Her eyesight must be worse than he thought. Rupert glanced out at the damp, dingy fields and the bare trees under a weepy, gray sky. "If you think it looks lovely now, you are in for a pleasant surprise over the next few weeks. When the trees unfurl their spring leaves and bluebells carpet the woodland hereabouts, it is a wondrous sight. It is kind of you to praise the beauty of Berkshire. I would have thought you spoiled for scenery, coming from the North Country."

She shook her head. "The moors and dales can be quite breathtaking, but they are too wild and forbidding for me. I prefer gentler country like this. It reminds me of my old home in Oxfordshire."

Oxfordshire? That explained another minor mystery that had stirred his suspicion—how a woman who had come from Lancashire could speak with so little trace of the broad northern accent. Perhaps there were equally innocent explanations for all his other questions about her, which he would discover in time if he was patient.

"You should feel quite at home at Nethercross, Miss Ellerby. Oxfordshire is but a short distance upriver. What part of that county do you hale from?"

She offered him a grudging answer, as if he were a highwayman demanding her prized locket. "I was raised in Witney, where my father was vicar."

How many clergymen's daughters ended up as governesses? Rupert had never given it much thought. Quite a number, he imagined. They would have the proper education and breeding for the task, while needing some respectable means of providing for themselves.

"Does your family still live in Oxfordshire?" he asked. "How did you come to be so far north?"

Again she answered reluctantly. "After my father died, I was sent to the Pendergast School, which was founded to educate the orphaned daughters of clergymen."

"Ah." Rupert wished he'd curbed his curiosity. But he could not help himself. The woman's air of mystery challenged him to discover all he could about her. "I am very sorry."

"There is no need, sir," she murmured. "It all happened long ago."

"Perhaps." He could not excuse himself so easily for prying into her past and dredging up unhappy memories. "But there is some grief no amount of time can heal completely."

A faint sigh escaped her lips. "That is true."

This new governess was a very singular creature, Rupert reflected as they drove the last few miles to Nethercross. One minute she roused his suspicion and the next his sympathy. Just now he'd been tempted to confide in her more than anyone since his wife's death. But for the sake of his daughters, he could not afford to let down his guard too easily.

He must keep a close watch on Miss Ellerby until he was certain she could be trusted.

It was clear Lord Steadwell did not altogether trust her. Grace could hardly blame the gentleman for she did not trust him, either.

It surprised her that she had let down her guard enough to fall asleep while the two of them were alone in the carriage. Exhaustion and relief must have overpowered her wariness—that could be the only explanation.

Fortunately for her, the baron had made no effort to take advantage of her vulnerability. Her disguise had protected her from any improper interest, as had an unexpected ally—his lordship's continued devotion to his late wife. The way he spoke of her, it was clear he cared more for his wife's memory than he could for any living woman.

Admiration and pity mingled in her heart as she contemplated his lingering grief. Though she knew such feelings would help keep her safe at Nethercross, part of her could not help wishing she had the power to ease them.

An awkward silence fell between her and Lord Steadwell. Grace knew it was no use pretending to sleep. She did not want him staring at her, perhaps seeing through her dowdy facade.

Neither did she want him asking more questions about her past. They roused too many painful memories she preferred to keep locked away. Besides, she could not abide having him know her too well. Once they reached Nethercross, he would become occupied with his duties and his pastimes, leaving the care of his daughters in her capable hands. If he was anything like the fathers of her past pupils, their paths would seldom cross, which was precisely how she wanted it.

For now, however, she would be cooped up in this carriage with him for a little while longer. If she wanted to prevent him quizzing her, then she must turn the tables. "Tell me, Lord Steadwell, are any of your daughters like their mother?"

Her question seemed to catch him off guard, but he

soon rallied. "All three remind me of her, each in their own way. I suspect Charlotte will be the very image of her mother when she grows up, though her temperament is more like mine. Phoebe has her mama's strong will and impulsiveness."

"And Sophie?" Grace prompted him. The more she heard about the girls, the more anxious she was to meet them. "How is she like her mother?"

"Sophie…" The warmth in Lord Steadwell's voice when he spoke of his youngest daughter made Grace peep at him over the top of her spectacles. His wide mouth was relaxed into a very appealing smile. "She is most like her mother of all—so full of fancy and curiosity."

The late Lady Steadwell sounded like a fascinating woman. Filling even part of the void she had left behind at Nethercross would be a daunting task.

Perhaps Lord Steadwell did not care to be further reminded of his loss. He averted his face from her to gaze out the carriage window.

"We are on Nethercross lands now." His voice rang with pride nearly as great as when he spoke of his children. "These are some of the farthest outlying farms of my tenants."

Again Grace glanced over her spectacles in order to get a clear view. She could not help but approve of the neat houses and barns, the well laid-out fields, the sturdy cattle and sheep grazing in the pastures. "You have a very fine estate, sir."

His lordship nodded. "It has been in my family for generations. When I stand in the shadow of one of the great oaks I often wonder which of my ancestors saw it as a sapling."

It must be a great blessing, Grace reflected as they drove past more snug, well-tended farms, to have such a strong sense of belonging. She knew very little about her ancestors. By the time she'd been old enough to take an interest in such matters, she was quite alone in the world. The only place she'd ever felt she belonged was among her circle of friends at school. They had not been envious of her appearance but understood what a burden it was to her. Rebecca and Marian had been quick to take her part when any of the older girls tried to bully her. Hannah always provided comfort and sympathy while Leah's high spirits never failed to lift hers.

The carriage soon turned up a long, winding lane with rows of well-grown trees on either side.

"This must be a delightful drive when the trees are green," Grace murmured. Why was beauty in nature universally admired, while in a woman it provoked envy and lust?

"Delightful indeed," his lordship agreed. "Only surpassed by that brief period when the lindens are in blossom. Then this lane smells as lovely as it looks. When the time comes, remind me to take you and the girls for a drive through it in an open carriage."

Grace looked forward to such a treat, though she wondered at the wistful note in Lord Steadwell's voice when he spoke of it.

That question fled her mind as the house came into view. It was a curious mixture of styles that had clearly been added to over the years. The front had a range of weathered pale stone set with bays of large mullioned windows. It was topped by Dutch gables, a red-tiled roof and clusters of tall chimneys. Beside it stood a quaint hall of checkered white and grey brick with a large stained-glass window.

When the carriage drew to a halt before the vaulted front entrance, Lord Steadwell swiftly alighted and inhaled a deep breath, as if the air of home were the only kind truly worth breathing.

As he helped Grace out, a young boy cantered up on his black pony. "So you found us a governess, did you, Papa? I hope you made a good choice!"

"Phoebe!" His lordship let out a half-stifled groan. "How many times have I told you not to borrow the stable boys' breeches and ride astride?"

The child laughed. "Counting this one, two hundred and thirty-seven. I keep hoping you will get discouraged and give up."

Phoebe scrambled down and pulled off her cap, releasing a cascade of dark curls. "You know I hate the side saddle. It's so much harder to mount and I can't ride as fast. You wouldn't want me getting hurt, would you?"

"Of course not." His lordship pulled her into a warm embrace. "Though I approve of anything that would make you ride a little slower."

With his arm draped around his daughter's shoulders, Lord Steadwell turned toward Grace. "This is indeed your new governess. You and your sisters may judge how well I have chosen. I hope Miss Ellerby will have better luck taming you than poor Mademoiselle Audet."

"I hope she doesn't." Phoebe pulled a face but thrust out her hand in a frank, eager fashion to shake Grace's. "Welcome to Nethercross. If you don't natter on at me about behaving like a *proper young lady,* we should get on very well."

Though she did not relish the idea of being put in the middle of a clash of wills between Phoebe and her father, Grace could not resist the girl's refreshing, forthright air. Even if they had their differences, she sensed Phoebe would take her own part rather than complain to her father.

"I expect you to mind Miss Ellerby," Lord Steadwell warned his daughter. "Now, go stable your pony and come inside. The next time I see you, it had better be in proper attire for a young lady."

"Yes, Papa." Phoebe rolled her eyes, forcing Grace to bite the inside of her cheek to keep from grinning.

Lord Steadwell appeared not to notice or pretended he didn't. "Come inside, Miss Ellerby. I will show you to the nursery and you can meet the other girls."

He held open one of a pair of thick, old doors that rose to a point in the middle. Then he ushered her into a high-ceilinged entry hall with a wide oak staircase running up the right-hand wall. The moment they entered, Grace heard footsteps descending—one set very light and quick, the other slower.

"Not so fast, Sophie." A girl's voice drifted down. "If you fall and break your neck I shall get the blame for it."

"I won't fall," came Sophie's breathless reply. "I want to see Papa and Mamzell."

"We talked about this, remember?" replied the other girl who must surely be Charlotte. "Papa is not bring-ing—"

Before Charlotte could finish, Sophie rounded the final landing and flew down the last flight of stairs. Grace had a fleeting impression of dainty features, wide-set eyes and a billow of ginger hair.

"Papa!" The child flung herself down the last few steps.

If her father had not caught her, she might have taken a nasty fall. But he managed to seize hold of her and clutch her to his heart. An instant later, Charlotte appeared. Apart from her darker auburn hair, she looked like an older version of her little sister. Though her mouth was tightened in an expression of annoyance, it was clear she would grow up to be a beauty.

Grace's first impulse was to pity the child on that account, though perhaps her looks would not be such a burden for a girl from a good family.

"You should listen to your sister, monkey!" Lord Steadwell scolded his youngest daughter fondly. "Stairs are not for running."

"But I wanted to see you, Papa." The child peppered his cheek with kisses. "I missed you! I was afraid you might get caught by a troll from under a bridge. I wanted to see *her,* too!"

Sophie left off kissing her father long enough to crane her neck and scan the entry hall.

Grace permitted herself a faint smile. She did not want her severe appearance to frighten the child.

But Sophie looked past her as if she were not there. "Where is she, Papa?"

Before her father could answer Charlotte piped up. "Our new governess is right there, you silly thing. I tried to tell you."

The child's gaze swung back to Grace and fixed on her with unnerving intensity.

"Good afternoon, Sophie…and Charlotte." Grace nodded to each of the girls in turn. "I am Miss Ellerby. Your father has told me quite a lot about you, and I look forward to learning more as we become better acquainted."

"Welcome to Nethercross, Miss Ellerby." Charlotte made a dignified curtsy. "I trust you had a pleasant journey."

"Quite pleasant, thank you." Grace had the uncomfortable feeling she was addressing a superior. "This is beautiful country."

She glanced back toward Sophie hopefully, but the child promptly burst into tears and buried her head in her father's shoulder. "She isn't Mamzell. I don't want her! Send her away, Papa, and fetch Mamzell back!"

Grace's spirits sank. She feared Lord Steadwell's daughters were far less eager than he to have her as their governess.

Had he been wrong to choose his daughters a governess so different from their previous one? Rupert pondered that question as little Sophie pressed her face into his shoulder and wept with a fierce mixture of sorrow and frustration.

The child was not only sad over losing her beloved *Mamzell,* but also vexed that her world had been turned upside down. Rupert suspected she might also feel a sense of helplessness at having no control over the situation.

He could sympathize, for Sophie's feelings mirrored his when her mother had been snatched away from them with such brutal suddenness.

"Hush now." He held the child close to let her know she still had him…and to satisfy his need to cling to the one part of Annabelle he had left. "I explained to you why Mademoiselle Audet could not be your governess anymore. She is married to Captain Rundell now and she will have her own family to look after. If you loved her as you claim, you should try to rejoice in her happiness."

Rupert glanced over Sophie's head toward the new governess. The poor creature looked painfully out of place in this elegant entry hall as Sophie tearfully protested her coming and Charlotte sized her up with a cool stare.

Was he a hypocrite for expecting his small daughter to accept this new situation with good grace after he had resented every well-intentioned effort to console him over the loss of his wife?

At least he could offer Sophie a crumb of hope. "You may still see Mademoiselle again, you know. Perhaps she and her husband will come for a visit and she'll pay a call on us."

"D-do you think she w-will?" Sophie responded to the possibility by quieting to a series of wet hiccoughs punctuated by sniffles. "Wh-when?"

Not any time soon. Rupert knew better than to voice such an opinion in Sophie's hearing. The young captain's family made no secret of being disgraced by his elopement with a French governess. It was also clear they held Rupert responsible for introducing Mademoiselle Audet into the neighborhood.

"I cannot predict when she might visit, so it will be a lovely surprise. In the meantime, we must all do our best to make Miss Ellerby welcome. She has come a very long way, you know. Let us show her to the nursery." He did not wait for Sophie to respond but pretended to take her agreement for granted. "This way, Miss Ellerby."

Still cradling Sophie in his arms, he strode toward the staircase. Charlotte hurried to catch up with him.

"Really, Papa," she chided him in a whisper. "Did you have to hire the homeliest dowdy you could find?"

He silenced her with a sharp look then cast a glance back, hoping Miss Ellerby was too far behind to have overheard. Satisfied that she was, he pitched his reply very low, for his daughters' ears alone. "In fact, I did, as you should well appreciate. The last thing I want is a repetition of recent events."

Sophie could not possibly understand his reasons for engaging Miss Ellerby, but he hoped Charlotte would.

"Besides," he murmured, "you should not judge by appearances. She may turn out to be very amiable and you'll all become fond of her."

Charlotte expressed her doubts with a muted sniff.

He wasn't setting much of an example in making the new governess welcome, Rupert realized with a prickle of guilt. Deliberately slowing his steps so she could catch up, he raised his voice to include her in the conversation. "Only a little farther, Miss Ellerby. I hope you will not find Nethercross too old and gloomy after some of the other houses in which you have lived."

For him, the dark paneled walls and parquet floors had a special beauty born of familiarity. But he could not expect a newcomer to regard them as he did. Even Annabelle had not appreciated the subtle delights of his beloved home at first.

Miss Ellerby's answer surprised him. "On the contrary, sir, this house has an air of having been well lived in and well loved for many years. The greatest fortune and the best architect in the world cannot duplicate that."

Perhaps there was hope for the new governess after all. "You have discovered half the secret of winning my approval, Miss Ellerby—sincere appreciation of my home."

"And the other half, sir?" Spoken in a different tone, by an altogether different type of woman, her question might have sounded flirtatious. But from Miss Ellerby it was severely earnest. "Do you intend to tell me or must I discover that for myself?"

Still her remarks amused him. "I doubt it will take you long to discover that I am well-disposed toward anyone who praises my children."

That might prove more difficult for the new governess, given what she had seen of his daughters so far. Fortunately, their arrival at the nursery prevented her from having to answer.

"This will be your realm, Miss Ellerby." He ushered her through the door Charlotte had opened. "Provided things are running smoothly, I will not interfere in your management of it."

Rupert kept his eye on the lady as she inspected the spacious area that served as the girls' playroom and schoolroom. Annabelle had insisted on papering over the wood paneling with a light, floral pattern. Entering this room from the dark corridor gave the impression of emerging into a sunny garden. It flustered him to realize how much he cared about Miss Ellerby's reaction to the place.

To his relief, it seemed favorable.

She did not smile. Rupert wondered whether she knew how. But her head moved up and down in one slow, continuous nod. "There is plenty of room, and the windows are oriented to provide a great deal of light in the morning but falling dark earlier in the evening. One might suppose the whole house had been arranged to the advantage of your nursery."

"It may have been." Her approval pleased Rupert, perhaps because he sensed she was not easily impressed. "Children have long been the treasure of Nethercross."

Through his aunts, great aunts and back through the generations, his family was connected with several of the most powerful dynasties in the kingdom. Though not as well-dowered as some, the Kendrick ladies had been sought-after brides for their looks, character and ability to bear sons. The direct line had never lacked for male heirs…until now.

Rupert shuddered to think of Nethercross falling into the hands of some distant cousin who might not appreciate its history and traditions as he did. It was his duty to remarry and sire a son or two. For the past few years he had permitted his grief to get in the way of that duty.

Now, for the sake of Nethercross and his young daughters, he must begin his search for a suitable bride.

Chapter Three

"Come girls, it is time for bed." Grace strove to keep her voice from betraying her bone-deep weariness.

It felt like several days since she'd woken at the inn in Reading when it had been only that morning. Her nap during the carriage ride to Nethercross had not helped to blunt her exhaustion. To make matters worse, her head ached from wearing those beastly spectacles.

The more she saw of Nethercross, the more it felt like the kind of sanctuary she'd been seeking. But her first few hours with her new pupils had made her fear she might lose this position if she failed to win *their* approval. It was clear Lord Steadwell doted on his daughters to an uncommon degree. Eager as he had been to engage her services, Grace had no illusions that he would continue to employ her against the protests of his children.

In reply to her mention of bedtime, Charlotte announced, "We are accustomed to staying up later than this."

Phoebe headed for the nursery door. "I'll go straight

to bed as soon as I make sure Jem is settled for the night."

Before Grace could forbid her, the girl was gone. Though her manner had been more cheerful and co-operative than her sisters', it was clear Phoebe did not intend to let a new governess stand in the way of her beloved pony's well-being.

Sophie said nothing at all but peered out at Grace from behind Charlotte's skirts as if she were a child-eating beast who might lunge at her any moment. Grace was not certain which bothered her more—Sophie's ex-cessive fear, Phoebe's breezy indifference or Charlotte's constant contradictions. None was conducive to a well-run nursery and a mixture of all three would be a recipe for disaster.

Thrusting those tormenting spectacles into her apron pocket, Grace rubbed her throbbing temples. "Ten min-utes more. That should give Phoebe time enough to bid her pony good-night."

"It might if that is all she would do." Charlotte wrapped her arms around Sophie as if to protect the child. "But Phoebe usually wants to curry Jem one last time and feed him an apple. I doubt she'll be back in less than an hour and then she'll stink of the stables."

It would have been helpful to know that before she let the child dash away. "In that case, I will speak to Phoebe when she returns. I expect the two of you to begin preparing for bed in ten minutes."

"I told you." Charlotte stroked Sophie's hair. "We are accustomed to staying up later."

"And I am accustomed to having my bidding obeyed by my pupils," Grace replied, more sharply than she in-tended.

All the changes of the day seemed to have caught up with her at once. She wanted nothing more than to retire to her own quarters and rally her composure.

Sophie gave a choked little sob and clung tighter to Charlotte, making Grace feel like a perfect ogre.

This was major change for the children, too, she reminded herself—a change that had been inflicted upon them by the actions of others. Though experience had taught her it was best to establish her authority early if she hoped to have any control over her pupils, she wondered if a gentler approach might work better in this case.

"Perhaps a compromise is in order," she suggested, deliberately softening her tone. "If the two of you get ready for bed now, I will read to you until your sister returns."

Charlotte gave a doubtful frown but Sophie responded swiftly. "What story will you read to us?"

Once the words were out of her mouth, the child seemed to realize she had spoken directly to her new governess for the first time. She hid her face against her sister once more, then peeped timidly back at Grace.

Recalling what his lordship had told her about his youngest daughter's active imagination, Grace hoped it might provide a way to reach the child. "I will leave the choice of story to you, Sophie. Do you have a particular favorite?"

The child gave an eager nod and the beginnings of a smile curled one corner of her mouth upward. "'The Little Glass Slipper.' Do you know that one? It is in our *Tales of Mother Goose* book."

Grace shook her head. "I'm not familiar with the

story, but if you have the book, I would be happy to read it to you."

"We have the book." Sophie wriggled out of her sister's arms. "Come, Charlotte. Help me find *Mother Goose* for Miss…Miss…?"

"Miss Ellerby," Grace allowed herself a brief smile, hoping to reassure the child she was not as severe as her appearance might suggest.

"Oh, very well." Charlotte heaved an exasperated sigh. "But I know that story by heart after all the times you made Mademoiselle read it to us. I could recite it to you."

"How fortunate. If I make a mistake, I can rely on you to correct me." Grace made it sound as if the girl would be doing her a favor. Perhaps that would make Charlotte a bit less eager to find fault with her at every opportunity.

As the girls headed off to get ready for bed, she called after them, "Charlotte."

The girl turned. "Yes. What is it?"

Grace struggled to subdue her impatience with Charlotte's attitude and focus on something positive instead. "Sophie is very fortunate to have such a kind, capable sister to help her through this time of change. When I was her age, I often wished I had an elder sister to look out for me."

Grace's comment seemed to take Charlotte aback. Two bright spots flared in her fair cheeks. "Someone had to take her in hand. It was no use expecting Phoebe to. She doesn't care about anything unless it has hooves and neighs."

She spun away again, fussing over Sophie more like a mother than a sister.

A short while later, the three of them huddled on the nursery settee while Grace made an effort to read the story in the way the girls were accustomed to hearing it. The tale itself appealed to her—it was about an orphan persecuted by her hard-hearted stepmother who was jealous of the girl's beauty. Though treated as the humblest of servants, the heroine eventually found security, success and love. It was pleasant to believe such wonders could come true against all odds. For herself, Grace had far more modest dreams.

The sound of the nursery door opening made all three of them look up. Grace was about to inform Phoebe that her time in the stables had made her miss the story when she realized it was not the child at all, but her father who had entered.

"Papa!" cried Sophie as both girls bounded up to greet him. "Miss Ellerby is reading us 'The Little Glass Slipper.'"

With a stab of panic, Grace remembered her spectacles. Rummaging in her apron pocket, she thrust them on, knocking the book from her lap onto the floor. She leaped from the settee to retrieve it, scooping up the fallen volume with one hand. With the other, she fumbled around the edge of her cap to check that no telltale wisps of hair had slipped free.

"G-good evening, sir." Her greeting emerged in a breathless rush, with no more warmth of welcome than Charlotte had shown her earlier. "I was about to put the girls to bed. Is there something I can do for you?"

It was his house, of course, she reminded herself. Lord Steadwell was free to go where and when he chose. But, in spite of his devotion to his daughters, Grace had hoped she might see little more of him in the nursery than she had any of her past employers…especially in the evenings.

What if he insisted on staying to speak with her after the girls went to bed?

"Not *you,* Miss Ellerby." His lordship scooped up Sophie in one arm and wrapped the other around Charlotte's shoulders. "I came to tuck my daughters in for the night…and hear their prayers."

He made it sound as if that were a nightly ritual at Nethercross.

"Have you, Papa?" Sophie flung her arms around his neck. "That would be lovely!"

The child's eager response made it clear her father's sudden appearance was an unexpected pleasure. What was the true reason he'd come?

Grace could guess. He was checking on her.

His mistrust sent a wave of scalding indignation surging through her. What had he expected to catch her doing to his precious daughters? Criticizing and ridiculing them? Sending them to bed hungry? Whipping them? Having suffered all those punishments and worse at the Pendergast School, Grace had vowed never to inflict them on her own pupils, no matter how disagreeable. It offended her to be suspected of such behavior!

If Lord Steadwell meant to make a habit of these surprise visits to the nursery, he would be worse than a hundred meddling mothers. It was going to be difficult enough getting his daughters to accept her without his constant vigilance. Charlotte was bright enough to soon guess that her father did not trust Grace—which would further erode her authority.

But what choice did she have other than accept the situation and try to make the best of it? Practicality won out over indignation. She could not afford to leave another position again so soon.

"Of course, sir." Grace kept her eyes downcast so they would not betray any glint of irritation.

"We have to hear the end of the story first, Papa," Sophie insisted. "Sit down beside Miss Ella and hold me on your knee."

"Very well." Though his lordship did not sound eager to do as his daughter bid, he was obviously accustomed to indulging her.

Grace was no happier than Lord Steadwell about the prospect of sitting next to him. When he bore Sophie to the settee and sank down on one end, she retreated to the other, leaving room for Charlotte in the middle.

His lordship seemed relieved, but Sophie would have none of it. "You must sit in the middle, Miss Ella, so I can see the words in the book. I know how to read some of them already."

Grace would rather have snuggled up to a snarling mastiff, but she could think of no excuse to object. Gingerly, she budged to the middle of the settee, every muscle as stiff as buckram while her stomach seethed and her heart hammered so hard she feared his lordship would hear it.

Charlotte flounced down on Grace's other side with a sulky air, perhaps because of all the attention her father was paying Sophie.

Grace tried to ignore Lord Steadwell's nearness but how could she when part of her was so preoccupied with keeping her arm from accidentally brushing against his? Even with no actual contact between them, she was intensely aware of his resolute strength tempered with deep devotion to his children.

Determined to get the story over with a soon as possible, Grace read quickly, her tongue tripping over the words in her haste. "The guards at the palace gate were asked if they had not seen a princess go out. They replied they had seen nobody but a young girl, very meanly dressed, who had more the air of a poor country girl of—"

"Wait a minute." Lord Steadwell interrupted her. "I am one daughter short. Where is Phoebe?"

Before Grace could stammer a reply, the nursery door flew open and Phoebe rushed in. She looked more like a scarecrow than a nobleman's daughter. Her ribbons had come undone, leaving her hair hanging in a wild tangle with bits of straw sticking out. Grace spied a scuff of dirt across her skirts at the knee and she seemed to have lost a button off her spencer. Charlotte had been right about her smelling of the stables.

At the sight of them staring at her, Phoebe froze and glanced down as if noticing her disheveled appearance for the first time. "Hullo, Papa. What are you doing here?"

"He came to say good-night and hear our prayers," Sophie piped up. "Isn't that nice?"

Grace sensed his lordship squirm a little on the settee beside her. Phoebe's question confirmed her suspicion that this bedtime nursery visit was an unusual occurrence.

"Why I am here matters a great deal less than why you were *not,* young lady," he snapped. "I hope you are prepared to give a good account of your whereabouts and why you have returned in this sorry state."

"It was that horrid stable boy, Peter." Phoebe scowled. "He acts as if Jem belongs to him instead of me. Just because he gets to spend so much more time with Jem. That's not my fault."

From her tone, it was clear she envied the stable boy and would have traded places with him in an instant.

"What did the lad do to you?" Lord Steadwell slid Sophie off his lap and surged to his feet. His voice fairly crackled with protective outrage. "If he dared lay a hand on my daughter, I'll—"

"He didn't!" Phoebe shook her head so hard it sent her hair into worse disarray. "I meant to box *his* ears for answering me back so impudently. But he kept dodging me until I fell down. Then he ran off, the beast."

"I see." His lordship sounded vexed at losing a target for his anger. "That does not explain what you were doing in the stables all alone at this hour."

He spun around to glower at Grace. "May I have a word with you in private, Miss Ellerby?"

As she rose from the settee, Grace tried not to look as guilty and intimidated as she felt. "Phoebe, go get into your nightclothes."

Grace turned and handed the book to Charlotte. "Will you please read Sophie the rest of the story? I reckon you will do a better job of it than I."

Keeping a tight hold on her emotions, she followed Lord Steadwell out into the corridor. Was he going to dismiss her on her very first day at Nethercross?

What was the use of having a governess who looked strict and severe if she meant to let the girls do whatever dangerous thing they fancied? Rupert stalked out of his daughters' nursery, not certain who he was more vexed with—Phoebe or Grace Ellerby.

When he first arrived to see how the new governess was getting on, he'd been pleasantly surprised to discover a cozy domestic scene with her reading his daughters a bedtime story. For a moment he'd felt almost guilty for his vague suspicions and tried to justify his presence with an excuse that fooled no one.

Phoebe's abrupt return had changed all that. Clearly he'd been right in his doubts about Miss Ellerby after all.

Hearing the nursery door close behind them, he swung around to confront the new governess. "What on earth possessed you to let my daughter run off to the stables at this hour?"

He expected her to offer some excuse for her actions, which he could refute, going back and forth until he'd relieved his feelings and impressed upon Miss Ellerby the error of her ways.

But she refused to be drawn.

"I'm sorry, sir." Keeping her mouth set in a tight line, she avoided his direct gaze. "I didn't realize… I can assure you, it will not happen again."

"It certainly must not." Rupert felt daft repeating himself but he could not help it. Miss Ellerby's flat apology had denied him the desired opportunity to vent his feelings. "Stables can be dangerous places. Horses are large, unpredictable beasts and you may have noticed that Phoebe tends to be impulsive and heedless. Without proper supervision, she could be badly injured."

Miss Ellerby made no effort to deny it but accepted his rebuke with sullen self-restraint that made him suspect she was well accustomed to censure. That thought nearly silenced him but he had more that needed to be said. "My daughter's physical safety is not the half of it. There may be an even greater threat to her future reputation if she makes a habit of such behavior. Today it was a harmless spat with a stableboy. Five years hence it could be altogether more serious."

That possibility had never occurred to Miss Ellerby. Rupert could tell by the way she flinched when he mentioned it. Subtle though her reaction was, it somehow satisfied him that he had impressed upon her the gravity of her lapse in judgment.

The instant he was certain of that he began to have second thoughts. Had he been wrong to rebuke the new governess? It was a serious matter, but this was only her first day. Besides, he had not given her any clear instructions as to what was expected of her. He'd assumed that with her years of experience she would know better than he what she should do. Now he found himself questioning whether that was fair.

Still Miss Ellerby remained mute.

While Rupert tried to think what to say next, the nursery door swung open and Phoebe charged out. She was clad in her nightdress with her hair sloppily braided for the night.

"What are you doing out here, young lady?" He tried to maintain a frosty frown, but she looked so much younger than her years just then. "As I recall, you were ordered to bed."

"No, I wasn't," she replied in a tone that was not insolent, only stating a plain fact. "Miss Ellerby said I should put on my nightclothes, which I did. Neither of you forbade me to come out here. Since you're talking about me, I reckon I *should* be here."

"What makes you so certain we're talking about you?" Rupert demanded.

Phoebe rolled her eyes. "You have been, though, haven't you?"

She had him there. Rupert shuddered to think what a formidable adversary she might become in another few years—a proper little rebel over whom he might have no control. "If you have been the subject of our conversation, that is between Miss Ellerby and me. You must get to bed at once."

The child stood her ground. "It wasn't Miss Ellerby's fault that I ended up in the stables. I didn't ask her permission. I just told her I was going and went. I've been going out to bid Jem good-night for weeks now, even before Mademoiselle went away."

Rupert almost staggered. Phoebe's imprudent behavior had been going on all this time without him ever suspecting? He was torn between indignation at the former governess and vexation with himself for having permitted it to happen.

"What on earth possessed Mademoiselle Audet to let you do that?" Once the question was out of his mouth, he realized it was the same one he'd put to Miss Ellerby a few moments ago. She'd remained so quiet and still since his daughter's sudden appearance he had almost forgotten she was there.

"I knew something about Mademoiselle," Phoebe admitted in a guilty mutter. "I saw her once on her half day, meeting that man—the one she ran away to marry."

"You blackmailed your governess?" This was far worse than he'd expected.

"I didn't!" Phoebe insisted. "I wouldn't have tattled on her the way Charlotte does. I didn't even know she was doing something she oughtn't. But after that she let me do whatever I wanted."

Could he believe her? Recent events had shaken his faith in womankind, even his young daughter. What else had been going on in the Nethercross nursery without his knowledge?

"I have heard quite enough." With a flick of his hand he gestured toward the nursery door. "To bed with you, young lady. I will deal with you later."

The child's lips set in a rebellious frown, but a look of hurt flickered in her eyes. Eyes so much like Annabelle's that he could not bear to glimpse such an expression in them.

"Miss Ellerby shouldn't be in trouble," she muttered as she retreated toward the nursery. "It was my fault and Mademoiselle's…and Peter's, the wretch."

Before her father could bid her away again, she slipped through the door and closed it behind her, leaving him alone with Miss Ellerby. Though the governess did not move or speak, her silent reproach threatened to deafen him.

He drew in a deep breath and forced out the words fairness demanded he speak. "It seems I was hasty and harsh in my judgment. I owe you an apology, Miss Ellerby."

She gave a shallow shrug that seemed to accept both his apology and his earlier rebuke. "I should not have let her go, sir, for all the reasons you mentioned."

Her forbearance should have made him feel less ashamed of the way he'd spoken…but it did not. Quite the opposite in fact. He pictured himself as the cruel tyrant in one of Sophie's stories. It was not a role he relished. "I should not have expected you to remedy a situation that appears to have been going on for quite some time right under my nose."

Miss Ellerby flicked a brief glance up at him as if she did not believe what she was hearing. Was it so difficult for her to accept that he was capable of offering an apology when it was so clearly warranted?

"It was wrong of me," he continued, "to assume you would know what I expect of you when we have never discussed the matter."

"It would help to know what the girls are permitted to do," she agreed, "and what they are not."

Somehow, that made him feel better. It might provide him with an opportunity to make up for his unfairness. "In a fortnight, the new session of Parliament begins and I shall be obliged to go to London during the week. It is vital that we are quite clear about my expectations before then. Come down to the drawing room tomorrow evening after you have put the girls to bed and we can discuss the matter."

"As you wish, sir," she replied.

But behind those thick, ugly spectacles, her eyes widened as if he had proposed something improper, even dangerous. But that was ridiculous. He must have misinterpreted her expression just as he had misjudged her actions.

This new governess was an exceedingly puzzling creature. Perhaps a meeting or two between them would help him understand her a little better, in addition to helping her understand what he expected of her. "I do wish it, Miss Ellerby. In fact, I insist. For the sake of my daughters, I believe it is vital that we confer."

He made a polite bow. "Until tomorrow evening, then."

As he strode away, she called after him in a quiet but insistent voice. "I beg your pardon, sir."

Rupert halted and turned on his heel.

"Yes?" He could not fully conceal his impatience. He wanted to put this whole awkward evening behind them as soon as possible.

"I thought you wanted to hear the girls' prayers."

Behind her dour facade, he sensed Miss Ellerby might be having a secret chuckle at his expense. Tempted as he was to resent it, Rupert had to admit he deserved it.

As she watched Lord Steadwell hearing his daughters' prayers, Grace strove to make sense of what had happened in the past half hour.

She had fully expected Lord Steadwell's rebuke for letting Phoebe run off to the stables right before bed. Though she wanted to excuse herself on account of her exhaustion and her uncertainty about how much freedom her new pupils were permitted, she knew she had made a serious lapse in judgment. A lapse for which her employer had every right to be vexed.

So she had done what she'd learned to do at school whenever one of her teachers scolded her for vanity or laziness or disobedience. She accepted the criticism in meek silence, heeding as much of it as she could bear in an effort to improve herself. But when it got to be more than she could absorb without breaking down in tears, she had imagined herself encased in a thick sheath of alabaster, which nothing could penetrate to harm her. It muffled the words until they became nothing more than a rumble of noise without any meaning.

She'd soon discovered it was more difficult to reduce Lord Steadwell's voice to a harmless babble. Its pitch and timbre were so very agreeable that she found herself compelled to listen carefully, even when she could not expect to hear anything good.

Phoebe's sudden appearance had jarred Grace out of her protective trance. The last thing she'd ever expected was for that willful girl to come to her defense at the risk of incurring her father's wrath. It reminded her of the times at school when Marian or Rebecca had stood up for her, deflecting the spiteful anger of the teachers. It made her feel worthy of something better than blame and belittlement.

Yet, as much as Phoebe's behavior had surprised her, Lord Steadwell's reaction amazed her even more. Upon hearing what Phoebe had to say, he had not only been diverted from his annoyance with Grace, but also admitted he was wrong to blame her. He'd gone so far as to beg *her* pardon.

That went contrary to all her previous experience. Even when it was proved that she had been unjustly punished, none of the teachers had ever shown the slightest remorse for *their* mistake. Lord Steadwell's apology was all the more difficult to fathom because she knew he was not entirely wrong to hold her responsible for what had happened.

If only he had left it at a simple apology.

Grace's stomach seethed at his suggestion that they meet late in the evening to discuss her duties. She would have preferred he stay vexed with her. At least that might have provided an extra layer of defense against any unwelcome attention from her new employer.

"God bless Papa." A fervent note in Sophie's small voice made it clear she believed she was speaking directly to her Heavenly Father, who listened with perfect attention, as ready to grant her requests as her doting Papa. "And God bless Charlotte and Phoebe and Mamzell…"

When Sophie paused, her father leaned close and whispered something in her ear, after which she continued, "God, bless Miss Ella and help us behave well so she will want to stay at Nethercross. Amen."

Did his lordship truly believe she might leave because his daughters behaved badly? If only he knew she was far more concerned about *his* behavior. Not that he had given her any reason to be…yet.

"Sleep well." Sophie's father tucked the bedclothes around her then pressed a kiss on her forehead. "And sweet dreams."

"Thank you, Papa." The child replied in a drowsy murmur. "Will you come and hear our prayers again tomorrow night?"

His lordship flinched slightly at his daughter's request and cast a furtive glance toward Grace. "Perhaps I will. I reckon I should visit the nursery more often. At least until Miss Ellerby grows more accustomed to our ways."

Much as Grace wished he would keep his distance, she knew she should welcome his presence for the sake of his children. It would not be easy for them when their father went away to London for days at a time while they tried to become accustomed to a new governess.

When Lord Steadwell bid her good-night, Grace bobbed a curtsy and wished him the same. The instant the door closed behind him, she pulled off her spectacles and rubbed her tired eyes. Would she ever grow accustomed to wearing this dowdy disguise? She comforted herself with the reminder that his lordship would soon be away from Nethercross during the week. She would not need to maintain such a heightened state of vigilance then.

Eager to get to bed after her long day, Grace checked to make certain the girls were settled for the night. She found Phoebe faced toward the wall, though she sensed the child was not asleep. For a moment she stood quietly watching and listening until a heave of Phoebe's shoulders and a covert sniffle betrayed the child's distress. Grace recognized the signs all too well. How often had she shed a few tears at the end of a hard day at school, forced to muffle her sobs from a dormitory full of girls?

Though part of her wanted to respect Phoebe's privacy, the need to relieve the child's misery was far stronger.

She settled herself on the edge of Phoebe's bed. "That was very brave of you to speak to your father on my behalf. Very brave and very kind."

The bedclothes over Phoebe's shoulder rippled as she gave a shrug. "I wish I didn't have to. Now Papa will never let me go say good-night to Jem. The last one he sees will always be P-Peter. My pony will think he belongs to the stable boy and not to m-me!"

"What made you speak up then if you knew there might be such unpleasant consequences?" Grace's gratitude was mixed with puzzlement.

Another shrug. "I knew Papa would put a stop to my stable visits anyway once he found out. And it wasn't fair for you to get in trouble for what I did. I'm sorry I made Papa angry with you on your first day here."

"Apology accepted." Grace ran a hand over the child's shoulder in a sympathetic caress. Already she felt more attached to Phoebe than to any of the children she'd taught before. None of them would have hesitated to make her the scapegoat for their misbehavior. "I understand how your feelings for your pony made you do what you might not have otherwise."

"You do?" Phoebe gave a loud sniffle.

"Yes." Much as she'd feared getting into trouble at school, she had broken a number of rules over the years for the sake of her friends. "I cannot promise anything, but I will speak to your father about finding a way to let you spend more time with Jem."

"You will? Why?" The child rolled toward Grace. Her eyes and nose were red and swollen and her hair a horrible tangle. Somehow it was a more endearing sight than any pampered, perfectly groomed poppet. "And why did you try to take part of the blame after I told Papa the truth?"

"For the same reason as you, I suppose—because it was fair and true." A thought popped into her mind of a lesson she'd learned at school—one the teachers had surely not intended to instill. "And perhaps because I thought your father could not be quite so angry at either of us if he was angry at both."

Phoebe seemed intrigued by that notion. "It worked... a little at least. Do you reckon you can persuade Papa about Jem?"

The last thing Grace wanted was to disappoint the child. "I'm not certain. Your father seems to be a very strong-willed man with firmly fixed ideas—especially when it comes to the welfare of you and your sisters. But I will try."

"Papa treats me as if I'm no older than Sophie," Phoebe grumbled, "when I'm almost eleven."

Brooding on grievances against her father would not help the child sleep well.

"Why don't you sit up and let me fix your hair," Grace suggested. "I'm sure you will rest much more comfortably if it is a bit neater."

Phoebe heaved herself up, wiping her eyes with the sleeve of her nightdress while Grace fetched a hairbrush. "I hope you will not be like Mademoiselle, always harping at me about my looks. There are lots more important things."

"There are, indeed." Grace breathed fervently as she brushed out the girl's wild dark locks and twined them into a pair of neat braids. "All I will ask is that you try to keep tidy. You wouldn't want to have your pony going about with his coat uncurried and his mane and tail all matted, would you?"

Phoebe shook her head violently as she lay back down. "Then people might think I didn't take proper care of Jem."

"Just so." Grace tucked the bedclothes around her new pupil. "I know I would hate to have people think I did not take proper care of you and your sisters—your father especially. You can understand that, can't you?"

Phoebe gave a vague murmur of agreement.

"I thought you would." Grace had an urge to kiss the child good-night but sensed it might be too soon for such familiarity. Instead, she settled for resting her hand on Phoebe's head. "That is the good sense I would expect from a young lady of nearly eleven."

Her comment seemed to please Phoebe, who snuggled into her pillow with a little grin.

As Grace retired to her own quarters and began to unpack her meager possessions, she congratulated herself on having made progress with at least one of Lord Steadwell's daughters. She knew better than to suppose the other two would be so easy to win over.

As for their father, she would feel a great deal more comfortable at Nethercross once he went away to London.

Chapter Four

"You seem to be settling in quite well at Nethercross, Miss Ellerby." Rupert gestured toward a brocade armchair in the drawing room. "After that regrettable incident last night, I hope Phoebe is minding you better."

"Yes, sir." The governess took the seat he had indicated, her posture as prim and stiff as her ugly starched cap, with her hands clasped tightly in her lap. "We are getting on quite well. She is a delightful child."

A note of genuine warmth crept into Miss Ellerby's voice.

"She is?" Rupert sank onto a nearby chair. "I mean, of course she is. Though I must admit I did not expect you to see that side of her quite so soon. Mademoiselle Audet found her something of a handful. And I have had more…difficulty with Phoebe than with her sisters. You may have noticed she is strong-willed and not particularly biddable."

"Phoebe has great spirit." Though Miss Ellerby seemed to agree with him, she put a rather different emphasis on his daughter's temperament. "She is open, brave and truthful. Not many girls her age would have risked your displeasure on behalf of a stranger as she did for me last night."

"I suppose not." He'd been so concerned with Phoebe's heedless behavior that he had not stopped to consider how admirable it was of her to confess the truth. "Still, I hope she has obeyed my orders to stay out of the stables in the evening. You made certain she did not sneak out?"

Miss Ellerby's pale brows knit together in an indignant frown. "I do not believe Phoebe would ever do that, sir. She might be pushed to outright defiance but not deception."

"Pushed? Are you insinuating that I provoke my daughter to misbehave?" Rupert bristled at the thought. "I have known Phoebe from the day she was born. You only met her yesterday."

The sharpness of his tone made Miss Ellerby recoil slightly, but she refused to back down. "That is true, sir. Perhaps your memories of her as a young child may have blinded you to the fact that Phoebe is growing up. When you give her orders or impose punishment without respecting her feelings, she thinks you are treating her like a much younger child and she resents it a good deal."

"Does she?" Much as he would have liked to dismiss Miss Ellerby's comments, Rupert could not deny their ring of truth. "My daughter needs to realize that respect must be earned."

The governess's tightly pursed lips relaxed a little. "That is what I told Phoebe, and she seemed to understand. Do you not think her truthfulness last night merits some respect? I certainly do."

"Perhaps." Rupert wondered where all this might lead. "What do you propose?"

Though Miss Ellerby seemed pleasantly surprised by his question, she had an answer ready. "I believe you should demonstrate your respect by giving Phoebe a little more freedom and allowing her to prove she can make responsible use of it."

"What sort of freedom?" Rupert could not hide his reluctance. He wanted to keep his daughters safe. With freedom came risks.

"Give her permission to visit her pony before bed."

"Out of the question." Rupert sprang to his feet and began to pace back and forth behind his chair. "Did you not heed a word I said last night about the trouble that could lead to?"

"I certainly did." Miss Ellerby sounded rather intimidated by his resistance but determined to prevail all the same. "That is why I would suggest a firm time limit, which might be extended if Phoebe proves she can abide by it. Of course, she would have to be accompanied by a trusted servant to make certain she does not come to any harm or get into fights with stable boys."

Rupert clenched his jaw in an effort to conceal any sign that he might be weakening. How was it that this mousy governess tested his stubborn resolution? Could it be because he sensed they both wanted the same thing, only their approach to the problem differed? Even then, she seemed to understand his concerns and tried to address them.

"I will give the matter some thought."

"Thank you, sir." Miss Ellerby's tight-pressed lips

blossomed into a radiant smile that disappeared as quickly as it had come, leaving Rupert to wonder if he had only imagined it.

"Do you mean it, Miss Ellerby?" The smile that illuminated Phoebe's face when she learned of Lord Steadwell's decision was so bright it made Grace's eyes sting a little. "I can go back to visiting Jem before bedtime?"

"That is what your father said."

Ever since Phoebe had woken that morning, she'd been aquiver to find out about Grace's conversation with her father. Grace thought a delay in satisfying the child's curiosity might help her understand what a valuable opportunity she'd been granted.

"Thank you!" The girl threw her arms around Grace and squeezed so hard it threatened to crack her ribs. "I *never* thought you'd be able to persuade Papa."

Grace gasped to recover the breath Phoebe's violent embrace had driven from her lungs. "He did set some conditions and it is very important you abide by them. You must always take Bessie with you and you can only stay ten minutes to begin with. If you prove you can be trusted to behave responsibly, he may be willing to grant you more privileges."

"I will!" Phoebe loosened her crushing grip. "I promise."

Grace adjusted her cap, which the child had knocked askew in her excitement. "I suspect your father would also like you to apply yourself to your studies."

His lordship had not mentioned any such thing, but surely it was worth making the most of Phoebe's gratitude.

The child nodded eagerly. "That won't be hard. You make studies more interesting than Mademoiselle ever did with all that tiresome needlework and music practice. I enjoy ciphering figures and learning about faraway places."

"Mademoiselle did a fine job." Charlotte muttered as she pulled on her gloves. "She taught us the sort of accomplishments young ladies require, not all that arithmetic, history and geography nonsense. Gentlemen do not admire dowdy bluestockings."

She looked up long enough to flick a dismissive glance from her governess to her sister. "Nor hoydens."

The child's barb stung Grace, though not because of the suggestion that no gentleman would ever take an interest in her. She could imagine no greater blessing than to be ignored by every man she ever met. What troubled her was the claim that learning must be a detriment to women. Most of her former employers would have agreed with Charlotte. If Grace's previous pupils had not included a few boys, her teaching skills might have been little challenged.

"Surely there must be some gentlemen who prefer ladies capable of clever conversation as well as the more conventional accomplishments." She tossed off the comment lightly as she looked the girls over to make certain they were properly dressed and groomed for church.

She did not want to be drawn into an argument with Charlotte, who seemed to enjoy contradicting her at every turn. Hard as she tried to focus on the child's good qualities, which were numerous, Charlotte seemed resolved to dislike her. Worse yet, she was encouraging Sophie to follow her example.

"Mademoiselle didn't think so." Charlotte fussed

over Sophie, fastening the buttons on her pelisse. "And she managed to get herself a good husband, so she must know."

Though the girl's tone made it sound as if she were not addressing anyone in particular, Grace felt the stab of her insinuation. Once upon a time, she had hoped that marriage might rescue her from the drudgery, indignity and insecurity of being a governess, the way the prince in Sophie's story had rescued the servant heroine. To her dismay and heartbreak, she had learned that men attracted by her appearance did not have honorable intentions toward a young woman without fortune or connections.

The pain of those memories made it impossible for Grace to let Charlotte's remark pass without rebuttal. "Your father seems to think otherwise. Besides our discussion about Phoebe, we also talked at some length about what manner of instruction I should give you girls. He feels you would benefit from more rigorous instruction and I reckon you are all clever enough to manage it."

Invoking their adored father seemed to silence Charlotte on the subject. But her features settled into a scowl of such ferocity that Grace feared she might have won the battle only to lose the war.

"How did you get Papa to agree, Miss Ellerby?" asked Phoebe as Grace retied her hair ribbons. "He hardly ever changes his mind once he's made it up."

"Indeed?" Grace recalled something his lordship had said during their interview in Reading, about being stubborn. Was that why he had insisted on hiring her in spite of their mutual misgivings—because he had made up his mind and would not—or *could* not—change it?

"I have found him to be a reasonable man who would do almost anything for the benefit of you and your sisters. I simply appealed to his reason and his affection for you."

It sounded so easy put that way. Grace recalled it had taken considerable persuasion on her part to overcome considerable reluctance on his. She was not certain which surprised her more—Lord Steadwell's willingness to reconsider his decision or her forceful insistence that he do so. She had never spoken out like that to any of her previous employers. Why had she risked it with him?

And what was it about *her* that had made him change his mind? Certainly she had not employed any feminine wiles, as she'd often seen women use on their husbands. Whatever the cause, Grace could not help feeling rather flattered that she had accomplished a feat few others had attempted and fewer still succeeded.

"If we don't get going soon, we'll be late for church." Charlotte's crisp pronouncement crashed upon Grace's musing, prompting a guilty start.

It was she who should have been watching the time and hurrying the girls along, not the other way around. In future, she must take care not to let her thoughts wander like that.

"You are quite right, Charlotte." She beckoned Phoebe and Sophie toward the door. "Come, girls. We do not want to keep your father waiting."

If she hoped her concession would soften Charlotte's aversion to her, she was mistaken. The girl grasped Sophie by the hand and flounced off, leaving Grace and Phoebe to follow.

"There you are." Lord Steadwell tucked away his

pocket watch when the four of them came trooping down the stairs. "I thought I might have to attend the service on my own."

"I beg your pardon, sir." Glancing at his lordship over the top of her spectacles, Grace could not help but notice how handsome he looked this morning in a well-cut blue coat that complimented his tall, spare figure and distinguished features. "I shall be more attentive to the time after this."

He opened the door to usher her and the girls out. "Do not fret, Miss Ellerby. I realize this was your first Sunday morning getting all three of the girls ready to go out. I am willing to make allowances."

"We were ready in plenty of time," Charlotte grumbled as they walked toward the carriage and climbed in. "At least Sophie and I were. Phoebe made a mess of her ribbons, as usual. Then Miss Ellerby stood there staring off until I reminded her of the time."

As Grace settled in the seat beside Phoebe, she braced for Lord Steadwell's rebuke.

Instead his lordship cast Charlotte a warm smile as he sat beside her and took Sophie onto his lap. "That was good of you to help Miss Ellerby out."

Grace could barely contain a sputter. Did he not realize that assisting her was the furthest thing from his daughter's mind?

"Thank you, Papa," Charlotte replied with feigned sweetness and a triumphant smirk. "You can always rely on me."

That much was true, Grace reflected bitterly. They could rely on Charlotte to undermine her authority at every turn and report every mistake she committed.

* * *

It seemed his daughters were as divided in their opinions of their new governess as he was. Rupert reflected on that thought as they drove to church.

Sophie still clearly missed Mademoiselle Audet and clung to Charlotte, who seemed to resent Miss Ellerby's presence. Would she have felt the same way about anyone he'd hired, or had the new governess done something particular to provoke his daughter's aversion? Phoebe, however, seemed to have taken a liking to Miss Ellerby after years of giving Mademoiselle nothing but trouble.

The child sat beside her new governess looking thoroughly pleased with herself and the world. "I want to thank you, Papa. Miss Ellerby told me what you decided about my visiting Jem. I will do everything you asked, I promise. I'll prove I can be responsible."

"I shall be happy if you do." He now understood what had placed Miss Ellerby in Phoebe's good graces. But the reason did not trouble him. This was such an agreeable change from the usual rebelliousness of his middle daughter. He only hoped it would last. "I cannot deny I had some reservations. But I thought it was good of you to speak up on Miss Ellerby's behalf the other evening. That demonstration of character persuaded me you deserve an opportunity to prove yourself further."

Phoebe's eyes glowed with affection, the likes of which she usually reserved for her pony. Since her mother's death, she and Rupert had been at odds more often than he cared to recall. She was so different from her sisters—so impulsive and willful. He did not love her any less for it. But he feared for her and felt compelled to protect her from her own recklessness. Had she mistaken that for disapproval or oppression?

Much as he disliked being wrong, Rupert hoped Phoebe would rise to the occasion and justify Miss Ellerby's faith in her. For now, he was pleased to enjoy the prospect of renewed closeness with his daughter— a blessing for which he had her governess to thank.

Rupert stole a brief glance from Phoebe to Miss Ellerby, for he sensed the governess did not like being stared at. He glimpsed a softening in the usual tight severity of her features, similar to her fleeting smile the previous night. Why did she seem to guard against such displays when they made her appearance so much more agreeable?

He had no time to ponder that puzzle, for just then the carriage pulled up in front of the parish church. "It seems we will not be late after all. The bells have not begun to toll yet."

They climbed out of the carriage and headed across the churchyard with Sophie and Charlotte clinging to his hands while Phoebe strode along beside their governess. Rupert bowed and nodded to the neighbors and tenants who greeted him.

He detected a number of curious, disapproving looks cast in Miss Ellerby's direction and found himself growing indignant on her behalf. Was that why she projected such a grim, forbidding air—because she was accustomed to people judging her harshly on account of her plainness? Now that she was a member of his household, he could not suppress an urge to defend her, even from the silent censure of his fellow parishioners. Christians, of all people, ought to recall that beauty was vain and favor fleeting.

"Yoo-hoo, Lord Steadwell!" A breathless feminine voice jarred Rupert from his thoughts.

He turned to see Mrs. Cadmore and her son hurrying to catch up with his family. The Cadmore estate bordered Nethercross and Rupert had been on cordial terms with its late owner.

"Good morning." He bowed. "Why, Henry, I believe you have grown an inch in the past fortnight. Soon you will tower over your mother."

"I fear he is outgrowing his strength," Mrs. Cadmore declared in a tone of anxious fondness. "That is why I cannot think of sending him back to school next term. Speaking of schooling, I see you have found a replacement for your French governess. I always thought there was something altogether too worldly about her. I hope you were able to engage a proper English governess this time."

Though Rupert doubted Mademoiselle Audet's nationality had anything to do with her elopement, he hastened to introduce Miss Ellerby.

Mrs. Cadmore regarded her with a stiff little smile and a rather critical gaze, but in the end she gave an approving nod. "Welcome to our quiet little corner of the kingdom, my dear. You seem just the sort of person his lordship's delightful daughters require. If you ever find yourself in need of a woman's advice on child-rearing, I should be only too happy to assist you."

"Thank you, ma'am," Miss Ellerby murmured.

"I doubt she will require much help of that nature." Rupert was not certain what compelled him to speak as if he were defending her. "Miss Ellerby has been teaching children for nearly as long as you and I have been parents."

Mrs. Cadmore laughed as if he had made a deliberate jest. "I have no doubt she is well-qualified, but one can scarcely compare the experience of a *paid* governess with that of a devoted mother."

His pretty neighbor seemed prepared to hold forth on the subject at some length. Fortunately, the peal of the church bell summoned them all to worship.

During brief moments between the various parts of the service, Rupert found his thoughts turning to Barbara Cadmore. Her husband had passed away a little over a year ago, yet she seemed to have put her grief behind her and moved sensibly forward with her life. Part of him envied her peace of mind. A year after Annabelle's death, the gaping wound in his heart had tormented him even more than in the beginning. Yet, he could not help wondering if his neighbor had recovered much faster from the loss of her husband because she had not cared for him to such a perilous degree.

Rupert shoved that thought to the back of his mind as the congregation rose for one of his favorite hymns.

"I sing the mighty power of God, that made the mountains rise." The familiar words poured out of him. Truth be told, he often felt closer to his Creator when he watched the first green shoots of corn rise from the earth, or listened to the song of a nightingale on a still spring evening, than in this handsome old building of stone and glass. The parts of the Bible that most stirred his soul were those that spoke of the glories of nature.

As the second verse began, Rupert became aware of a pure, sweet voice trilling the meaningful words of the hymn. As he listened to Miss Ellerby sing, something stirred within him, just like when he heard a nightingale. For a moment it struck him as ironic that such beautiful music should issue from such a drab source. Then again, he reminded himself, it was not the magnificent peacock or the elegant swan that produced the loveliest songs in nature but little brown larks and thrushes.

That thought made him smile to himself. For a moment, his heart felt whole and lightened in a way it had not for a very long time.

Lord Steadwell had a fine singing voice. Grace secretly admired it as they joined in the hymn. It had a warm, rich depth that lent the words special meaning. Somehow, it drew her closer to him and his daughters, making her feel more a part of the family than she had in any of her previous positions.

Then the final chords of the hymn died away and that fragile illusion shattered. Phoebe and her father seemed willing to accept Grace, and Sophie might give her a chance...if not for Charlotte. Thinking back over her earlier exchange with Lord Steadwell's eldest daughter, Grace silently implored the Almighty to give her more patience and help her find a way to gain the child's respect, if not her affection.

No brilliant revelation came to her, yet she left the service feeling strengthened and encouraged. As the closing words of the hymn had assured her—everywhere she would be in the coming week, God's presence would be with her.

On the way out of the church, Lord Steadwell introduced her to the vicar, who greeted her cordially. "Ellerby? Not by any chance related to the Reverend Jonah Ellerby, late of Witney?"

"His daughter, sir. Did you know my father?"

The vicar beamed. "We were at school together. He was a fine man and a most inspiring preacher. His passing was a sad loss for the church and his friends. But it is a pleasure to meet his daughter. I must ask my sister to invite you to tea at the vicarage so we may become better acquainted."

A rare sensation of happiness swelled in Grace's heart. She could imagine few things more agreeable than the opportunity to converse with an old friend of her father's.

"Why, thank you, sir!" Grace forgot all about her resolution not to smile in Lord Steadwell's presence. "I would welcome—"

"That is very kind of you, Vicar," his lordship interrupted. "Perhaps once Parliament recesses next summer, Miss Ellerby will not have her hands quite so full with my daughters in my absence."

"Yes, of course." The vicar offered an apologetic smile. "I should have given thought to your duties, Miss Ellerby. When you are less occupied, perhaps."

Though she agreed meekly enough, in her heart Grace bristled. Why had his lordship broken in on her conversation in such an imperious manner? Was he trying to imply that one brief visit to the vicarage would interfere with her duties?

She maintained a frosty silence as they crossed the churchyard, but his lordship appeared not to notice or care that she was vexed with him.

Most of the other parishioners had departed for home but Mrs. Cadmore and her son lingered at the gate. She was a handsome woman who looked a few years older than Grace, with abundant dark hair elaborately styled. Her lavender-colored pelisse and elegant grey hat suggested that she had recently emerged from the traditional period of mourning. Her son looked a good deal like her.

Though Mrs. Cadmore had been polite enough, in a rather patronizing way, her manner reminded Grace far too much of her stepmother. She sensed that his lordship's neighbor only approved of her because she appeared so unattractive. If Grace had attended church that morning without her cap and spectacles and wearing fashionable clothes, she had no doubt Mrs. Cadmore's response to her would have been very different.

"Oh, Lord Steadwell." The lady raised one grey-gloved hand and waggled her fingers in a flirtatious wave. "I had a most delightful idea. Now that you have hired a governess, you should bring your daughters to Dungrove for a visit. I know Henry would be pleased to have some company, wouldn't you, dear?"

The boy nodded, though without any great enthusiasm.

"Can we go, please, Papa?" asked Charlotte.

Lord Steadwell shook his head. "I'm afraid I must go to London next week and I have a hundred tasks to attend to before then. But Miss Ellerby is welcome to take the girls for a visit whenever you wish."

"That would be...delightful." Mrs. Cadmore sounded no more pleased at the prospect than Grace felt.

Clearly Lord Steadwell was the guest for whom her invitation had been intended. That notion irritated Grace, though she could not decide why. She had never considered the possibility that his lordship might remarry at some point. Prudence told her such an event would be to her advantage. Yet she was becoming accustomed to serving in a household with no mistress and found it suited her better than she'd expected. Hopefully once Lord Steadwell returned to Parliament, her situation would improve even further. For several days a week, she would have sole charge of the girls. Perhaps that would encourage Charlotte and Sophie to accept her as an inevitable part of their lives.

Besides, having suffered a most disagreeable stepmother in her youth, she would not wish such a trial upon Lord Steadwell's daughters.

Not even Charlotte.

Chapter Five

How had the girls fared in his absence? Rupert wondered as he drove home after his first week back in the House of Lords.

It had been a busy one with a good deal of new legislation pending now that the war *was* over…if, indeed, it was over. There were disturbing rumors circulating that Bonaparte had slipped away from the island of Elba. How on earth the Royal Navy had permitted that to happen, Rupert could not fathom. What confounded him even more was how few people seemed to regard the news as cause for alarm. He certainly did, though for the moment his thoughts turned to a potential conflict of more intimate scale.

It had not been easy to bid his daughters goodbye when he departed for London. Sophie had clung to him in tears, begging him not to go, while Charlotte had urged him to take them with him. Only Phoebe seemed resigned to his departure, though she bid him farewell with a more affectionate embrace than she'd given him in quite a while. He hoped Miss Ellerby had not let the child run wild, while being too strict with her sisters.

During his last week at Nethercross, the new governess seemed more tight-lipped and steely-eyed than ever.

Once again Rupert questioned whether it might have been a mistake to choose a governess for his daughters based principally on her being unmarriageable. Recalling how much attention the vicar had paid Miss Ellerby, it seemed he could not even rely upon that. Perhaps it was not romantic interest—the man was old enough to be her father. Yet all the more reason the vicar could not afford to be particular if he was looking for a wife.

Caution had urged Rupert to discourage any closer acquaintance between the two. If Miss Ellerby needed adult companionship, she would do better to cultivate Mrs. Cadmore, who seemed to have taken a liking to her.

As he stared out at the darkened countryside, a faint scowl tightened Rupert's features. The Lords had been late to adjourn and one of the carriage horses had picked up a stone near Slough. The delays had sunk his hope of reaching home in time to see the girls off to bed and hear all the news about their week.

Of course he could always visit with his daughters tomorrow, but he would have a busy day conferring with his steward about the spring planting and riding out to check on the progress of some improvements he was making to the estate. Part of him envied his fellow peers, who could swan off to London for months at a time, leaving the management of their lands entirely to hirelings. That had never been his family's practice.

When his carriage pulled up in front of Nethercross, Rupert could not help glancing toward the nursery windows, even though he knew it was far too late. Perhaps the girls had begged to wait up past their usual bedtime to welcome him home.

But the nursery windows were dark.

Rupert stifled a pang of disappointment. Had his daughters doubted he would return home tonight? Had they gone to bed feeling he'd let them down? Dependability was a quality he prized in others and strove to cultivate in himself. It would grieve him if his daughters viewed him otherwise.

As he climbed out of the carriage and quietly entered the house, a more palatable possibility occurred to him. What if the girls had expected him to return tonight but Miss Ellerby had disregarded their pleas, sending them to bed at the usual hour? That seemed far more likely. The new governess struck him as strict and rigid, without a proper appreciation for the sensitive feelings of children. He would have to speak to her about that. At Nethercross, he expected healthy routine and discipline to be tempered with understanding and kindness.

Rupert mulled over those thoughts as he climbed the stairs and strode down the dim corridor to the nursery. He would not dream of disturbing his daughters if they were asleep, yet he still felt compelled to look in on them.

With slow, patient stealth, he let himself into the nursery then stood silent, listening for the tranquil drone of the girls' breathing to assure him all was well. Instead, the first sound he heard was a sniffle from the direction of Sophie's bed. It seemed to reach into his chest and give his heart a hard squeeze.

But before he could fly to her bedside, another sound stopped him.

It was a low, comforting murmur. "I'm here, Sophie.

Everything will be all right. You had a bad dream. I know they can be frightening, but I promise they aren't real."

Could that be the child's stern governess?

"It f-felt real," Sophie's plaintive whimper made Rupert long to wrap her securely in his arms and never let her go.

But it sounded as if his daughter was being comforted quite well without him.

"Perhaps it would help if you tell me about your dream," Miss Ellerby urged her. "Then you might see that it could not possibly be true."

Sophie hesitated a moment then began to speak. Already her voice sounded less tearful—as if the effort to recall her dream helped release her from its dark thrall. "I was exploring the house, looking for everyone, but some of the rooms didn't belong. What should have been the drawing room looked like the inside of the church and Papa's study looked like a shop in the village. I didn't know how they could have got into Nethercross."

"They couldn't, could they?" Miss Ellerby sounded nothing like he had ever heard her before…except when she'd sung hymns on Sundays. "That means none of it could be real."

"I called for Mamzell and Papa," Sophie continued. "I thought I heard their voices behind the doors. But when I opened them, the rooms were always empty."

He'd had a dream like that. As Rupert listened to what Sophie told her governess, the frustration and disappointment came flooding back to overwhelm him. Wandering through an empty house searching in vain for Annabelle, sometimes he caught a tantalizing whisper of her voice from behind a closed door. But when he opened it, she would always be gone save for a distant echo of footsteps to beckon him on.

"That must have frightened you." Miss Ellerby's voice held a note of deep understanding, as if she too had been lost in that baffling, lonely dream. "No one wants to be all alone without the people we love."

Again he sensed Miss Ellerby spoke from painful experience. She was all alone in the world and had been for many years. How old had she been when she lost her parents—Charlotte's age? Sophie's? Hard as it had been to endure his own bereavement, the loss had been compounded by his daughters' grief for their mother. Rupert had faith enough not to fear death on his own account. But he could not bear the thought of leaving his girls orphaned. Even then, at least they would have each other. Grace Ellerby had no one.

Was it any wonder she seemed so secretive and solitary? Perhaps she was afraid to let anyone too close for fear of losing them. He could understand that self-protective instinct all too well. A pang of regret nagged at him when he recalled discouraging her from visiting the vicarage.

"But you are not alone, Sophie," Miss Ellerby crooned. Rupert could vaguely make out her shape, hovering over his daughter, perhaps smoothing back her hair or caressing her cheek. "Your father will soon be home. Charlotte and Phoebe are asleep nearby and I am right here with you. I will stay for as long as you need me."

"You will?" Sophie sniffled again. "Mamzell used to get cross with me when I woke her in the night."

"I doubt she was truly angry with you," Miss Ellerby assured the child. "Some people get out of sorts when they're woken suddenly."

"Do you?"

"Sometimes. But not tonight and not ever when you need me. Now would you like to hear what I do to help me get back to sleep after I've had a bad dream?"

Sophie must have nodded because her governess continued, "I close my eyes and imagine myself back in my dream. Only this time, I am still a little awake, so I can make it come out the way I choose."

"You can?" His daughter sounded doubtful. Rupert could not blame her. "But I don't want to go back to that dream."

"I know, but if you try, I promise it will make you feel much better. Just listen to my voice and picture what I tell you. I'm certain you can because you are very good at imagining. Think of it like one of your Mother Goose tales. Only this time, the story is about you instead of Cinderella or Puss in Boots."

"All right," Sophie murmured after a hesitant pause. "I'll try."

"Brave girl." The reassuring fondness in Miss Ellerby's voice made Rupert smile to himself in the darkness.

"Now picture yourself in one of those rooms. Which one will you choose?"

Sophie thought for a moment. "The music room. I'm outside the door and someone is playing the pianoforte. It's a piece Mamzell used to play. But when I open the door, no one is there."

"Don't get ahead of yourself now. You are just outside the music room and you hear someone playing. You don't barge in. You knock politely and wait a moment."

"All right. I've knocked."

"Very good." A suppressed chuckle bubbled beneath Miss Ellerby's reply. "Now the pianoforte goes quiet and you hear footsteps coming toward the door. Can you hear them?"

"I think so." Sophie ended her answer with a yawn.

Might her governess's unorthodox idea actually help Sophie get back to sleep?

"Are they light, graceful footsteps like Charlotte's or running steps like Phoebe's or—"

"They're Papa's steps," Sophie sounded surprised at the details her imagination could produce. "Heavier than the girls but still quiet and not too fast."

That *was* his accustomed tread, Rupert realized— measured and muted.

"Excellent." Miss Ellerby's voice grew quieter. "Listen to the footsteps. They're coming closer. Now the door swings open and there is your Papa, looking very handsome in his blue coat and black breeches."

The lady considered him handsome? Rupert stood a little taller and his chest expanded.

"He smiles at you," Miss Ellerby continued, "and his dark eyes sparkle. He holds out his hand and says, *Sophie, thank goodness you are here at last. I was about to come looking for you. We are having a little concert and you are the guest of honor.*"

"I am?" Sophie asked in a drowsy murmur. Rupert sensed she was speaking to her vision of him.

"But of course." Miss Ellerby provided his answer. *"Come in and sit on my lap and listen to the music. Afterward we will retire to the dining room for cake and punch."*

"Will Miss Ella sing, too?" asked Sophie. She sounded half asleep.

"Would you like her to?" The governess inquired, so

softly Rupert had to strain to catch her words. Did he detect a catch of emotion in her voice?

"Oh, yes." Sophie yawned again. "I like her singing."

"Then we must send for her to join us. Phoebe, go fetch Miss Ellerby. Sophie wishes to hear her sing." When the governess spoke for him, Rupert fancied he could hear the words in his own voice.

"You take your Papa's hand and step into the music room. Mademoiselle smiles at you from the pianoforte and begins to play your favorite tune." As she described the scene, Miss Ellerby's voice grew quieter and quieter until Rupert could no longer make out her words. Soon, even the low murmur of her voice died away. He had no doubt Sophie must have gone back to sleep.

Miss Ellerby's idea seemed to have worked perfectly. Who would have thought the lady had such a capacity for comfort and nurturing?

Not he, Rupert acknowledged to his chagrin. Instead, he had done precisely what he'd cautioned Charlotte against—judging her governess based on appearances. After tonight, he doubted he would ever look at Miss Ellerby in quite the same way again.

Had she won Sophie over? As Grace perched on the edge of the child's bed listening to her peaceful breathing, she hoped the process had begun at least. The fact that Sophie had wanted to include her in the dream with her family boded well.

Grace shivered and yawned. Now that her small charge had fallen back to sleep, it was time she returned to her bed and tried to get some rest. But something made her linger near the sleeping child, savoring the memory of holding Sophie in her arms. Even as it helped to fill a void within her heart, it reminded her that such emptiness existed—something she had tried very hard to deny.

With the latest upheaval in her life it had been a great while since she'd heard from any of her friends. She had begun writing to them all with news of her new position and where they could reach her, but it was still too soon to expect answers. Now she yearned for any scrap of news of their doings or fond greetings to let her know they still cared about her after so many years apart.

Gingerly, so as not to disturb her young pupil's rest, Grace dropped a whisper-light kiss on Sophie's forehead. Then she rose quietly from her perch to steal back to her own bed. She had only gone a few steps when a large, dark form reared up from the shadows in her path.

A strangled scream caught in her throat as she jumped back.

The form started, too, and issued an urgent whisper. "Forgive me, Miss Ellerby! I did not mean to give you a fright."

Whether he'd meant to or not, that was what Lord Steadwell had done. Grace's heart beat at such a wild gallop that she feared it would run away with her. She gasped in shallow snatches of air that never seemed to be enough. She could spare no breath to speak, which was just as well perhaps, for she feared what words might spurt out.

His lordship seemed to feel obliged to fill the silence. "I just returned from London and wanted to check that all was well with the girls. I should have made my presence known right away, but I was afraid it would only prevent you from getting Sophie back to sleep."

It probably would have done, Grace was forced to admit as her jangling nerves began to settle.

"I regret giving you such a shock. Are you feeling faint?" He must be thinking of their interview at the coffeehouse in Reading. His hand reached out of the darkness, brushed against her arm and latched onto it. "Perhaps you should come downstairs and I will fetch a cup of warm milk to soothe your nerves."

Go downstairs into the light, where he would see her without her spectacles, cap or any of her usual defenses? Perilous as that might be at any time, Grace could least afford to let it happen at this dark hour, in her vulnerable state of undress. "No! Er...thank you, sir. That will not be necessary. I am in no danger...of fainting, I assure you."

As she forced out those words in a breathless whisper, Grace wrenched her arm from his grasp and stumbled back. Some foolish part of her resisted the necessity of breaking contact with him so abruptly. His touch had not felt the least bit threatening, only concerned and protective. And she had responded to it with something more than panic.

"You do not sound well," his lordship countered. "You sound frightened half out of your wits, for which I am to blame. Please tell me what I can do to atone."

"Nothing, sir. I mean...it is not necessary." She had recovered her breath at last and her heart had slowed to something approaching its usual beat.

Yet her senses all seemed heightened. Even in the darkness she could pick out the contours of Lord Steadwell's profile. Her ears caught his every breath and her arm tingled with the memory of his touch.

"I know you did not intend to frighten me. I should

have heard you come in, but I was so preoccupied with Sophie…"

"You were indeed." His approving tone promised to satisfy a longing within her if she would let it. "And a fine job you did getting her settled. The next time I wake from a bad dream, I must try your trick of going back and making it come out better."

"You have bad dreams?" Grace was not certain why that should come as such a surprise. Did she assume because men had so much more power and choice in their lives that they could never fall prey to baffling, baseless fears?

"I wish I did not, but I do," he admitted. "That dream of Sophie's is all too familiar to me. I roam through this house, searching for what I have lost and can never recover."

The edge of that loss was sharp in his voice. He must have loved his late wife very much to still miss her so keenly. Though that knowledge made Grace feel safer in his company, it also troubled her vaguely.

As flustered by the intimate tenor of their exchange as she had been by his touch, Grace did not know how to reply. Part of her wanted to change the subject—to inquire how his first week back in London had gone. To her surprise, his absence was not as much of a relief as she'd expected. More than once during the week, she'd found herself listening for his footsteps in the hallway at the girls' bedtime. Now, in spite of the fright he'd given her, she was glad to have him home…for his daughters' sake, of course. They had missed their father and that feeling seemed to be contagious.

But duty and caution prevented her from indulging in a late-night chat with his lordship that might risk waking his sleeping daughters. "The girls will be very happy to see you tomorrow, sir. Now, if you will excuse me, I must retire for the night."

"Of course, Miss Ellerby. I did not mean to detain you. I hope your dreams will be as pleasant as the ones you helped Sophie to."

He backed away, leaving Grace room to get past him and make her way to her adjoining chamber. Once there, she shut the door quietly behind her and debated whether to bolt it. In the end she decided not to. She was satisfied Lord Steadwell had no interest of that kind in his daughters' drab, aloof governess. Even if he'd managed to see through her disguise, she was beginning to trust that he would not do anything dishonorable.

What was it about Miss Ellerby that made him feel free to talk about Annabelle? When he woke the next morning after a surprisingly refreshing sleep Rupert reflected on their whispered conversation. Could it be because she was a stranger who had never known his late wife? Or was it his sense that she had experienced deep loss in her own life and might understand the feelings that often puzzled him as much as they hurt?

Whatever the reason, he had too busy a day ahead to lie about pondering such questions. Rupert climbed out of bed to shave and dress. As he pulled on his clothes, it occurred to him that he ought to have breakfast in the nursery with his daughters. He had to eat somewhere and that would give him an opportunity to spend some time with them.

He arrived to find the girls dressed and having their hair combed.

"Papa, you're home!" Sophie tore away from Miss

Ellerby and hurled herself into his arms. "Did you just get here? Why did you not come last evening?"

"I'm sorry I was late." Rupert held the child tight as he bent to kiss her sisters who also flocked toward him when he arrived. He explained the circumstances that delayed him. "I looked in on you but you were already asleep. May I stay for breakfast so we can visit before I start to work on estate business?"

He cast a glance toward Miss Ellerby, one eyebrow raised in a silent request for permission. This was her domain, after all.

But before the governess could answer, Charlotte spoke. "Of course, Papa! Why would anyone object to that? We have missed you so much this week."

Soon they were all squeezed around the nursery table enjoying a hearty country breakfast. Miss Ellerby seemed hesitant to join the girls with their father there, but Rupert insisted. He could not tell whether she was pleased to be included with the family or put out by the disruption he'd created. Perhaps a little of both.

"Where did your poor horse pick up the stone, Papa?" Phoebe seemed much more interested in that than any other part of his account.

Sophie tugged on her father's coat sleeve as he was relating all the details of the lame horse. "I had a bad dream last night, Papa. But Miss Ella came and made it better."

Rupert listened attentively as if it was all new to him. Yet he could not help stealing a glance at Miss Ellerby. Somehow he expected her to look or act differently after last night, yet she seemed as guarded as ever. If not for his daughter's account of what had happened, he might have wondered if he had only dreamed everything he'd overheard.

"There was no need to wake anyone else, Sophie." Charlotte picked at her breakfast with an offended frown. "You should have come to me if you had a bad dream."

Sophie shook her head. "I called and called but you didn't come. Miss Ella did and she told me how to make my bad dream better."

The child's explanation did not appear to please Charlotte, who changed the subject abruptly. "Did you have a nice week in London, Papa? What did you do?"

He told them about some of the business before the House of Lords but did not mention any of the worrisome rumors about Napoleon. "And I attended an assembly on Wednesday evening."

"Did you enjoy it, Papa?" Charlotte perked up. "Was there dancing? Did the ladies have beautiful gowns?"

"There is always dancing at these events." He had taken a few turns on the floor to be sociable. "And everyone was very well-dressed."

His daughter managed to coax a few more details out of him but Rupert refrained from mentioning the point of the evening—to scout for a prospective bride. In that respect it had been a disappointment. Everywhere he'd turned, ambitious mothers threw their debutante daughters into his path. He had never met such a lot of tiresome chits in one night—all with their heads full of romantic expectations about marriage. He knew better than to encourage them.

What he needed in a wife was maturity, compatibility and practical willingness to settle for the kind of marriage he could give her. That did not include the deep closeness he and Annabelle had shared. Now that he had poked his nose around the marriage market, he wondered if he was asking too much.

"Tell me about *your* week," he urged the girls.

"Nothing exciting happened," Charlotte muttered, "except we got an invitation from Mrs. Cadmore to visit Dungrove next Thursday. It will be pleasant to visit, though we would much rather go to London with you, Papa."

"Speak for yourself, Charlotte." Phoebe pulled a face that made Miss Ellerby bite her lip and raise her teacup for a very long drink. "I'm much happier in the country."

While the girls bickered over the merits of town versus country, Rupert found himself thinking about Barbara Cadmore. She was a fine-looking woman who possessed most of the qualities he was looking for in a wife. The mother of one child, she was still young enough to have more. A union between them would benefit her, as well. He would be able to help look after Dungrove until young Henry came of age to take over. The more he considered the lady as a matrimonial candidate, the more sensible a choice she seemed.

When his heart protested, he resolutely silenced it.

"Girls," Miss Ellerby interrupted Charlotte and Phoebe as their argument threatened to escalate to a bitter quarrel. "Kindly make an effort to be civil or your father may be reluctant to join us for meals in the future. Isn't that so, sir?"

"Definitely." Even if he had not agreed, Rupert would have felt obliged to support her. "I cannot abide squabbling. I get more than enough of that in Parliament. Enjoy the freedom of the country while you can,

Charlotte. All too soon I shall be forced to take you to London to be presented."

"I thought the week passed quickly." Phoebe tossed her head in defiance of her elder sister. "I like all the new things Miss Ellerby is teaching us. I learned such a lot."

A fleeting smile lit the governess's face before she could prevent it. "I am pleased with their progress. Your daughters are very clever, Lord Steadwell."

He had once told Miss Ellerby that praising his children was a sure way to win his approval. But he sensed she was sincere, which only made her tribute please him more.

"Besides being an attentive student," the governess continued, "Phoebe has faithfully followed your instructions about going to the stables. I believe she has earned a longer visiting time."

"I am delighted to hear it." Rupert reached over and gave his daughter's shoulder an affectionate pat. In this case he did not mind being proved wrong. "Very well, Miss Ellerby. If you reckon Phoebe has shown sufficient responsibility to merit more time, then she shall have more."

"Thank you, Papa!" The child seized his hand and pressed it to her lips. "I won't let you down."

"I have every faith in you." He beamed at his daughter then turned the smile upon her governess, grateful for the way she had handled his rebellious child. It was as if she had managed to gentle a headstrong filly and begun training it to be a champion.

The lady's gaze skittered away from his, focusing on the children, her breakfast—anywhere but at him. Ah well, he could tolerate her unsociable manner as long as she managed so well with the girls.

"I learned, too, Papa." Sophie's eyes sparkled with her mother's lively intelligence. "I can read twenty new words and find a dozen countries on the globe. I want to visit all of them some day."

"Don't be silly," Charlotte muttered. "When you grow up, you'll go to London and perhaps a fine country house if your husband has one. You won't need all this useless information that's being crammed into our heads."

Though he hated to contradict his daughter, Rupert felt obliged to point out, "I do not believe any information is entirely useless. Better to be over-informed than ignorant."

Charlotte paled as if he had struck her, which made Rupert's stomach contract in a tight ball of guilt. Miss Ellerby was doing so well with the younger girls. What had she done to alienate his eldest? Or was it *his* fault for relying so much on Charlotte after Mademoiselle's abrupt departure that the child was bound to feel displaced by *any* new governess?

The mantel clock chimed just then, reminding him of his duties as a landowner, which warred with his desire to be an attentive father. "I'm afraid I must be on my way. A great many matters require my attention."

His daughters' fallen faces reproached him. "But... perhaps you could come with me. Charlotte and Phoebe can ride their ponies and Sophie can ride with me. Would you like that?"

Phoebe let out a most unladylike whoop of joy while Sophie bobbed her head eagerly. Only Charlotte did not appear eager to accept his invitation. "I would rather stay home and catch up on my needlework. I have had far too little time for it lately."

"As you wish." Rupert tried to ignore a pang of disappointment. "Another time perhaps."

His daughter was growing up far too quickly and he feared he might have accelerated the process. She needed a mother to guide her through these next awkward years to womanhood. They all did.

Perhaps during their travels today, he and Phoebe and Sophie could pay a brief call on the Cadmores.

Chapter Six

Would Charlotte *ever* accept her?

Grace heaved a sigh and dipped the tip of her pen in the ink well to begin a letter to her friend Hannah Fletcher. Having put the girls to bed not long ago, she was now free to indulge in the pleasure of correspondence. Only yesterday she had received a long letter from Hannah, every word of which seemed to reach across the miles that separated them with tender concern and sympathy. It was not the same as being able to sit down for a long heart-to-heart talk, but it was the closest thing they had.

How Grace longed to see her friends again! After leaving school, she had never found another person in whom she could confide so freely. Governesses lived in a twilight position, beneath the families who employed them yet above the servants. Any familiarity between the two was frowned upon. She had not minded a great deal, until recently.

But now she found herself growing to care for Phoebe and Sophie Kendrick more deeply than she had for any of her past pupils. Was that because they were growing up without a mother, as she had? She sensed what they needed and longed to supply it. She would like to have done the same for Charlotte, if only the girl would let her. But the harder she tried, the tighter Charlotte closed herself off. Perhaps Hannah would have some advice on how to handle the situation. She'd always had a sensible head on her shoulders.

Writing feverishly, pouring out her frustration, Grace reminded herself she ought to be grateful that she had won over two of the girls. She had also been fortunate to gain their father's support, though she was not certain how far that might extend.

The nib of her pen scratched softly over the paper as she wrote about the day Charlotte had coldly refused to ride around the estate with her father and sisters.

Later I heard muffled weeping and found Charlotte curled up on the window seat watching the rest of the family ride off. I spoke to her as gently as I could and asked if she had changed her mind about going.

She jumped up with such a glare I feared she might strike me. Then she replied that her feelings were none of my concern and demanded to be left alone. Yet, much as her harshness vexed me, I was moved by the hurt and sadness in her eyes. I believe the poor child makes herself more miserable than anyone with her spite against me.

Ever since that day, she and Charlotte seemed to be in a state of armed truce that threatened to erupt in open warfare at any moment—rather like the tense situation in Europe as Napoleon returned to power. Grace did not want war to come again so soon. She thought of Hannah, whose master was an officer recently returned home after years of service in the cavalry. Neither did she want hostilities with Charlotte to escalate. But she could not purchase peace at the cost of her authority over the Nethercross nursery.

As Grace paused to let the ink dry she heard faint sounds from the nursery. Ever since Sophie's nightmare, she had left her bedroom door slightly ajar at night in case the child called out for her.

Though that was not what Grace heard now, she wondered if it might be Sophie murmuring in her sleep, begging those she had lost to come back. Laying aside her pen, Grace rose and crept toward the door, her ears straining to make sense of the whispers drifting in from the nursery.

It wasn't Sophie talking, at least not *only* her. All three of the girls seemed to be carrying on a hushed but emphatic conversation that was growing louder than they could have intended. Grace was about to call out for them to get to sleep when she suddenly picked out a familiar word from the girls' furtive exchange. That seemed to be the key, making the rest come clear.

"...must stand up to Miss Ellerby," Charlotte urged her sisters in a fierce whisper that carried clearly to Grace's ears. Was the child so intent on making her point that she did not notice her voice had risen? Or did she not care if the governess overheard her? "Otherwise she'll do just as she likes and turn Papa against us."

"You're just put out," Phoebe countered, "because Papa sided with her the other day and because he's pleased with me instead of you for a change."

"I didn't care for Miss Ella at first." Sophie scarcely

bothered to lower her voice at all. "But I do now. She understands about things."

"You two are impossible!" Charlotte hissed. "She's turned you against me, as well."

"She has not," Phoebe snapped. "You're doing that all by yourself."

"I'm not against you, Charlotte." Sophie's plaintive little voice sounded choked with tears. "Why are you so angry with me? I'll try not to like Miss Ella if you don't want me to."

Grace had heard quite enough. She'd overlooked Charlotte's criticism and insolence, hoping to win her cooperation with kindness. Clearly that had not worked. Grace was not about to let the child take out her frustration upon her sisters.

Striving to sound more confident and controlled than she felt, Grace pushed open her door and strode into the nursery. "Girls, I'm afraid your whispering has grown too loud to ignore."

She headed straight toward Sophie's bed and put her arms around the tearful child. "Charlotte, I am not prepared to tolerate any more of your troublemaking. I know you do not want me at Nethercross, but that is your father's decision, not yours. You are wrong if you suppose I am trying to turn him against you."

The child did not argue with her openly as Phoebe would have done. Instead, she retreated into petulant silence that seemed to crackle like thin ice beneath Grace's feet.

"Hush, Sophie." Grace stroked the child's hair. "Your sister is not angry at you and I'm certain she did not mean to upset you. Isn't that right, Charlotte?"

After a long, fraught moment, Charlotte spoke. "I'm

sorry, Sophie. I didn't mean to make you cry. I know *you* aren't against me."

"No one is against you, Charlotte," Grace insisted as she continued to comfort Sophie. "But I must insist you give me your obedience and respect. Otherwise, I shall not be able to take you with us when we visit the Cadmores."

She tried to keep her voice calm, so as not to provoke the child or further distress her sister. But her statement of the consequences Charlotte would suffer for her continued insolence roused the girl from her petulant silence. "Keep me home from the Cadmores? You wouldn't dare! I would tell Papa the instant he returns from London and he would dismiss you at once for treating me like that."

Might this action cost her the position she was coming to enjoy more every day? Charlotte's threat made Grace hesitate. Up to this point Lord Steadwell had been surprisingly supportive. But that support must have limits. Past experience warned Grace that parents always came to the defense of an aggrieved child, without a thought for how difficult it made her job. Why should her new employer be any different?

Yet she could not bring herself to back down. She was not asking anything unreasonable, after all. Charlotte's attitude was not only causing trouble for Grace, but also upsetting her sisters. It was also for her own good. If Charlotte continued on, expecting to have her own way without regard for the feelings of others, she would one day find herself much worse off.

"I'm sorry you feel that way." Grace chose her words with care. "But I must stand firm. I do not mean this as a punishment but a choice you are free to make through your actions. If you wish to accompany us to the Cadmores, I have made clear what sort of behavior I expect from you. I hope you will make the wise choice."

Charlotte gave an angry "Hmph!" Then she pitched down onto her bed and turned her back on Grace with as much noise as possible.

"That didn't sound very promising, did it?" Grace whispered to Sophie.

The child shook her head.

"Thank you for speaking up for me," Grace pressed a kiss upon Sophie's forehead. "That was kind and brave of you."

First Phoebe, now Sophie—not since her friends at school had others come to her defense like that. Surely she owed them and herself the same. She only hoped that standing up to Charlotte would not cost her this opportunity to care for children she was rapidly coming to love.

After a tumultuous week in Parliament, Rupert was more eager than ever to get back to the peace of the countryside and the loving company of his children. Having ignored the danger of Napoleon's return to power, the government had finally come to its senses and committed to putting troops in the field. Rupert feared their reluctance to act might have given the little tyrant a worrisome advantage.

As his carriage drew up to the house, he spied Charlotte waiting by the front door. She must have been watching for his arrival so she could come out to meet him, bless her heart.

When he climbed out of the carriage, however, he

was not greeted with the warm smile he expected but by a pale countenance and flashing eyes.

"What is wrong, dearest?" He held his arms open to her. "Is one of your sisters hurt or ill?"

The thought of harm coming to any of his daughters threatened to rip his heart out.

"Oh, Papa!" Charlotte hurled herself into his arms, her slender frame heaving with sobs. "It's M-Miss Ellerby. She's…h-horrible! Why did you h-hire her?"

So this tearful outburst was Miss Ellerby's fault? All Rupert's earlier misgivings about the governess came roaring back.

"There now." He sought to comfort his daughter. "What has Miss Ellerby done to upset you so?"

He wrapped his arm around her shoulders and ushered her into the house. It took little encouragement for Charlotte to unburden herself. The upshot seemed to be that the governess had denied her the opportunity to visit Dungrove.

"Surely it was not her place to say whether I could go. You were the one who accepted the invitation for all three of us, weren't you, Papa? Miss Ellerby should never have forced me to stay home without consulting you."

What could Charlotte have done to merit such punishment? In the past, his eldest daughter had always been impeccably behaved, never giving Mademoiselle Audet any trouble. Missing out on that visit would have been a severe deprivation for her. Charlotte had talked about little else since Mrs. Cadmore extended the invitation.

Pulling out a handkerchief, Rupert pressed it into his

daughter's hand. "Never fear. I will get this sorted out. Go tell Miss Ellerby I wish to speak to her in my study."

"Thank you, Papa." The child wiped her eyes and immediately brightened. "I knew I could rely on you."

Rely on him to do what? Rupert wondered.

Charlotte ran off up the stairs at a pace for which she might have scolded her younger sisters. Meanwhile, Rupert headed to his study with a sigh. He had hoped to escape all the trouble in London by coming home to peaceful Nethercross, but it seemed there had been conflict brewing here also.

He had barely reached his study when Charlotte returned, followed by her worried-looking governess.

"You wished to see me, sir?"

"I did, Miss Ellerby." He rose and gestured for her to take a seat.

When Charlotte headed away again with an ill-concealed air of triumph, he motioned her to stay. "I understand there has been some…difficulty in the nursery this week, which resulted in you forbidding Charlotte to accompany the other girls to Dungrove. Is that correct?"

Miss Ellerby's brow furrowed deeper. "Not entirely, sir."

"Then perhaps you could explain what occurred."

"Very well." Miss Ellery shifted in her seat. "For some time, I have felt that Charlotte resents my presence at Nethercross. She often complains of my teaching methods and finds fault with much that I do."

"That's not true!" Charlotte cried. "Besides, it has nothing to do with what happened."

Rupert was inclined to agree, but Miss Ellerby spoke up with quiet insistence. "I beg your pardon, sir, but I believe your daughter's attitude toward me has a great deal to do with this situation. May I continue?"

When Charlotte tried to protest, Rupert silenced her. "You were able to tell me your side of the story without interruption. Your governess deserves the same opportunity. Pray go on, Miss Ellerby."

She gave a nod of thanks. "Matters came to a head on Monday evening, when I overheard Charlotte criticizing me to her sisters and urging them to disobey me."

"Did you hear that, Papa?" Charlotte demanded. "She admits to eavesdropping on us."

"The girls were supposed to be asleep at the time," Miss Ellerby explained. "But their whispers grew so loud, they became impossible to ignore."

While Rupert kept Charlotte quiet with a sharp look, Miss Ellerby explained the choice she had given his daughter. When she finished, he stood silent for several tense moments, digesting all he had heard from both sides and deciding what to do.

At last he spoke. "I must apologize, Miss Ellerby, for my daughter's conduct."

It was difficult to judge which of the two was more shocked by his words, Charlotte or her governess. Both regarded him with open mouths and wide, wary eyes.

Taking advantage of their silence, he continued, "Perhaps I also owe you an apology, Charlotte, for placing so much responsibility on your young shoulders that you became reluctant to surrender it. That was not fair to you."

"But, Papa," Charlotte wailed. "How can you take her part over mine? She has turned you against me, just as I feared she would."

Rupert shook his head. "Nothing could be further

from the truth, my dear. This is not a case of taking sides. I am trying to do what is best for everyone. You are a clever girl and mature beyond your years, so I hope you will understand that I am thinking of you as much as anyone. I do not want you to be unhappy, but as Miss Ellerby tried to make you see, that will be your choice. From now on, I expect you to obey her as you would me and respect her likewise."

"But, Papa..."

"Is that understood, Charlotte?"

"Yes, Papa." The child's obedient but resentful tone made Rupert hope he had not lost her affection altogether. "May I go now?"

"You may."

Charlotte rose and curtsied to him, then to her governess, like a wooden puppet. Her features were frozen in a neutral expression that he feared might mask turbulent feelings. It reminded him of Miss Ellerby. Might that be another reason the two had gotten off to a difficult start—because they were too much alike?

As soon as his daughter left the room, her governess let out a shaky breath. "Thank you for what you said to Charlotte. I know it cannot have been easy for you to disoblige her."

Rupert made an effort to chuckle but it came out more like a sigh. "I only hope I have not made matters worse for you."

When she thought back on it a full fortnight later, Grace still had trouble believing Lord Steadwell had stood up for her when his daughter all but demanded her dismissal.

Not that his actions signified he had any particular

liking for her, she insisted to herself. He had been defending the principle that his daughters should respect the governess he had hired to care for them. No doubt he also recognized that Charlotte needed to learn more consideration for others. All the same, his defense of her gave Grace added confidence in her authority. It made her feel valued at Nethercross in a way she had not in any of her previous positions. If only his lordship's actions had had as positive an effect upon his daughter.

On the surface, Charlotte appeared to do everything her father had asked. She had not criticized or corrected Grace once since that evening and there had been no more late-night whispers against her. Charlotte seemed to have grown even more protective of Sophie, perhaps to reassure the child that she was not vexed with her. Or could it be a covert tug-of-war for Sophie's affection? Grace would not have put it past her, for she sensed Charlotte was biding her time, watching for a mistake she could exploit.

For her part, Grace tried not to appear as if she exulted in Lord Steadwell's confidence. Instead, she made an effort to let bygones be bygones. And every night, she prayed that Charlotte would lower her bristling defenses and give her an opportunity to draw closer.

Hearing the nursery door close softly behind her, Grace spun away from the window, where she had been staring out at the drizzly day brightened here and there by blooming crocuses. The girls had worked so hard of late on their studies that she had promised them a whole afternoon to do as they pleased. She'd hoped the weather would be fine so they could go outdoors, but it had not turned out that way.

Phoebe had gone off to the stables. Charlotte asked

politely if she might go to the kitchen for a cookery lesson. Grace consented, though she wondered whether it was only an excuse for Charlotte to get as far away as possible from the nursery. Sophie had not been able to decide what she wanted to do. Or perhaps she refused to say, hoping to steal off on her own.

"Sophie!" Grace scrambled toward the door. She recalled a story Lord Steadwell had told her during their first meeting about how the child had wandered off once before and not been found for hours.

Her heart seemed to seize in her chest when she looked down the corridor and saw no sign of her youngest pupil.

"Where are you off to, Sophie?" she called. "Please let me come with you!"

An instant later, a small fair head popped out from around the corner. "I decided to go exploring. Would you really like to come along?"

"I would." As Grace advanced toward the child, her pulse gradually slowed. "This is such an interesting old house but I have seen little of it beyond the nursery."

Sophie seemed pleased with the idea of having a companion for her explorations. She held out her hand to clasp Grace's. "I can show you heaps of things you've never seen before. There are lots of pictures of people. Papa says they're relations of ours who lived long ago. Some of them wore such odd clothes."

As the child chattered on, Grace had an idea of how she might teach history to Sophie and her sisters by relating dates and events to their oddly dressed ancestors. No doubt the family had played a part in shaping their times, just as Lord Steadwell did now, faithfully attending Parliament when he would rather have remained in the country with his children. Grace had come to admire his diligence and sense of duty.

Sophie led her along narrow corridors and wider galleries, up unexpected staircases. In one room, Grace marveled at an enormous bed hung with rich brocade draperies.

"Who sleeps here?" she asked Sophie. "Your father?"

His lordship never put on any great display of his wealth. Grace often forgot what an enormous gulf separated her position from his.

"Papa doesn't sleep here." Sophie giggled as if her governess had made a deliberate jest. "Nobody does. This is the King's bed. I can't remember which king, but one visited Nethercross and slept here long ago. Papa told me. You can ask him."

"Indeed I will," Grace mused. Perhaps his lordship could explain to her how the history of his family connected with that of the kingdom.

"That is my favorite picture." Sophie pointed to a magnificent portrait that hung above the marble mantelpiece. It showed a lady wearing a coral-colored gown in the style of the Stuart royal court with voluminous skirts and lavishly puffed sleeves. Her dark hair hung in masses of thick ringlets with a fringe of wispy curls over her brow.

"Papa told me her name was Sophia—almost like me. She was my great-great-great-great-great-grandmama."

Grace smiled as Sophie counted off the number of "greats" on her fingers. Now that Lord Steadwell was away in London so much, she no longer made such an effort to keep from smiling. Nor did she bother to wear her father's old spectacles during the week. The girls all took it for granted that she was plain and never seemed to notice her appearance anymore.

"She is lovely." Grace noted a strong resemblance to Sophie's father in the lady's raven hair, dark eyes and elegant features. "And such a gown. It may look odd to you but I imagine Cinderella might have worn one like it to the prince's ball in your story."

"Do you think so?" Sophie's eyes grew wide. "Would you like to see it?"

"See what?" asked Grace. "I can see the painting already."

"Not that. The gown." Sophie seized her hand and drew her into a smaller chamber that must once have been a dressing room.

Two sides of the room were lined with tall cupboards that almost reached the ceiling. A third wall was hung with two large looking glasses. Sophie moved from cupboard to cupboard, peeping inside each.

"I think this is the one," she announced at last.

"One what?" Grace threw wide the cupboard door to find Sophie lifting the lid of a large trunk. "Careful you don't jam your fingers. Are you allowed to be in here, going through all these old things?"

"This is it." Sophie lifted up the bodice of the elaborate lace-trimmed gown from the portrait. "Smell."

The child inhaled deeply, prompting Grace to do likewise. The wholesome sweetness of dried lavender wafted up from the open trunk along with the faint pungency of cedar, which must have kept the moths at bay all these years.

"It is very fine." Grace took one of the sleeves between her fingers and caressed the rich fabric. "Just imagine wearing something like this." Her voice trailed off in a wistful sigh.

"You don't need to imagine." Sophie thrust the gown toward Grace. "Put it on."

Grace drew back in shock as if she'd been invited to commit murder. "I couldn't possibly."

"Why not?" The child looked perplexed.

"Because…it doesn't belong to me."

"You aren't going to *steal* it," Sophie persisted. "And nobody has worn it for years and years. Poor gown! Imagine how sad it must have been to lie in a trunk all this time, even if it does smell nice."

Grace tried to return the gown to its proper resting place, but her hands refused to cooperate. "Sophie, you know gowns aren't living things with thoughts and feelings."

"I know." The child did not sound persuaded. "But I wonder what it might be like if they did. What if the gown remembered being worn and taken out places? Wouldn't that make a good story?"

Such were Sophie's powers of invention that Grace fancied she could hear the rustling pleas of the old gown, begging to be worn and admired one more time, if only for a few moments. What would it hurt, after all, to indulge the child's harmless whim?

"Very well, then," she murmured. "I will put it on, but only for a few moments over the dress I'm wearing."

As it turned out, that looked ridiculous—the tight, long sleeves and prim neck of her rust-brown dress protruding from that luxurious confection of damask and lace. The gown might as well have stayed in its trunk as be worn that way. At Sophie's urging, Grace slid off the bodice of her dress and let it fall around her hips, hidden by the volume of the old-fashioned skirts.

"Kneel down," said Sophie. "I'll fasten your hooks."

Though part of her protested, Grace obeyed.

"Look in the glass." Sophie clapped her hands as Grace rose from the floor. "You are like Cinderella. That means I must be your godmother."

Grace turned and looked at the reflection of a woman she barely recognized. The vivid coral hue of the fabric brought out the color of her eyes and brightened her complexion, making it look more like fresh cream than cold wax. The delicacy of the lacework highlighted her fine features. The unexpected pleasure she found in her appearance made her eyes sparkle and her lips relax into a winsome smile.

Was it wicked vanity, as she'd so often been told, to be pleased by her reflection in the glass? It did not feel wicked. It felt joyful and free, as if she had been released from a tight, dingy prison.

Her fragile bubble of happiness did not last long.

"Do you hear footsteps?" She spun toward the door, her heart hammering so hard it made the lace trim around the gown's neckline tremble. "Someone is coming. I must get out of this!"

How could she have forgotten the danger of casting off her protective disguise?

"I don't hear anything. And your cap doesn't look right with that gown." Before Grace could stop her, the child reached up and grasped one of the long white lappets. Then she pulled it off, bringing down Grace's tightly pinned hair in the process.

"Sophie!" she cried in dismay.

"Sophie?" another voice echoed. "Are you in there?"

Panic froze Grace to the spot as the door swung open and Charlotte rushed in.

The instant she caught sight of Grace, her eyes bulged and she let out a piercing scream. Grace's nerves were wound so tight, she screamed, too.

"Run, Sophie!" Charlotte tried to drag her sister toward the door.

But Sophie dug her feet in. "What's wrong with you, Charlotte? It's only Miss Ella. I think she looks as pretty as a princess, don't you?"

Charlotte peered at Grace in stunned disbelief. "Miss…Ellerby?"

"That's right." Grace snatched up her cap from the floor and tried to cover her hair with it again.

If she had been caught committing a dreadful crime, she could not have been more consumed with shame or fear for her future. She had no doubt Charlotte would seize this opportunity to get rid of her.

Chapter Seven

"I don't understand." Charlotte crossed her arms over her chest and shot Grace a scowl that seemed more wary and bewildered than angry. "Why do you pretend to be plain and dowdy when you're…beautiful?"

She sounded reluctant to use that word in reference to the governess she heartily disliked.

It was now evening, several hours after Charlotte had burst in on Grace and Sophie in the dressing room. To her credit, she had not yet mentioned the incident to anyone else at Nethercross. But her father would return from London the day after tomorrow and Grace knew better than to hope Charlotte would remain silent then. If something like this had happened at one of her previous posts, Grace would have packed her bags and fled before his lordship's return. This time she could not bear to give up a position she had come to enjoy so much without making some appeal.

That was why she'd asked to speak with Charlotte after her sisters had gone to sleep. Given the girl's hostility toward her, Grace doubted any explanation would satisfy Charlotte. But she had to try.

"It is a long story." Grace pulled off her cap. Lately it had begun to feel stifling and there was no longer any use maintaining her disguise in front of Charlotte. "Suffice to say that your beauty and your sisters' will be a benefit to you as you grow older. For a woman like me, without fortune or family, attractive looks can be more of a burden."

As she spoke, Charlotte's scowl seemed to soften.

"It can make others envious," she continued, determined to tell Charlotte as much of the truth as was proper for her young ears. "It can make them assume I must be vain…selfish…foolish."

How many times had she been accused of those vices by her teachers? "I cannot claim to be perfect, but I do not believe my appearance makes me a bad person. By making myself look plain, I hope others will be able to see my character for what it truly is, rather than what they judge it to be based on my looks."

Grace had expected Charlotte to interrupt her with questions, perhaps even contradiction. But even after she'd finished speaking, the child remained silent.

"I wish you would not mention any of this to your father." Grace hated to beg, but she hated the thought of leaving Nethercross even more. "I'm afraid he might not understand."

"He would so." The need to defend her father forced Charlotte to speak. "When you first came here, he told me not to judge you by your looks."

Part of Grace wanted to believe that Charlotte was right and Lord Steadwell might not be like other men in that respect. But she had been too often mistaken about people in the past to trust that vulnerable hope.

"I believe one of the reasons your father hired me was because I looked plain. If he found out that was not my true appearance, he might suspect I had set out to deceive him."

But hadn't she? her conscience whispered. Perhaps, but only as a last resort and not in a way that would do any harm to him or his children.

"Who called you vain?" Charlotte demanded.

Grace hesitated, for this was not a subject she cared to discuss any more than she'd been forced to already. "My stepmother was the first. But not the last or the worst."

"Who was the worst?"

Why did Charlotte want to know all this? So she could gloat over the governess she detested and now had in her power to destroy?

"My teachers at school," Grace admitted, uncertain what compelled her to answer. Perhaps it was because she had so little to lose. Or could it be that she was tired of hiding her past and her true self? "And the great girls. That was what we called the older pupils who bullied and tormented us younger ones. I was a favorite target because they envied my looks, I suppose. Or perhaps they could tell I was not very good at standing up for myself."

Could that be part of the reason she and Charlotte had gotten off on the wrong foot—because Charlotte sensed Grace's weakness from the beginning?

"That school sounds dreadful," Charlotte insisted fiercely. "Why didn't you just go home?"

Grace hesitated, but she could not suppress the truth. "I had no home to go to. The school was an institution for the orphaned daughters of clergymen. My stepmother sent me there after my father died. I doubt she would have taken me back even if I'd wanted to go home…which I did not. Harsh as conditions were at the school, at least there I had a few friends."

"Is that who you write letters to all the time?" asked Charlotte.

Grace nodded. "We are all scattered about now. I have not seen any of the others since we left school. You are very fortunate to have your sisters so close."

"Too close sometimes," Charlotte muttered. "Tell me about these friends of yours."

Grace was sorely tempted to declare that her friends were none of Charlotte's business, but she could not risk vexing the child. "There was Marian from Scotland. The great girls made fun of the way she talked, but I liked it. She was one of the smallest girls in our year but fierce as a lion if the great girls picked on any of us."

If Marian were here now, she would find a way to keep Charlotte from tattling to Lord Steadwell. But Marian was far away in Nottinghamshire with troubles of her own. Her young pupils had been orphaned with the prospect of a disreputable aunt taking charge of them.

Grace did not intend to tell Charlotte too much, but once she began talking about her friends, it seemed to bring them closer. She was in the middle of a funny story about Leah Shaw when she noticed Charlotte trying to smother a yawn.

"That is a great deal more than you wanted to know, I'm sure. You should get to bed."

Charlotte nodded as she got to her feet. "I am tired. Good night, Miss Ellerby."

Was it her imagination, or did the child's tone sound more amiable? Probably the former because Charlotte had given no promise that she intended to keep Grace's secret.

Something had changed this week while he'd been in London. As Rupert stood at the window of his study staring down toward the river, he was not certain *what* had changed or how it had come about, yet he sensed the altered atmosphere. In general, he mistrusted change. Its results could be positive, but all too often they were not. Which result this change would yield remained to be seen.

He had left London early on Friday because there was no pressing legislation before the House of Lords. After his talk with Charlotte the previous week, he'd wanted to make certain she was giving her governess the cooperation he'd insisted upon. When he reached home, he'd found all three girls busy with their lessons.

To his surprise, Phoebe was engrossed in a book on a mild afternoon that would have been perfect for riding. Sophie was not off in some daydream world, but eagerly relating a story that the governess copied down for her. Charlotte seemed too absorbed in a composition she was writing to cause Miss Ellerby any trouble.

All three girls started up with ready smiles when he appeared.

"Forgive me for interrupting," he begged their governess. "After getting home so late the other week, I wanted to make it up to my daughters at the first opportunity."

"You needn't apologize, sir." Miss Ellerby fiddled

with her spectacles, which he could have sworn she had not been wearing a moment ago. "The girls have been working very hard at their studies. They deserve some time away from their books to be with you."

"That's the second time this week we've had a break from lessons," cried Phoebe.

The governess winced at the child's words, as if she expected Rupert to chide her for neglecting her duty. In fact, he could not be better happier with her work. Though Phoebe still talked constantly of her pony, she often mentioned new things she'd learned in a tone that conveyed enthusiasm for her studies. Sophie seemed happier than she had been since Mademoiselle Audet left. Charlotte was quieter than usual and not so quick to boss her younger sisters.

At first Rupert wondered if she might still be vexed with him for insisting she obey Miss Ellerby. But she seemed affectionate enough, in spite of her subdued manner. Perhaps she was simply maturing—discovering that he could question her behavior yet still love her as much as ever.

The thought of his daughters growing up triggered an insistent voice in the back of Rupert's mind. It urged him to get busy courting Barbara Cadmore. The lady was out of mourning and eligible to remarry without violating propriety. She was a handsome woman of property and still relatively young. If he did not soon signal his intentions, some other suitor might steal the march on him.

Though he knew it was the sensible course of action, part of him remained reluctant. The same part that mistrusted change, no doubt.

As he passed several pleasant hours in the nursery

with his daughters, Rupert sensed a change in Miss Ellerby also. She seemed more guarded and aloof, less like the sensitive, nurturing lady he'd glimpsed of late.

The girls were delighted when he suggesting dining with them in the nursery. While Rupert quizzed them about the things they'd done that week, their governess perched on the edge of her seat, as if she expected disaster to befall at any moment.

After he'd helped her settle his daughters for the night, Rupert drew Miss Ellerby aside for a quiet word. "Charlotte hasn't given you any more trouble, has she?"

"Not in the least, sir," she replied in a tone that sounded sincere in spite of the uneasy glance she cast toward his daughter's bed.

"I hope not." He pitched his voice lower still to be certain Charlotte would not overhear. That meant he had to draw closer to Miss Ellerby. "If she is, I will back you up in whatever measures you see fit to take. If you think it would help, I can have another talk with her."

"That will not be necessary, sir," she assured him in a tight, emphatic whisper. "But I thank you for your concern. Whatever happens, I shall always be grateful for your support."

With that, she slipped away, leaving Rupert to wander back to his study, more puzzled than ever. What had she meant by *whatever happens*? Would he ever be able to understand this enigmatic woman who shared his home and cared for his children?

As he stared out his study window over the darkening countryside, a flicker of movement caught his eye. He recognized Miss Ellerby walking along the footpath by the river. What was she doing out at this hour? Not sneaking off to meet some man, surely. Somehow that suspicion did not seem quite so ridiculous as when he'd first hired her. Or might there be a more ominous explanation that also accounted for the changes he'd sensed at Nethercross?

Could his daughters' governess be so unhappy here that she wanted to do herself harm? Difficult as it had been for the girls to lose their first governess in the way they had, he could not bear for them to lose a second so soon under tragic circumstances.

But it was not only the well-being of his children that propelled Rupert out of his study, down a flight of stairs and through a side door that opened onto the garden. He also felt responsible for the woman he had hired, perhaps for the wrong reasons, then discouraged from socializing outside his household. He should have taken more care to ensure she was settling in well at Nethercross.

By the pale light of the rising moon, he picked his way through the flowerbeds toward the footpath where he had spied the governess.

"Miss Ellerby!" he called out, rushing toward her.

She jumped back with a cry of alarm when he came bounding out of the shadows. "Sir, you startled me!"

"Forgive me. I saw you from my study and wondered what brought you out here at this hour."

His inquiry seemed to catch her off guard, as if she'd expected him to say something else. "The evening is mild and the hyacinths are in bloom, so I thought I would take a walk in the fresh air before I retire to help me sleep."

That sounded reasonable, yet Rupert sensed she had other motives. "Have you had difficulty sleeping?"

"A little in the past few days." She began to walk away slowly.

Rupert fell in step with her. "When I saw you out here, I was worried something might be troubling you."

"You were worried…about me?" Miss Ellerby sounded as if she could scarcely believe it. Then she inhaled sharply and her tone grew brusque. "You need not, sir. I am quite well. I told you at the beginning of our acquaintance that I enjoy solitary walks."

Now that she mentioned it, he did recall. But was her mention of *solitary* walks a hint that he was trespassing on her cherished privacy? "I fear this may not be the safest time or place to walk alone, Miss Ellerby."

"Are you ordering me back inside?"

"No." Rupert chose his next words with care. "I am only offering to accompany you, if that would not be too disagreeable."

The governess ignored his final question, perhaps because she did not dare give an honest answer. "But would I not be taking you away from your own pursuits? You spend all week in London attending to the business of the nation then you come home to be with your daughters and tend your estate. That leaves little time for activities you enjoy."

What pursuits did he enjoy? Rupert could scarcely recall. Anything in the company of his late wife—riding around the estate, playing backgammon by the fire on a winter evening, reading aloud to her while she did needlework. They had brought him a sense of sweet contentment.

Rupert tried to ignore a pang that skewered his heart. "The time I spend with my children is not a duty, Miss Ellerby. I only wish I had more time to be with them."

"Have you considered taking them to London with you?" Before he could protest, she rushed on. "Not all the time. I understand why you want them to be at Nethercross. But a week now and then would do them no harm, surely? Perhaps you could take them to places of interest in the city. I am certain it would please Charlotte. She is eager to see more of the world. Would it not be better for her to do that under your supervision? Otherwise I fear she may come to think of Nethercross as captivity she needs to escape."

"For someone with whom my daughter has not gotten on, you seem to understand her very well, Miss Ellerby."

His rueful jest seemed to fluster her. "I believe I could understand Charlotte better if she would let me."

Did Miss Ellerby think he was criticizing her for failing to gain his eldest daughter's confidence as quickly as she had that of the other girls? "Do not give up on Charlotte. She will come around in time. I fear she is too much like me in that respect, taking a while to trust new acquaintances. Once we do, I can assure you we make loyal friends."

"Does that mean you will consider my latest suggestion, sir?"

"I suppose I will have to, won't I?" Rupert pretended to be disgruntled. "Do you reckon you have developed a knack for managing me, Miss Ellerby? I must warn you, I do not care to be managed."

"Not at all, sir," she protested. "You are a perfect enigma to me. I have never met a man quite like you before."

Did she mean that as a compliment, Rupert wondered, or a criticism? He could not be certain. He only knew he felt flattered.

* * *

His lordship was quite unlike most other men she'd known, Grace reflected as they continued their walk on that mild spring evening.

His sudden appearance had alarmed her but once she collected her wits, she'd braced to hear that Charlotte had revealed her secret. She expected Lord Steadwell to demand an explanation, perhaps even her resignation. Instead, he'd expressed concern for her welfare and offered to keep her company.

After her experiences with men, his offer had made her uneasy. But as the minutes wore on and Lord Steadwell kept his distance, she began to relax. Of course no man would think of making advances to plain, prim Miss Ellerby, she reminded herself. Yet, the better she came to know his lordship, the more she began to think he might be a man she could trust.

Even with the truth of her appearance? A reckless impulse urged her to confess and hope he might understand the reasons for her ruse. But caution was far stronger in her than courage. If she held her tongue, it was possible Charlotte might not betray her. But if she confessed, there was no way of predicting what the consequences might be.

"How did you spend your week?" his lordship asked. "Is my daughter correct that nothing exciting ever happens at Nethercross?"

Grace thrust her uncertainty to the back of her mind, determined to savor a few moments of adult conversation. "I suppose it depends upon what one considers exciting. I find it exciting that spring arrives earlier here than in Lancashire. I find it exciting that you have so many fine portraits of your ancestors. It gave me an idea for how I might make the study of history more meaningful to your daughters."

"Pray, tell me this idea," he urged. "I suffered far too many tiresome lectures on the subject at school. Anything that promises to spare my daughters that drudgery will have my full support."

Pleased to hear him sound so receptive, Grace explained her plan to make the connection between his ancestors and the times in which they lived.

"A fine idea!" he declared when she had finished. "My grandfather told me many stories about the people in those portraits. I never thought of them in connection with all those dry dates and battles and kings my history masters droned on about."

"To my mind, history *is* those stories of people from bygone days, all woven together into a grand tapestry." Grace looked forward to teaching the subject that way to his daughters. "It would be a great help to me, sir, if you would share those stories with me, so I can place them in their proper historical perspective."

"There was Augustus Kendrick." His lordship sounded as eager to tell his stories as she was to hear them. "He was a courtier of James I. You may have noticed his portrait in the Great Parlor. He even played host to the king at Nethercross on one occasion. The bed His Majesty slept in remains in the State Apartment in the west range."

Grace was on the verge of telling him she had seen the King's bed when she caught herself. Such an admission could lead to awkward questions.

"When I was Phoebe's age," he continued, "I slept on it one night, just so I could say I had. But between the protests of my guilty conscience and the musty smell of the bed curtains, I did not get much rest."

Grace knew all about the pangs of a guilty conscience.

"Then there was Augustus Kendrick's grandson, James," his lordship continued. "He smuggled supplies to the Royalists during the Siege of Reading by floating them downstream in baskets after dark. His portrait hangs in the entry hall."

"The man with the enormous hat?" asked Grace.

"And the nose to match." Lord Steadwell chuckled. "Thank goodness I did not inherit that along with the estate."

Grace could not suppress a bubble of laughter. She thought his lordship had a fine nose—straight and well-proportioned to the rest of his features. He was a most handsome man, though his looks mattered far less to her than his character, which appealed to her more and more.

"What about the other portrait in the entry hall—the auburn-haired lady? Was she his wife?"

"No, indeed. That is the notorious Lady Althea. She was married to James Kendrick's grandson."

"Notorious?" Grace could not recall the last time she had been so well entertained in conversation. "What did she do?"

"It is said Lady Althea took a violent fancy to my great-grandfather Rupert. She challenged him to a duel unless he married her. I cannot imagine why she felt driven to such lengths to secure him when it was an advantageous match. She brought a very generous dowry and added some fine property to the estate."

Of course families like the Kendricks must keep dynastic considerations in mind when they wed, Grace reminded herself. "Were they happy together, after all that?"

"They were for as long as their marriage lasted." His tone grew subdued. "My great-grandfather died twelve years later. Lady Althea survived him by another forty years. She never remarried, though she had a number of suitors."

His voice trailed off on a wistful note. Clearly he sympathized with his great-grandmother, who had also lost a beloved spouse at a young age. Grace wished she had never mentioned Lady Althea.

That regret made her aware of her surroundings. A breeze had picked up, bringing a chill to the unseasonably mild night.

A shiver ran through her. "This has been an enjoyable stroll, sir, but we should be getting back. I hope I can prevail upon you to tell me more family stories when I have the means at hand to copy them down."

Her request seemed to rouse his lordship from the melancholy musing into which he had slipped. "It would be my pleasure, Miss Ellerby."

He led her back to the house by a route that brought them to the front entrance. Grace knew the entry hall was always well lit until the butler locked up for the night. Not expecting to encounter Lord Steadwell, she had left her spectacles back on her dressing table. The night air would surely have brought color to her cheeks, perhaps teasing wisps of hair out from under her cap. She mustn't let his lordship see her like this or it might not matter whether Charlotte kept her secret.

"Thank you for accompanying me on my walk, sir." She spoke in a high-pitched rush. "Good night."

When he opened the door for her, Grace bolted inside and darted up the stairs as fast as her feet would carry her. She resisted the dangerous urge to indulge in a quick glance back at his lordship.

The nursery was dark and peaceful when she stole in, with only the crackle of embers in the hearth and the faint drone of the girls' breathing. When she tiptoed into her chamber, Grace found a piece of paper pinned to her pillow. What could it be and who could have left it there?

She lit a candle and examined the page more closely. The words on it were written in Charlotte's hand. It must be the composition over which the child had labored the past few days. But why had she not simply handed it over during study hours?

As Grace read, she began to understand. In her composition, Charlotte apologized for making her governess's job so difficult since she'd come to Nethercross. Apparently the things she'd learned about Grace's past had brought about a profound change of heart.

"I did not know how cruelly you had been persecuted by your horrid stepmother and all those beastly teachers and 'great girls' at your school. I would never want to be like them. You have my word I will say nothing to my father or anyone."

With touch of adolescent melodrama she closed, "I will keep your secret until my dying breath. I pray you can find it in your heart to forgive one who has wronged you but now repents it bitterly. Your respectful and affectionate pupil, C.K."

A deep sigh of relief gusted out of Grace. It appeared her place at Nethercross was safe now and all would be well.

Yet even as she knelt by her bed to offer a prayer of thanks, the harsh experiences of a lifetime made Grace fear her good fortune could not last.

Chapter Eight

It had taken some time, but domestic arrangements at Nethercross were finally back in order. As April swathed the Berkshire countryside in spring blossoms, Rupert reflected on the situation with satisfaction.

To be sure, the new governess was a rather odd creature—solemn and aloof at times and strangely engaging at others. But his daughters were growing more devoted to Miss Ellerby by the day, especially Charlotte, who had been the last of the three to come around. They were all learning a great deal, on their way to becoming clever and accomplished young ladies. Rupert congratulated himself on having made such an excellent choice in Grace Ellerby.

Gratified by that success, he knew he must move forward with the next step of his plan—courting Mrs. Cadmore. He sensed she would be receptive. She always made a point of speaking to him at church and praising his daughters. She had asked his advice about a minor matter regarding her son's estate and mentioned her regret that Henry was growing up without a father's guidance.

As he drove home from London, Rupert's resolve overcame his unaccountable hesitation. Knocking on the carriage ceiling he ordered his coachman to make a brief stop at Dungrove.

"Upon my word, Lord Steadwell," Mrs. Cadmore cried when he was ushered into her sitting room, "to what do I owe the unexpected pleasure of your visit?"

Rupert tried to concentrate on how attractive she looked in a yellow day dress with her dark hair elaborately styled and not how her effusive manner grated on his nerves. "I stopped on my way home to inquire if you and Master Henry might care to dine at Nethercross tomorrow evening. Or is it too late notice? Perhaps next Saturday would be better."

"Tomorrow would be perfectly convenient." Mrs. Cadmore flashed a delighted smile. "Henry and I live so quietly. I have only begun accepting invitations again. I am certain the dear boy will be pleased to spend time with your charming daughters. It was kind of you to think of him."

"Capital." Though he sensed she would like him to stay longer, Rupert was anxious to get home. "Until tomorrow evening, then."

With a polite bow and a sense of duty done, he took his leave.

When his carriage rolled down the lane toward Nethercross a short while later, he noticed the linden trees on either side had burst into bloom. Rupert recalled the promise he'd made to take Miss Ellerby for a ride beneath that blossoming archway. Perhaps the experience might coax forth one of her rare smiles.

He could not fathom why the thought of showing the linden lane to his daughters' plain, solitary governess appealed to him more than the prospect of dining with the Cadmores. Perhaps because it was not burdened with any expectations for the future, only an opportunity to enjoy the fleeting delights of springtime.

He was about to enter the house when the sound of girlish laughter drew his attention toward the riverbank. Rupert could make out his daughters and Miss Ellerby sitting on the ground.

Sophie spied him and cried out, "Papa!"

All three girls scrambled up from the picnic rug where they'd been clustered around their governess. They ran toward him, throwing their arms around him at various heights while he tried to distribute kisses and endearments equally among them. During all this commotion, he was vaguely aware of Miss Ellerby rising to her feet and adjusting her spectacles as she watched the girls' demonstrative greeting.

"Did you have a good week, Papa?" Charlotte rested her head against his arm, alarming him with the realization of how much taller she'd grown over the winter. "Is there any more news from abroad?"

Rupert winced at her mention of the renewed conflict in Europe. He had tried to keep that worrisome news from his daughters but it had proved impossible because several of the servants had relatives in uniform. "Troops are massing at the French borders preparing to invade. No doubt Wellington will make quick work of it."

"We've been busy, Papa." Sophie gazed up at him with such an endearing smile that he could not resist hoisting her into his arms.

He only regretted that Charlotte and Phoebe had grown too big to carry. "What have you been busy doing? Much more agreeable occupations than mine, I dare say."

Phoebe chimed in with an answer. "Miss Ellerby has brought us outdoors to sketch. Wait until you see the one I drew of Jem."

"Her work is very good." The governess took a few steps closer to Rupert and his daughters. "I believe it deserves to be framed and put on display. I hope you don't mind my bringing the girls outside for their lessons, sir. The weather has been so fine and the grounds of Nethercross are lovely at this time of year."

"Mind?" Rupert shook his head. "I heartily approve. They are shut indoors for too much of the year. I reckon country air, sunshine and the beauties of nature are essential to children's health and happiness. Besides, it does not sound as if you have neglected their studies. What book are you reading them?"

She clutched the brown leather-covered volume in her arms. "*Gulliver's Travels,* sir."

"Have you read it, Papa?" asked Phoebe. "It is such an exciting adventure!"

"And so fan-tast-ical." Sophie glowed with pride at having produced that impressive word. "I like it almost as much as Mother Goose."

"It is an excellent work," he agreed. "No doubt Phoebe will enjoy the part where Gulliver visits the land of the horse-people."

An excited squeal from his daughter confirmed that guess.

Miss Ellerby held out the book. "Would you care to join us and read the rest of this chapter to the girls?"

"Would you like me to?" Rupert asked his daughters. They responded with unanimous approval.

"That settles it then." Rupert set Sophie back on her feet and took the book from Miss Ellerby.

They sank onto the picnic rug, the girls snuggled close around him.

"You, too, Miss Ella." Sophie bounded up and seized her governess by the hand.

"There is not enough room," she protested.

"We can budge up." Phoebe squeezed closer to her father. "And you can take Sophie on your lap."

Seeing the girls were determined to include her in their tight little family group, Miss Ellerby gave in with obvious reluctance.

Rupert began to read about how Gulliver was bought by the giant queen of Brobdingnag and became her favorite. As he read, he found himself aware of Miss Ellerby so nearby. Her presence seemed to restore the family circle that had been shattered so painfully. But she was only a hired member of his staff. Surely a wife and mother would be even better.

When he concluded the chapter, the girls all pleaded for "just one more."

Their governess's response was kind but firm. "It will soon be time for dinner. But if you come quietly, your father might agree to read you another chapter before you go to bed."

Both Rupert and his daughters agreed to that suggestion.

He dined with them in the nursery, as had become his custom on Friday evenings.

"What would you say to joining *me* for dinner tomorrow evening?" he asked as they ate with hearty appetites of which he approved. "I have invited Mrs. Cadmore and Henry to dine with us."

Phoebe and Sophie were quick to say yes, but Charlotte asked, "Why did you invite them, Papa?"

"They are our neighbors and Mrs. Cadmore did invite you girls to Dungrove."

By the way Charlotte stared at him, Rupert wondered if she guessed there was something more behind his invitation.

When Lord Steadwell had first gone off to London to attend Parliament, Grace was relieved to hear his carriage drive away very early on Monday mornings. As Friday approached, she'd grown more anxious, anticipating his return. But lately that pattern had begun to reverse itself. The girls were so happy to have their father home and Grace had come to care for them so much, she could not dislike anything that pleased them.

At least that was what she told herself whenever she reflected on the change in her attitude.

"With your permission, Miss Ellerby," said his lordship as they finished their supper in the nursery, "I should like the girls to have an early bedtime tonight—"

His request was interrupted by groans of protest, Phoebe's loudest of all.

"Because," he continued, fixing the girls with a firm look, "they shall be staying up later tomorrow night when we dine with the Cadmores. I do not want them to be tired and ill-humored with our guests."

"What about Jem?" Phoebe demanded before Grace could answer. "He looks for me to say good-night to him now. I can't disappoint him."

"Go then." His lordship nodded toward the door. "But for this one evening, try to keep it brief."

"Thank you, Papa!" The child jumped up and gave him a vigorous kiss on the cheek before dashing away.

As the nursery door banged shut behind Phoebe, her father glanced at Grace with a rueful grin. "I beg your pardon, Miss Ellerby. I should not have presumed you would grant my request."

"There is no need to apologize, sir," she replied. "This is your house and these are your daughters. Unless you propose something that might harm them, you may always take my approval for granted."

"That is most obliging of you." The sincere respect and gratitude in his tone warmed her. "But I meant what I said when you first came here, about the nursery being under your authority. I do not wish to trespass upon that authority, especially considering what a fine job you have done."

"Thank you, sir." His praise flustered her, but not in the way a compliment to her appearance would have done. "It is not difficult to succeed with such clever, agreeable pupils and with the support I have received from you. It is an excellent idea for the girls to retire early so they will be fresh and rested for when they dine with guests. I should have thought of it myself."

"Will you still read to us before bed, Papa?" Sophie begged.

"Of course." His lordship ruffled the child's red-gold hair. "As soon as you are ready we can begin."

Charlotte and Sophie had scarcely finished changing into their nightclothes when Phoebe returned from the stables. Her father greeted her with an approving smile.

When his daughters were snuggled on either side of him on the nursery settee, Lord Steadwell read them more about Gulliver's adventures in the land of the giants.

Grace resisted the girls' entreaties to join them. That afternoon on the picnic rug had been as close to Lord Steadwell as she could bear to be for one day, even though he had behaved with perfect propriety. It was nothing he had done that made her uneasy but rather her own bewildering feelings.

Now as he read to the girls, Grace moved quietly about the nursery, putting everything in order. Yet she was acutely conscious of his lordship's deep, smooth voice and his strong masculine presence in this feminine domain. His devotion to his daughters was so strong, it seemed to envelop her, like the scent of fresh-baked bread or the warmth of a glowing fire. It promised to restore something lost long ago and deeply missed ever since.

Once his lordship had finished reading the chapter, heard his daughters' prayers and tucked them into bed, he approached Grace. To bid her good-night, she assumed, and perhaps leave instructions on dressing the girls for tomorrow's dinner.

But his words surprised her. "I pride myself on keeping my promises, Miss Ellerby, and I promised you a ride down the lane under the linden trees when they blossomed."

Had he? Grace recalled him saying something to that effect on the winter day she'd arrived at Nethercross. Looking back now, it felt like years ago rather than months.

"That is kind of you, sir." His invitation made her pulse race. "But you must have better things to do with your brief time at home. I would not think of holding you to an offer made so long ago."

"I cannot deny there are other things I might be doing." His smile was too appealing to resist. "But would they be better use of my time than savoring the beauty of nature at its best? It seems to me that failing to admire God's exquisite handiwork would be ungrateful."

His comment about admiring God's handiwork made Grace consider her appearance in a way she never had before. For most of her life, other people had made her feel ashamed of her beauty and view it as a burden she ought to hide. Yet she admired beauty in nature and other people as much as anyone. Perhaps it was not vain to be grateful for the form and features with which she'd been blessed.

"When you put it that way, how can I refuse?" She risked raising her downcast gaze and was rewarded with a glimpse of satisfaction in the dark depths of his eyes. "Are you this persuasive when you speak in Parliament?"

He shook his head. "I am not much of a speechmaker. But if I have persuaded you, then come along while there is still light for us to see the trees."

"Yes, sir." Grace hastened to fetch her cloak and bonnet.

While tying the ribbons of her unflattering bonnet, she glanced into the small looking glass behind her washstand. She recalled the much different reflection of herself she had glimpsed on the day she played dress-up for Sophie. Part of her wished Lord Steadwell could see her like that, making the most of her God-given appearance rather than hiding her light under pinched spectacles and drab clothes.

Reason and caution put a stop to such thoughts. His lordship *might* understand her reasons for deceiving him, but Grace could not be certain. She had grown too fond of Nethercross and her young pupils to risk losing her safe, congenial position.

The spring daylight was quickly fading when she and Lord Steadwell emerged from the house.

"As I recall, I promised you a *drive* under the lindens, Miss Ellerby. But I fear by the time a gig is harnessed, we may be too late to see much. Would you mind if we went on foot instead?" He offered her his arm.

Grace hesitated, but her inclination overcame her misgivings. With the lightest of touches, she tucked her hand into the crook of his elbow. "I would not mind at all. If we walk, it will give us more time to savor the experience."

"Very sensible." His lordship set off down the lane at a stiff pace, forcing Grace to scurry to keep up. But once they reached the tree-lined avenue, he slowed to a leisurely stroll. For several moments, Grace became less aware of his nearness and the light, chaste contact between them. For the past several days, she had seen the blossoming trees from a distance. But that was nothing compared to walking beneath them

Gazing up at the vault of white and yellow blossoms, she gave a gasp of wonder. That intake of breath carried the scented air deep into her lungs. The aroma of the linden blossoms was one of the sweetest she had ever smelled, yet it had a mellow warmth and freshness that prevented it from cloying.

Her fears were no match for this banquet for the

senses. Her lips blossomed into a smile of profound enjoyment.

"Do you suppose this is a foretaste of paradise?" The question came straight from her heart, without conscious thought.

"I hope so." His lordship gave a soft sigh that whispered of loving sorrow untainted by regret. "It would comfort me to think of Annabelle in a place like this."

"You still miss her very much." Grace wished it were in her power to restore what he and the girls had lost. Even though it would diminish her position at Nethercross. Even though it would mean she could not be here with him like this, tasting a flavor of happiness unlike any she'd known before.

Grace did not expect him to answer, but he did.

"Miss my wife? Oh, yes. Sometimes more than I did at first, when disbelief numbed the worst of it. When I experience something that might have pleased her, I would give anything to share it with her. When I see our daughters growing and learning, I want her to share my pride in them."

Grace's hand pressed against his arm in an attempt to offer comfort, though she knew it would be in vain. At the same time, her heart ached with a hollow pang almost like grief. She wished someone could care for her the way Rupert Kendrick loved his late wife, with tenderness that survived longer than life itself.

"And yet," he mused in a voice that seemed to come from deep within him, "those feelings are not so raw and bitter as they once were. I do not know how it came about, but it is a blessing for which I am grateful beyond measure."

The words had scarcely left his mouth before a shudder ran through his frame. "Forgive me, Miss Ellerby. I did not invite you here to depress your spirits with such sad talk. Tell me, how are my daughters enjoying your history lessons?"

For his sake more than hers, Grace went along with his abrupt change of subject. "They seem to like it very well. They ask many questions that are quite perceptive for their ages. By the time we are finished, I reckon they will know at least as much history of the past few centuries as any boy from a good school."

"And a great deal more than most." Lord Steadwell gave a rumbling chuckle. "Myself included. Once Parliament recesses, I may have to join my daughters in their history lessons to learn what I missed at school."

Though Grace knew he was only in jest, she could not help imagining with pleasure what it might be like to have him as her pupil. "As a practice in composition I asked your daughters to write down those family stories so they can be preserved for future generations at Nethercross. I wonder if you might look the compositions over to make certain the information is accurate?"

She had thought her project would please him, but his reply sounded preoccupied. "Yes…of course. I should be happy to assist you in any way."

Having strolled to the end of the tree-lined lane, they turned and started back toward the house in the falling darkness. The lights in the windows beckoned Grace with a promise of home and belonging she had not known for many years.

Though she and Lord Steadwell continued to talk about his daughters, Grace could not help feeling his thoughts were elsewhere. What could she have said to affect him so? Was it her mention of paradise that had provoked thoughts of his late wife? In spite of his claim that the anguish of his grief had eased of late, she sensed his heart would always belong to the mother of his daughters.

When Saturday evening arrived, Charlotte, Phoebe and Sophie were all dressed, groomed and on their best behavior. Despite the short notice, the cook had risen valiantly to the occasion and prepared a fine dinner. Mrs. Cadmore and Henry seemed pleased with the invitation and determined to enjoy this family evening out.

Yet even as Rupert strove to make polite conversation and put everyone at ease, he found himself preoccupied with thoughts of the previous evening. Watching Miss Ellerby's wonder as they strolled beneath the arch of blossoming trees, he'd felt almost as if he were experiencing it for the first time. Why had he spoiled it by raising the morbid subject of his grief? Could it have been a qualm of guilt that for the first time in four years, he had enjoyed a pleasant experience *without* immediately wishing Annabelle was there to share it?

Perhaps that was a natural development, fostered by the kindness of time. Rupert knew he should be grateful for anything that made it easier for him to move on with his life and fulfill his duty to Nethercross and his daughters. Yet it still felt disloyal to the memory of his late wife and the love they'd shared.

Talking about Annabelle to Miss Ellerby had helped soothe his conflicted feelings, though he regretted casting a shadow over what was meant to be a pleasant outing for her. His attempt to recapture their initial enjoyment had worked for a while, until she mentioned handing down the history of Nethercross to future generations. Her words reminded him that if he failed to produce a male heir, his title and estate would go to distant cousins who knew nothing of country life or the proud traditions of his family.

With a start, Rupert roused from his abstraction to realize Mrs. Cadmore had just spoken to him. "I beg your pardon, ma'am?"

"I was saying what a credit your lovely daughters are to you." She practically shouted down the table. "You have done an excellent job of rearing them. I look to you as a model of how to bring up children without a spouse."

It irked him that she should raise the subject in front of the children. His girls had been without their mother long enough that this reminder of their loss might not trouble them greatly, but her son had been without his father for little more than a year.

"I have been fortunate to have such able assistance in raising my daughters. Their governesses deserve more credit than I for how well they have turned out." He looked around the table at his girls, casting a warm smile to thank them for their exemplary behavior.

Mrs. Cadmore chuckled as if he had made a jest. "However excellent a governess, they are surely no substitute for a mother. When I think how that French chit up and deserted you without—"

"That was regrettable," Rupert interrupted. Her mention of their late mother might not bother his daughters, but Mademoiselle Audet had only been gone a few months. Somehow it seemed a great deal longer. "But I have no fear of a repetition with Miss Ellerby."

"I should think not!" The lady laughed again, even

louder. "You were wise to hire such a plain mouse who would pose no danger of attracting secret suitors."

What Mrs. Cadmore said was perfectly true, yet Rupert could not suppress a surge of defensiveness that rose within him.

Before he had a chance to say something he might regret, Sophie burst out, "Miss Ella isn't a plain mouse! She's—"

"What my sister means," Charlotte broke in, "is that Miss Ellerby is a fine governess and we do not judge her upon her appearance."

"Of course you don't, my dears." Mrs. Cadmore beamed at Charlotte and her sister, clearly unperturbed that they had intruded upon an adult conversation. "How charitable of you. That is not the sort of virtue a child learns from a hired teacher, no matter what other accomplishments she instills."

Just then, Rupert wished he was up in the nursery eating an informal meal with his daughters and their governess. But duty demanded certain sacrifices and this was not such an onerous one.

Not prepared to abide any more subtle jabs at Miss Ellerby, he changed the subject to crops and weather, matters of mutual interest to their neighboring estates. After dinner had concluded, he and the girls bid their guests a good night. Then Phoebe ran off to visit the stables, as she had been promised as a reward for her good behavior. Sophie's eyes were growing heavy so Rupert carried her up to bed while Charlotte walked along beside him.

"Papa," she asked "are you certain you only invited the Cadmores to be neighborly?"

His daughter's question made Rupert uneasy, as if he

were planning something shameful, when he was doing this for her benefit.

"There is another reason." He glanced down at Sophie who had already fallen asleep in his arms. "The fact is…I should like us all to become better acquainted with the Cadmores because…I believe it might be in everyone's best interests to…unite our two families… eventually."

"Unite?" Charlotte stopped abruptly. "You mean—?"

At that moment, the nursery door swung open and Miss Ellerby peeped out. "I thought I heard voices. Charlotte, what is the matter? You look ill!"

"It's Papa." The child dodged past her governess into the nursery. "He's going to marry Mrs. Cadmore!"

Miss Ellerby's mouth fell open and she stared at Rupert over the tops of her spectacles. Her air of disapproval made him more determined than ever to do what he must.

Chapter Nine

"**M**arried!" Charlotte groaned and rested her head upon a page of the book she was supposed to be reading during Monday morning lessons. Clearly the child had too much on her mind to concentrate on her studies. "Why does he have to get married again? We're perfectly fine as we are."

Since Saturday evening, the girls had talked constantly of their father's plans whenever he was out of earshot. When he was nearby, they'd been stiff and guarded, as if expecting him to announce more bad news.

Now that he had returned to London, they seemed determined to give the subject a thorough airing. Grace sensed that any attempt to turn their attention back to their studies would only prolong their preoccupation. It might be better if she let them vent their feelings then do her best to calm their fears. Not that it would be easy. She had her own misgivings about Lord Steadwell's marriage plans.

Charlotte's abrupt announcement of her father's intentions toward Mrs. Cadmore had hit Grace like a hard blow to the belly. Perhaps it was because the situation reminded her of all the unhappiness her father's remarriage had caused. She could not bear to think of her young pupils having to endure what she had. That must be why her heart ached a little with every beat.

In answer to Charlotte's outburst, Grace set aside the story she'd been copying for Sophie and replied, "I know you dislike change. So do I. But it comes whether we like it or not. Each day we grow older. People are born, marry…die. Governments come and go. Wars are won or lost. Nothing stays the same forever except God's love. All we can do is pray for strength to make the best of whatever comes."

It was sound advice, learned from years of bitter experience. Yet even as she spoke, Grace felt her words rang hollow. It would be wrong for his lordship to marry Mrs. Cadmore, and all the prayers in the world could not make her accept such a great mistake with patient resignation.

"Besides," she added before the girls could challenge her sincerity. "I thought you liked Mrs. Cadmore. You were so eager to visit Dungrove a while back, remember?"

"I didn't want to go because I like *that woman*." Charlotte gave a mutinous scowl. "I wanted to get out for a visit. Anywhere would have done just as well. I wish I'd known she only invited us to worm her way into Papa's affections."

Though Grace knew it was her duty to deny the child's suspicions, she could not for she had entertained the same doubts.

"I don't know why Papa wants to marry her." For

once Phoebe seemed to care about something other than her pony. "I don't believe he likes her very much."

Grace could not dispute that, either. "It is best when people marry for love. But sometimes there may be other reasons they believe are more important."

"What other reasons?" Phoebe demanded.

"You would have to ask your father about that."

"I tried," Charlotte muttered. "He said I was too young to understand and he didn't wish to discuss it with me. He seems to think this is none of our business."

Phoebe slammed her book down. "If he marries Mrs. Cadmore, we will be the ones saddled with a stepmother. I should say that makes it our business."

"Will Mrs. Cadmore be our stepmother?" Sophie's lower lip began to quiver.

"Of course she will," Phoebe snapped. "What did you suppose we've been on about all this time?"

Before Grace could reproach Phoebe for taking out her frustration on her little sister, Sophie wailed, "I don't want a stepmother! She'll make me clean the cinders and never let me go to parties!"

The child threw herself into Grace's arms, sobbing.

"Hush now." Grace stroked Sophie's hair as she cast the two older girls a warning look. However anxious they might be about their father remarrying, it was no excuse for upsetting their sensitive little sister. "You know Mother Goose stories aren't true. Pumpkins cannot turn into coaches nor mice into footmen."

"But stepmothers *can* be cruel," Charlotte insisted. "Yours said horrid things to you and sent you away to that dreadful school. That was much worse than cleaning cinders!"

What Charlotte said was true, Grace acknowledged

as she tried to comfort Sophie. How could she tell the girls not to worry about something that troubled her so deeply?

"Will you talk to Papa, Miss Ella?" Phoebe pleaded. "He listens to your advice more than anyone else's. He won't be able to claim you're too young to understand."

"I couldn't." Grace fished out a handkerchief to wipe Sophie's dribbling nose. "It is not my place to interfere in your father's personal business."

"Phoebe's right," Charlotte declared. "Papa does listen to you. He did about Phoebe and her pony. He did about me even when I tried to persuade him otherwise. He told me he trusts your judgment."

Had he said that? In the midst of Grace's turmoil a flicker of satisfaction stirred.

"That is not the same." She dared not encourage the girls. "He only followed my advice about matters that affect your upbringing because that is the job he hired me to do."

"Does Papa inflicting a stepmother on us have no affect on our upbringing?" demanded Charlotte, her voice shrill.

The girls were far too persuasive—Sophie with her tears quite as much as the other two with their words. Grace could not deny their father had listened to her advice in the past. She might persuade him to think more carefully about the consequences of his proposed actions. At the very least, she could listen to his reasons for wanting to marry and explain them to the girls in a way that might calm their fears.

"Very well." She raised her palms in surrender. "I can see no more work will get done until I agree. If I promise to speak to your father on the matter, will you all try to put it out of your minds and concentrate on your studies?"

"Yes, Miss Ellerby." Charlotte and Phoebe looked as if they were swearing a blood oath.

Sophie gave a loud sniff and an emphatic nod.

All three girls gazed at her with glowing confidence. They seemed to believe she had only to speak to their father and he would immediately abandon his plans to remarry. Though she appreciated their faith in her, Grace had no such optimistic hopes.

For the first time since he had returned to Parliament, Rupert was grateful to have had a week away from his beloved daughters. He had not expected them to react with such hostility to the news of his marriage plans. He might have been wiser to keep them to himself until the girls had a chance to become better acquainted with Mrs. Cadmore.

Ah well, there was no going back now. He would simply have to be firm with the girls and make it clear his mind was made up. He was doing this for their benefit and he knew best. Still, he feared the next few days would be awkward between them.

When he arrived home, he found the girls out riding in the paddock. Phoebe cantered about on Jem, natural and confident in the saddle. Charlotte was riding a full-grown mare at a sedate walk, her posture stiffly erect. It was clear she considered riding a necessary skill she must master, rather than the joy her sister found it. Sophie perched on the back of a smaller pony being led around by her governess. She looked a bit unsteady but excited to be taking part in an activity with her elder sisters.

"Welcome home, Papa!" Phoebe spotted him and rode swiftly to the paddock fence. "How was your week in London?"

His daughter's eager greeting came as a vast relief.

He gave a cheerful shrug. "Well enough. Plenty of debates to listen to. I went out to the theatre on Wednesday evening. The play was rather good. How was *your* week?"

Before Phoebe could answer, Sophie waved and called out, "Look at me, Papa! I'm learning to ride just like the big girls."

Rupert smiled and waved back. "Well done. And a fine seat you have."

"We had a good week," Phoebe continued with her interrupted reply as Charlotte rode gingerly over to join them at the fence. "Miss Ellerby is teaching us all about the Civil War. We looked all over the house for paintings from that time. I think James Kendrick was very brave and clever to float those supplies into Reading during the siege."

"Welcome home, Papa." Charlotte's tone was not quite as enthusiastic as her sisters but warm enough to suggest she did not intend to sulk over his plans to remarry. "The weather has been lovely this week. We played pall mall one day and went for a punt on the river."

"I am pleased to hear it." Rupert glanced toward Grace Ellerby, who was leading Sophie's pony toward them. "The fresh air and sunshine will do you good."

Their activities must have provided a diversion for the girls. No doubt their governess had talked some sense into his daughters, making them understand the advantages of Nethercross having a mistress again.

More than ever, he was grateful to Grace Ellerby and pleased with himself for having hired her. He looked forward to dining in the nursery then having a talk with her once his daughters were tucked in for the night.

After their first evening stroll by the river, those discussions had become a custom to which he looked forward. They provided an opportunity to hear from her about everything his girls had been learning and doing in his absence—especially things they might not remember to tell him over dinner. It was also a chance to hear whether she had any concerns about the girls' health, spirits or behavior.

At first the governess seemed very guarded during their meetings—perhaps thinking he was judging her performance. Lately, however, she'd appeared more at ease.

After the girls returned their mounts to the stables, they joined their father and governess for a relaxed dinner in the nursery. His daughters were all in good spirits and no one said a word about marriage or Mrs. Cadmore.

"I beg your pardon, sir," said Miss Ellerby after the girls were tucked up in bed. "Might I have a word with you if it would not be inconvenient?"

Her stiff stance and shifting gaze suggested that she expected him to refuse…perhaps even *hoped* he would.

"My dear Miss Ellerby, it is never an inconvenient time for you to speak with me." Rupert strove to put her at ease. "I would be disappointed to miss one of our Friday evening chats. I noticed a few of the linden trees have kept their blossoms. Would you care to walk there with me again?"

The lady flinched at his suggestion, which troubled

him more than it should have. "Thank you, sir, but I have been out of doors a great deal this week. Perhaps we could speak in your study instead?"

"Yes, of course, if that is what you wish." He tried to ignore a foolish pang of disappointment.

Being in his study would emphasize the gulf between them as master of the house and employee, rather than two people who cared a great deal for his young daughters. Still, he tried to strike up a friendly conversation as they walked down to his study, talking about events in London and preparations under way to confront Napoleon. Miss Ellerby listened with polite interest but said very little in reply. Rupert wondered if something was bothering her. But what? The children all seemed well and happy.

Once they reached his study and were seated, Miss Ellerby did not keep him guessing what was on her mind. "I wished to speak with you, sir, about the matter you discussed with Charlotte last week."

"My intention to court Mrs. Cadmore, you mean?" Suddenly Rupert guessed what might be weighing on Miss Ellerby's mind. "If you are worried that my remarriage will affect your position at Nethercross, you may put your mind at ease. Mrs. Cadmore thinks quite as highly of you as I do. I am certain she will be only too happy to have you continue in charge of my daughters. There may even be more young Kendricks coming along for you to teach in future years. Given our agreement regarding your salary, you could end up quite handsomely paid for a year's service—and worth every farthing, to my mind."

His reassurance did not appear to have the effect he'd hoped for.

"Thank you, sir. I appreciate the confidence you place in me. It is not for myself that I am concerned but for your daughters. They are terribly upset at the prospect of you marrying Mrs. Cadmore and they begged me to speak with you on their behalf."

"Terribly upset? Nonsense! Perhaps the news came as a bit of a shock last week. But today they are all in fine spirits. None of them said a peep about Mrs. Cadmore."

The governess heaved an impatient sigh. "That is because you forbade them to mention the subject. And the only reason they seem happy is because they have faith in my ability to persuade you to reconsider your decision before it is too late."

"Before it is too late?" Rupert sprang from his chair and circled behind it. He felt as if he had come under attack and needed to take up a strong defensive position. "You make it sound as if I intend to commit a crime when I am only seeking to do right by my daughters and my estate."

"Forgive me, Lord Steadwell." She looked sincerely grieved at having offended him. "I am certain you have excellent reasons for what you intend to do."

"But you think I am wrong all the same. I suppose you share my daughters' belief that you can bring me to my senses." He infused those final words with bitter scorn.

Miss Ellerby shook her head. "I wish I could, but I fear your decision is irrevocable."

Well, that was better. At least she recognized his resolve. "Then let us waste no more time in fruitless argument."

"I wish I could oblige you." Her mouth settled into a

stubborn line. "But I promised the girls I would try and I must keep my promise."

Hang it all! Mousy Miss Ellerby was nearly as stubborn as he. "Let us get it over with, then. What objections do my daughters have to my marrying Mrs. Cadmore?"

"First perhaps you could explain why you want to make the lady your wife."

"I do not need to justify my decision to my daughters," he snapped, "and certainly not to you, Miss Ellerby."

She shrank back in her chair, making Rupert regret his harsh tone. She was only doing what his daughters had bidden her, after all. "I do not feel entitled to an explanation, sir. But surely your children deserve one. Perhaps if they understand your reasons, they might become reconciled to the idea in time."

When she put the matter that way, it seemed unreasonable to refuse. "It is not a decision I made lightly. Nor have I considered only my own interests—but those of everyone involved."

"I would never take you for a selfish man, sir."

Somehow that meant a great deal to him. "If I had only myself to consider, I would be content to remain a widower to the end of my days."

Miss Ellerby's pale brows kit together. "Then why...?"

"Because my daughters need a mother, for one thing."

When he saw the look of hurt that gripped her features, Rupert hastened to add, "You have done an excellent job with the girls—better than I ever hoped. But they will not remain this age forever. When the time comes for Charlotte to make her debut or Phoebe to give up her pony in favor of a young gentleman, those situations will require something more than even the best governess can provide."

Miss Ellerby opened her mouth to contradict him, then seemed to acknowledge the truth of what he'd said by shutting it again.

Rupert took advantage of her silence to continue. "There is also the question of who would care for the girls if something were to happen to me before they come of age. They have godparents, of course, but that might make it necessary to split them up."

"And you think a stepmother would be any better?" The question burst from Miss Ellerby's lips.

"I do," he replied. "Otherwise I would not think of remarrying. Finally, there is the matter of Nethercross and what will become of it when I am gone. Unless I have a son to succeed me, the heir to my title and this estate would be a feckless cousin. I would not trust him with anything of value."

"Oh." That appeared to be the only reply Miss Ellerby was capable of making just then.

Had he shocked her speechless with his indelicate reference to expanding his family?

After an awkward silence, the governess recovered her voice. "Are those your only reasons for wanting to marry Mrs. Cadmore?"

"Are they not sufficient?" Rupert demanded. "What more do you want?"

"Only the most important reason of all—that you care for the lady and want to share your life with her. Your daughters do not believe you are in love with Mrs. Cadmore and I have seen nothing to suggest otherwise."

In love with…? The very notion sent a cold trickle of fear slithering down his back. It provoked him to lash out.

"Are you so knowledgeable about being in love that you can recognize its absence? I would not have supposed you knew any more about the subject than my daughters. Have you ever been in love to speak from experience?"

It was not the sort of question a gentleman should ask a lady, but Rupert could not help himself. Besides, now that it was out, he found himself more than usually curious about her answer.

The red spots in Miss Ellerby's cheeks expanded until her whole face looked badly sunburnt. She hung her head. "I am no expert in matters of the heart, sir. I did fancy myself in love once, but now I am not certain I truly was."

Her reply surprised Rupert. It had not occurred to him that a woman like her had ever known the stirrings of love. Perhaps it had not occurred to the man she'd cared for, either. Which made them a pair of fools, Rupert acknowledged to his chagrin. Just because Grace Ellerby was no beauty did not mean her heart was incapable of beautiful feelings. He should know, for he had seen and heard the tenderness she lavished upon his children.

Was that the reason she behaved so guardedly—because her tender heart had been injured by a man who judged her too plain and poor to entertain feelings for him?

Before Rupert could summon the words to apologize for jumping to that same conclusion, Miss Ellerby raised her head to skewer him with a challenging glare. "Perhaps I was mistaken in my ignorance, Lord Steadwell. *Are* you in love with Mrs. Cadmore after all?"

Was Lord Steadwell in love with the woman he intended to court and marry? Grace wondered what had made her press him on such an intrusive question.

"My feelings toward Mrs. Cadmore are no business of yours or anyone else's," he replied at last. "But since you insist on knowing—no, I am not 'in love' with Barbara Cadmore."

His brutal candor surprised Grace. Yet part of her greeted his response with a flicker of relief.

"However," he continued, "I find the lady attractive and compatible, which is sufficient for me, as I believe it will be for her. We are not a pair of sentimental youngsters seeking the sort of endless romantic idyll in one of Sophie's Mother Goose tales. We both have children and property and responsibilities to consider ahead of our feelings. I have known love and discovered the high toll it exacts when lost. Even if I believed it were possible for me to recapture that kind of feeling, I would not care to try. I have no desire to plumb that depth of grief again. I doubt Mrs. Cadmore does, either."

A brief quiver of doubt in his eyes made Grace wonder what part of all that he did not truly believe. Much as it troubled her to hear him renounce love once and for all, she could understand his reasons. Had she not vowed to protect her heart from further injury after Captain Townsend had broken it?

Grace recalled the torment she'd suffered as if it were only yesterday. The engaging brother of her very first employer had spent one winter at his sister's home recovering from a wound he'd received while fighting in

Spain. Fresh out of school and desperately lonely, she had been flattered by the gallant captain's admiration. Like a naive little fool, she had allowed herself to dream of a future with him—that endless romantic idyll at which Lord Steadwell had sneered.

Only when the captain tried to tempt her into a dishonorable connection had she understood that he did not share her feelings. He'd scarcely regarded her as a person at all, only a pretty bauble to amuse him until he wed a lady of sufficient fortune to keep him in comfort. After that, she had never felt anything but fear and loathing of the men who had pursued her.

Grace stirred from her painful musing to find Lord Steadwell staring at her in expectant silence. Did her face betray as much of her feelings as his had a few moments ago?

"Well?" he prompted her. "Do you not intend to argue me out of my decision?"

Of course she did, though she now realized it would be even more difficult than she'd first believed. She owed it to his daughters to do everything in her power to keep him from making a mistake for which they might all pay dearly.

"I beg your pardon, sir. But what you said reminded me of another man who wed a woman he did not love for similar reasons."

"Who are you talking about?" his lordship demanded. "I assume his second marriage did not turn out well."

Grace gave a rueful nod. "The man was my father. A few years after my mother died he married a lady of some fortune, the better to provide for me."

She forced the words past a barrier of long-standing

reluctance to speak about the events of her childhood. Having recently told Charlotte about some of her experiences at school, she found it easier to confide in his lordship that she had expected.

"I sympathize with your father's motives." Lord Steadwell's tone seemed to question why Grace could not do the same.

"I know he meant well, as you do. Nevertheless, that marriage was a mistake. Our home was not a happy one. When I quarreled with my stepmother's children, she and Papa each took the part of their own offspring. Papa tried to hide his unhappiness and pretend all was well. To make up for my stepmother's coldness, he doted on me, which only vexed her and made the situation worse."

Was the cautionary tale of her childhood giving his lordship second thoughts? If so, perhaps it would be worth the heartache that had crawled out of some dark cupboard to gnaw at her again. "I believe the strain of all that frustration and regret was what made him ill. When he died, I was left at the mercy of my stepmother."

Her voice broke as stinging tears welled up in her eyes.

Old feelings trampled her heart in their fierce delight at being set free. She might have been able to subdue them if she'd believed her painful confession was having the desired result. Instead, she feared his lordship would not be swayed from his decision, no matter how much he pitied her past troubles. Futility threatened to overwhelm her.

Grace bowed her head and raised her hand to her brow. She was concentrating so hard to keep from breaking down that she scarcely noticed Lord Steadwell moving toward her. Suddenly he knelt beside her chair, pressing a handkerchief into her hand.

She started and shrank from him. But besides the usual flare of panic at having a man so dangerously near, Grace also experienced an unaccustomed yearning.

Chapter Ten

He could not bear to see Miss Ellerby so upset.

The sight of her hunched over, fighting back tears, tore at Rupert with an intense mixture of pity, helplessness and a jagged shard of guilt. It was his fault she had felt compelled to dredge up all those wrenching memories.

He ached to comfort her, but the nature of their connection made that improper, even if she had not cowered from his sudden approach.

"Do not fret," he pleaded, offering her a handkerchief. "I am sorry for all you suffered during your youth."

"You need not pity me!" She snatched the handkerchief from him and tipped up her spectacles to press the cloth to her eyes. "Save your pity for your children if you go ahead with your plan to remarry."

Deeply as her distress moved him, Rupert refused to believe Barbara Cadmore would behave toward his daughters as Grace Ellerby's stepmother had toward her. Mrs. Cadmore was a devoted mother to her son as she surely would be to his girls and any future children.

It was one of the qualities that had most recommended her to him. Besides, he had no intention of letting any harm come to him until his daughters were grown and he had sired a son to carry on at Nethercross.

Perhaps sensing his resistance, Miss Ellerby gathered her composure and continued. "My father was barely in his grave before my stepmother shipped me off to the Pendergast School. It is a wonder I did not die from grief and homesickness and the wretched conditions there."

As she told him about the scarce, bad food; the cold and dampness; the harsh teachers and bullying older girls, Rupert's jaw tensed and his face began to burn. He wished he could go back and whisk her away from that miserable institution. At the same time, he could not help admiring the strength with which she had carried on in the face of such unrelenting adversity. That must have been when she had developed her severe facade to protect the wounded child beneath. Yet everything she'd endured seemed only to have strengthened her character and faith.

"Did you never blame God for what happened to you?" he asked when she finished speaking and slumped in the chair, spent from the effort it had cost her. "Did you never feel He had abandoned you?"

It was an intrusive question, but he knew she might never be willing to confide in him so fully again. And he had an urgent need to hear her answer.

She thought for a moment, perhaps searching her heart for the feelings he had mentioned. Then Grace Ellerby shook her head. "Faith and friendship were all that sustained me during those dark days. I took great comfort from the certainty that our Heavenly Father does not judge by outward appearances, as others do, but can see past that to beauty of the spirit."

Rupert did not believe she was referring to him when she spoke of people judging by appearance. Yet his conscience troubled him for failing to look deeper to the strong, fine woman she was at heart. He reminded himself that if it were not for her drab appearance, he might never have brought her into his home and permitted the comradeship between them to grow as close as it had. That would have been a grave misfortune for him and for his daughters.

Seeing him grow so thoughtful must have given Miss Ellerby hope. "Has hearing of my experiences persuaded you to reconsider your decision, sir?"

Much as he hated to disappoint her, Rupert could not deceive her. "I am sorry that you have distressed yourself in vain, but I am as determined as ever to proceed with my plans."

After all she had put herself through, Miss Ellerby deserved an explanation. "You must see that my daughters' situation is quite different from yours. I believe the potential benefits of my remarriage, to them and to Nethercross, outweigh any risk."

He spoke in a firm tone to assure her of his resolve in the matter. The sooner she accepted the inevitable, the better it would be for his daughters. At the same time, he strove to infuse his words with warmth so she would know he did not resent her for making the effort.

"I appreciate that you want to protect my daughters from what you consider a threat. But I believe the kindest service you can do is to help them understand why I must remarry and urge them to accept it. Can I rely on you to do that, for their sake and for mine?"

"I will try, sir." A faint sigh escaped her. "That is the best I can promise you."

Rupert patted her hand, which had come to rest on the arm of the chair. "That will be good enough for me."

Would it, though? He sensed that Miss Ellerby was still not convinced he was doing the right thing. He feared that when it came to his daughters' well-being, their unassuming governess might be almost as stubborn as he.

"Can you try speaking to Papa again, Miss Ella?" Charlotte pleaded as she and her sisters practiced sketching in the garden on a sunny afternoon late in May.

"He's been to visit her every week since the end of April." Phoebe frowned at her sketching pad. "If we don't put a stop to it soon, I'm afraid he will propose to her. Then there will be nothing we can do."

Grace gave a rueful shrug. "I would try if I thought it might do any good. But you know better than I, your father can be a very stubborn man. Especially when he believes he is acting in the best interests of those he loves."

She had kept her promise to his lordship by explaining his reasons for wanting to remarry and trying to persuade the girls to accept the situation. But they seemed no more inclined to heed her than their father was. It could not help that they seemed to sense her misgivings.

"If he won't listen to you, then we must take drastic action," said Charlotte.

"I know!" said Phoebe. "Why don't we invite Mrs. Cadmore to Nethercross while Papa is in London and behave abominably? We could run about and pretend to quarrel at the top of our lungs. Then she won't want to marry Papa and have to live with us."

"We could throw food at teatime," suggested Sophie, entering into the spirit of her sister's plan, "and slide down the stairs on a big silver tray. I've always wanted to do that!"

"No!" Grace burst out before Charlotte could suggest further misbehavior. "You must not think of such a thing! Your father would be very cross with you when he learned what you had done. And you do not want to prejudice Mrs. Cadmore against you in case she does become your stepmother. She could make your lives quite miserable."

"Let her try," grumbled Charlotte. "Papa would not allow it."

"If she stayed at Nethercross through the week while he went to London, you would be at her mercy for five days out of seven."

Sophie dropped her sketching pencil and ran to Grace. "You won't let her be cruel to us, will you, Miss Ella?"

It had taken weeks to persuade the child that her future stepmother would not force her to sweep the cinders and sleep in the cellar.

"Of course not." Grace caught Sophie in a comforting embrace. "But if you behave as badly as you plan, she might persuade you father to dismiss me because I'd let you run wild."

"I hadn't thought of that. If we must have a stepmother, we do not want to lose you, Miss Ella." Phoebe's features clenched in a look of intense concentration, then after a moment she snapped her fingers. "I know! What if we tell Mrs. Cadmore that Papa drinks a great deal of brandy? I heard our cook tell Bessie no sensible woman would marry a man who drinks."

Charlotte shook her head. "I can't tell such lies about Papa."

Phoebe crumpled onto the grass. "What *can* we do then?"

"We have to keep thinking," Charlotte tried to encourage her.

"In the meantime," suggested Grace, "you might as well put your sketching materials away. It does not appear to be holding your interest. Perhaps a game of pall mall would suit you better."

The girls could take out their frustration on wooden balls with their mallets. It might be less hazardous than Phoebe's schemes to disrupt her father's courtship.

A short while later, Grace sat in the shade of a towering old elm tree, watching the girls play. On her lap lay a letter which had arrived that morning from her friend Rebecca. She was still trying to digest the astonishing news it contained.

Rebecca was engaged to be married. And her betrothed was not a humble clerk or curate to which a penniless governess might aspire but a wealthy viscount! The last Grace had heard from her friend, Viscount Benedict had been trying to break an engagement between his half brother and the young lady Rebecca served as companion. Though Grace had suspected her friend liked the gentleman far better than she would admit, it had never occurred to her their acquaintance might blossom into a romantic attachment.

Rebecca deserved all the happiness and security such a fine match would provide for she was one of the kindest, most loyal souls Grace had ever known. She also had the proper background to be the wife of a peer, for she came from aristocratic stock on her mother's side. Still it was a long way from the Pendergast School to a viscount's mansion.

"We have set the date for the final week of June," Rebecca wrote in her familiar neat hand.. "It would make me so very happy if you could come to the wedding. I long to see you and our other school friends again."

Much as Grace wished she could go to the Cotswolds to attend Rebecca's wedding, and perhaps visit with some of their other friends, she feared it would be impossible. With their father's courtship moving relentlessly toward a betrothal, her young pupils needed her more than ever to keep their spirits up and prevent them from taking any reckless action to keep his lordship from marrying Mrs. Cadmore.

As she pictured herself in the Cotswold church watching Rebecca's nuptials, Grace found her daydream changing until the bride looked like Mrs. Cadmore and the groom like Lord Steadwell. The imagined sight provoked an intense pang. That must be on account of what such a marriage would mean for her dear pupils... mustn't it? Somehow the sensation felt even more personal and painful than that.

It couldn't be! Surely not! Grace struggled to catch her breath, which that alarming possibility had snatched away. What she felt for Lord Steadwell could *not* be that perilous emotion she refused to name, even in the privacy of her own thoughts. It was nothing like the thrilling romantic fancy she'd once conceived for Captain Townsend.

Upon the stern inquisition of her conscience, Grace had to admit her feelings toward Lord Steadwell ran deeper than those she'd once had for the charming, dishonorable captain. What started out as wariness and fear had mellowed into gratitude, admiration and eventually trust. Because those feelings had ripened so slowly from such an unpromising beginning, she had only dimly suspected they might be straying in a dangerous direction.

Was it too late to root them out, like weeds that threatened to grow into pernicious vines, capable of twining around her heart and strangling it? She must try, for the consequences of permitting them to flourish did not bear thinking of.

For so many reasons, the baron could never return her feelings. Even if their backgrounds and positions were not impossibly far apart, he had told her in plain terms that he wanted nothing more to do with love. His heart still belonged to his late wife and he refused to risk it again. He had decided to select a wife with his stubborn head rather than with his wounded, wary heart.

Grace had experienced the pain of rejection before— by a man who wanted her favors but not her love. Then at least she had been able to go away and start afresh in a place where she'd been in no danger of encountering the object of her affections. Now, she had come to love Nethercross and the baron's daughters too much to desert them when they needed her most. Unless she wanted to suffer the secret torment of living in the same house as the man she cared for when he belonged to another woman, she would have no choice but to root out these improper feelings for her master.

But first she must take up her pen and write a tactful letter of congratulations to Rebecca, with regrets that she could not attend the wedding.

* * *

If Grace Ellerby presumed she could make him give up his marriage plans simply by acting cool toward him, she was in for an unpleasant surprise.

As Rupert neared home one day in late June, he strove to keep his mind on more pleasant matters, like the excellent news he was eager to share with his family. Somehow, thoughts of his daughters' governess kept intruding. That was quite the opposite of how the lady herself behaved toward him of late. Though she still maintained a polite, professional manner toward him, Miss Ellerby managed to convey the sense that a barrier had risen between them.

When he joined her and his daughters for dinner in the nursery on Fridays, she made every effort to smooth over any awkwardness between him and the girls. Yet once the children had been put to bed for the night, she always had some excuse not to go out for a stroll with him or to discuss how his daughters had got on that week. It came as an unsettling surprise to Rupert how much he missed those innocent conversations.

Surely once he was wed Miss Ellerby would realize his marriage was not the sort of disaster she anticipated. She and the children would adapt to the new situation and she would warm to him again…so far as she was able. In the meantime, he tried not to resent her behavior toward him and her disapproval of his plans. He knew they both sprang from her concern for his daughters. Misplaced though that concern might be, it still touched him.

It was becoming clear that the sooner he and Mrs. Cadmore got married, the better it would be for all concerned. There was no longer any excuse for delay. He had been calling at Dungrove regularly for the past several weeks. Barbara Cadmore could hardly be blind to his intentions. Indeed, she gave every sign of encouraging him. He had allowed his daughters plenty of time to become accustomed to the idea. Too much more might only increase their apprehension. He needed to show them their fears were unfounded. The only way to do that would be to let them experience the new family situation.

The next few weeks would be the ideal time to proceed. It would give everyone a few months to grow accustomed to the change before he was obliged to return to London for the brief autumn session of Parliament. Now that the uncertainty over matters on the Continent had been resolved, this was surely the proper time for new beginnings.

The thought reminded Rupert of the good tidings he had to convey to his family when he reached Nethercross. Though he had tried to conceal the gravity of the situation from his young daughters, they knew more about the conflict than he would have liked. No doubt they would be as relieved and happy about the outcome as he.

He managed to keep his mind fixed on that happy thought over the final mile of his journey. His anticipation grew as the familiar fields of Nethercross came in sight and he watched his tenants out making hay.

When his carriage rolled up the lane, he spied his daughters cavorting in the shade of a towering elm tree. Charlotte and Phoebe were batting a shuttlecock back and forth with Sophie and their governess. The girls turned at the sound of his carriage, dropped their battledore rackets and ran to greet him.

"Good news!" Rupert cried as he surged out of the carriage. "Wellington and Blucher have put the boots to the French army at a place called Waterloo. Boney has fled and there will finally be lasting peace!"

The girls cheered.

"That is splendid news, Papa!" Charlotte hurled herself into his arms, the warmest embrace she had given him since he'd announced his intention to remarry.

Out of the corner of his eye, Rupert spied Phoebe hugging her governess while Sophie jumped up and down with excitement.

When Charlotte released him to hug Miss Ellerby, Sophie ran over and took her sister's place in his arms. The round of joyful embraces continued among the five of them until suddenly Rupert found his arms around Grace Ellerby, not quite certain how it had happened. The governess seemed equally astonished. After a convulsive squeeze, they sprang apart as if the physical contact burned them.

Rupert's pulse thundered in his ears and his cheek tingled where that ugly cap of hers had brushed against it. He found himself wishing he could see her hair just once or her face without those wretched spectacles. For someone who seemed to resent being judged by her appearance, she did nothing to make herself look more attractive. Did she think it would be futile?

"There is great rejoicing in London over the news, as you can imagine." His tongue tripped over itself in his haste to distract attention—not least his own—from what had just happened. "People are planning all manner of celebrations. Before I left London, I received an invitation from the Countess of Maidenhead to a grand masked ball at Winterhill the week after next. What sort of costume do you think I should wear?"

He usually wore the same costume to every masquerade he attended, but perhaps the time had come for a change.

"You could go as a prince!" squealed Sophie, more excited by the notion of a masquerade than the great battle victory it was meant to celebrate.

Rupert shook his head with an indulgent smile. "The Prince Regent may be among the guests and take it ill if I try to rival him."

"What about Robin Hood, then?" Sophie countered. "Or a pirate?"

Rupert did not fancy himself an outlaw, either, not even a heroic one. He glanced toward his elder daughters, hoping they might be able to offer some additional suggestions. Instead, he caught Charlotte and Phoebe exchanging a worried look.

"I'm certain Papa means to propose to Mrs. Cadmore at that masked ball," Charlotte announced for the tenth time since her father had returned to London earlier in the week.

Grace and the girls had just returned from a boat ride on the river. On fine days, she liked to keep them out of doors as much as possible. Physical activity was much better than their studies for keeping their minds off the worrisome subject of their father's remarriage. Grace found it a welcome distraction from her own thoughts about Lord Steadwell.

Ever since she'd realized the perilous direction in which her feelings for him were moving, she had tried to reverse course or, at the very least, keep her heart from becoming any more engaged. She might as well have tried to walk against a violent wind or swim free of a powerful current.

Again and again she reminded herself that he had no intention of losing his heart again. Instead he wanted a marriage of convenience with Mrs. Cadmore. Even if he did not love his new wife, their union would bind him to her for the rest of their days.

If Grace remained at Nethercross while continuing to cherish this futile fancy for him, she would make herself more miserable than she had ever been at the school or after her father's remarriage. It would be even worse if his lordship's union proved unhappy, as she feared it might. She would long to offer him comfort, but that would be improper, if not downright wicked.

"Stop saying that, Charlotte." Phoebe picked up a stone and sent it skipping over the water. "There's no use talking about it if there is nothing we can do to stop Papa."

"We just haven't come up with the right idea yet." Charlotte tried to skip a stone but it hit the water and sank with a loud *plop*. "If we stop thinking about it, we never will."

"I've had all sorts of good ideas," Phoebe grumbled as she searched the riverbank for another stone. "But everyone keeps finding things wrong with them."

"If we cannot stop Papa," Charlotte mused, "we must try to delay him. Give him time to come to his senses."

Sophie had been unusually quiet during her sisters' exchange but now she piped up, "Whose carriage is that coming up the lane? It can't be Papa. Today is only Wednesday."

"Is it the Cadmores?" Charlotte peered toward the

lane. "If it is, I'm going to hide so I don't have to speak to her. I hate the way she looks the house over as if she can't wait to change things around, and the way she coos over us as if we're babies!"

"Charlotte, come back!" Grace called as she moved toward the approaching carriage, beckoning Phoebe and Sophie to her. "You cannot afford to antagonize Mrs. Cadmore."

Charlotte paid no heed.

"I don't think it is the Cadmores," said Phoebe. "I saw a man look out of the carriage window and a lady I didn't recognize."

The carriage came to a halt and a man climbed out. Grace did not recognize him, either. The lady he helped out of the carriage box was another matter. Though she wore a fashionable blue traveling dress rather than the drab garb of a charity pupil, Grace would have known Rebecca Beaton anywhere.

No longer Rebecca Beaton, she reminded herself, but *Lady Benedict.* Seeing her dear friend again made a lump rise in Grace's throat that prevented her from speaking.

But Rebecca showed no sign of recognizing Grace.

"I beg your pardon," she called, as if to a perfect stranger. "Is this the estate of Lord Steadwell?"

"Yes, it is," Sophie replied before Grace had a chance to recover her voice. "Who are you and what do you want with my Papa?"

"Sophie, mind your manners." Grace shushed the child.

But Lord and Lady Benedict gave an indulgent chuckle.

"It is not your Papa we came to call upon, Sophie,

but your governess." Rebecca bent down closer to the child's level. "Where might I find Miss Ellerby?"

Sophie's features clenched in a puzzled frown.

"This is Miss Ella." She pointed to Grace. "What do you want with *her*?"

Rebecca started up from her crouch. Her eyes grew wide with astonishment then narrowed as she peered at her old friend, seeking some familiar feature. "Grace Ellerby, is that truly you?"

"It is." Grace pulled off her cap and took a few stumbling steps toward her friend. "What brings you to Nethercross, Rebecca? It is so good to see you again!"

She'd had no idea what a jolt of joy it would bring her to see one of her school friends in the flesh again after so many years.

"Grace, it is you!" At last, a smile of recognition lit Rebecca's face.

The two friends fell into an affectionate embrace.

When at last they pulled apart, Rebecca introduced her new husband. "It is thanks to Sebastian that I am here. I was disappointed that none of my school friends could come to our wedding, though I quite understood your reasons. Sebastian suggested we take our bridal tour through the kingdom and call upon each of you. It was the most thoughtful wedding present he could have given me."

Grace smiled at Viscount Benedict without the slightest qualm. His obvious devotion to Rebecca made it safe for her to indulge in that innocent pleasantry without worrying where it might lead.

But she addressed her words to Rebecca. "You seem to have found as kind a husband as I could wish for you.

I did so long to attend your wedding, but I had my responsibilities."

She drew the girls forward. "This is Phoebe and Sophie. Their elder sister is around somewhere. Phoebe, will you go find Charlotte and tell her who is here?"

"Yes, Miss Ella." Phoebe dashed off in the direction her sister had gone.

"Charming children." Lord Benedict winked at Sophie. "Miss Ellerby, you appear to have done as fine a job raising them as my dear Rebecca did with her charge, who is now my sister-in-law."

It pleased Grace to hear his lordship praise Hermione, with whom she felt well-acquainted from Rebecca's letters over the years. "I cannot take nearly as much credit for my pupils, sir. I have only been at Nethercross a few months, whereas your wife spent many years at Rose Grange."

"But I had only one pupil to your three," Rebecca protested. "It is obvious the children like you very much, even after such a short time. Isn't that right, Sophie?"

The child gave a vigorous nod. "She doesn't get cross when I wake up with bad dreams. She rubs my head and helps me get back to sleep."

"She used to do the same thing for me when we were at school," said Rebecca. "Even then she had a tender heart for anyone who was upset or lonely."

Her friend's praise touched Grace deeply. "It was the least I could do after the number of times you and Marian stuck up for me. Speaking of Marian, have you heard her news? She managed to get herself a husband before you."

Rebecca did not appear to begrudge their friend getting to the altar ahead of her. "I hope we shall be able to make her husband's acquaintance when we reach Nottinghamshire. From what she told me, I gather their acquaintance began on an even less promising note than Sebastian's and mine. Can you imagine what our old teachers would say if they knew Marian and I had wed two such fine husbands? After all their efforts to impress upon us that we were too poor and plain to aspire to marriage. I'm certain they thought you were the only one of us with the looks to attract a husband."

Her friend's kindly meant remark stung Grace. Her looks had never secured the sincere regard Lord Benedict clearly felt for Rebecca. And no wonder. Superficial charms were only capable of attracting superficial interest.

Fortunately she was spared the necessity of answering when Phoebe returned with Charlotte. Grace introduced Lord Steadwell's eldest daughter to her guests.

"Will Lord and Lady Benedict stay to tea, Miss Ella?" The tone of Charlotte's question was more like a hint.

Grace realized how long she had kept the Benedicts standing outdoors. She hoped they would not feel unwelcome. However, she felt awkward offering them the hospitality of a house that was not hers.

Once again Charlotte came to her rescue. "I hope they will. I should like to hear how you became friends at school and about the others in your circle."

That was all the reassurance Grace needed. With Lord Steadwell away in London, Charlotte was lady of the house. Her wish to have their visitors stay to tea gave Grace the authority she needed to extend the invitation, which was readily accepted.

"Splendid." Charlotte looked in better spirits than she had for weeks. Perhaps Rebecca's visit was just the diversion she and her sisters needed to take their minds off their father's marriage plans. "I'll go along and tell Cook."

"I hope you will tell us all about your wedding," Grace begged Rebecca as they made their way into the house.

While her friend described her joyous nuptials, Grace pulled on her unbecoming cap with a faint stab of regret. It had been such a pleasant sensation to feel the summer breeze ruffle her hair. But she hoped none of the servants had spied her from the house. The last thing she needed was to become the subject of gossip that might reach the ears of Lord Steadwell.

As Grace replaced her cap, Rebecca shot her a questioning glance. Grace replied with a subtle shrug to communicate that she would explain later if they could find a private moment.

The six of them enjoyed a convivial tea. Lord Benedict seemed a trifle awkward to be the only gentleman among five females, but the girls soon drew him out, asking where he lived, how he had come to meet his bride and how many horses he owned. Under cover of their lively conversation, Rebecca and Grace were able to exchange a few quiet words—enough for Grace to learn that her friend was deeply in love with her new husband.

"Every morning I'm afraid I will open my eyes to discover all this happiness is only a dream," Rebecca whispered. "But I am always grateful to discover it is true. Even when I was at odds with Sebastian over his brother's engagement, I could tell what a good man he was. I never imagined he would think of someone like me for a wife."

"I think he is fortunate to have you." Grace reached under the table to give her friend's hand a warm squeeze. "And I am delighted he recognizes his good fortune and makes you so happy."

Her friend's joy in her marriage forced Grace to acknowledge a yearning for that sort of connection with a good man. Though she must admit there was only one man she thought of in that way. Unfortunately, he had no interest in any relationship that might put his heart at risk.

After tea, Lord and Lady Benedict took their leave.

"I know you have your duties," said Rebecca as they departed, "but I hope we can see each other as much as possible while I am in the neighborhood. Would you and the girls care to take a carriage ride with us tomorrow?"

She went on to suggest a number of other outings to which Charlotte, Phoebe and Sophie responded eagerly.

"Don't forget Lord Maidenhead's masquerade," Rebecca's husband reminded her. "We took the liberty of securing you an invitation, Miss Ellerby." The earl reached into his pocket and drew out a handsomely engraved card.

When he offered it to her, Grace drew back as if he were trying to give her a giant spider. "That is kind of you, but I couldn't possibly attend."

"Why not?" Phoebe snatched the invitation from Lord Benedict's hand.

When Grace cried out the child's name in a sharp

tone, Charlotte sprang to her sister's defense. "Phoebe is right, Miss Ella. You must go to the ball!"

Grace could tell by the looks they exchanged that they had some scheme in mind—one that would involve her.

Chapter Eleven

"**Y**ou *have* to go to that ball, Miss Ella!" The girls' pleas grew more and more insistent as the week wore on. "In case Papa tries to propose to Mrs. Cadmore, you must stop him."

"How do you expect me to do that?" Grace tried to resist, though the prospect of dressing up and attending a masquerade tempted her far more than she dared admit. "And how will I even recognize them?"

"It won't be difficult to pick out Papa," Charlotte assured her. "He always wears the same costume. I can draw you a sketch of it. And we can ask Mrs. Cadmore what she means to wear, just for good measure. As for how to stop Papa proposing, I'm sure you will think of something."

"Cause a distraction," Phoebe suggested.

"Spill something on her gown." Sophie's sweet young face twisted in a devious grin.

Grace hated to admit how much the girls' outrageous plan appealed to her. For weeks she had felt helpless to prevent Lord Steadwell from making a grave mistake. The temptation to take some action, no matter how futile, threatened to overcome her scruples.

She made one last attempt to dissuade the girls...and herself. "Even if I do what you ask, it would only delay the inevitable. Your father could still propose to Mrs. Cadmore the next day or the next."

"Perhaps." Charlotte shrugged. "But any delay will give Papa a chance to reconsider. Please say you'll do it, Miss Ella!"

The younger girls joined in a beseeching chorus that Grace could not have withstood even if she'd been far more determined. She did put up a token resistance by reminding them she had no costume fit to attend such a lavish gathering.

"That old gown from the painting fits you very well," Sophie reminded her.

"But surely you father would recognize it from the painting," Grace protested.

"Men never pay that much attention to clothes." Charlotte replied airily.

When Rebecca added her persuasive voice to those of the children, Grace soon found herself talked into doing what she secretly wanted.

The evening of the ball found her gowned and masked, her hair freed from the confines of that ugly old cap and dressed in a becoming style that matched the era of her costume. For the first little while she stuck close to Rebecca and Lord Benedict, but gradually she grew braver. Among the crowd of masked guests, she felt anonymous and free to be herself for the first time since coming to Nethercross.

She had not accepted the invitation for her own amusement, Grace reminded herself. The girls were counting on her to keep watch on their father and prevent him from doing something they all might bitterly regret.

At that moment she spied a lady in a Columbine costume, which was what Mrs. Cadmore had told the girls she would be wearing. Casting a backward glance at her friends on the dance floor, Grace slipped off through the crowd in pursuit. She followed the lady out of the ballroom, down a long gallery and into a large drawing room. When she finally managed to get close enough for a good look at Columbine's escort her spirits sank, for the gentleman was dressed as Punch and stood a full head shorter than Lord Steadwell.

Grace headed back to the ballroom, all the while scanning the crowd for the couple she sought. Suddenly, a man stepped into her path. A little taller than she and rather stout, he wore the flowing robes of an eastern sultan in the most garish mix of colors. His head was swathed in an enormous purple turban.

"Looking for someone, are you, fair lady?" Predatory eyes glittered through the slits of his black mask. "Has your escort been so negligent as to lose you in the crowd?"

"I have no escort, sir. I came with friends. I thought I saw someone I recognized and followed to speak with them, but I was mistaken. Pray excuse me." Grace darted past him, out of the drawing room and back down the gallery.

Then another Columbine caught her eye. Though her brush with the sultan had unnerved her, Grace knew she must concentrate on her mission. Changing course, she made her way back through the gallery to the music room, where a string consort was playing for a dozen couples to dance. After a moment, Grace picked out

Columbine and her partner. This one was a gangly stork of a gentleman dressed as Robin Hood.

"Such a lovely lady, attending a ball with no escort?" A suggestive murmur in her ear made Grace recoil from the odious sultan once again. "That is an unpardonable shame. Pray do me the honor of a dance, fair one, so we may become better acquainted."

"I do not wish to dance, sir." Grace's throat tightened. "I only want to find my friends. Good evening to you."

She spun away and fled to the ballroom only to find no sign of Lord and Lady Benedict. Suddenly the gaze of every gentleman in the room seemed to be following her. Striving to subdue her mounting alarm, she approached a lady in a ruff and farthingale.

"Pardon me. Have you seen a couple who were dancing here a short time ago?" She described the costumes her friends were wearing.

To her relief the woman nodded. "They left after the last dance. In that direction, I believe. Likely in search of refreshment."

Grace thanked the lady and headed off the way she'd been pointed. She almost bumped into another Columbine, but this one was far too tiny to be Mrs. Cadmore. Even if she had answered the lady's description in every particular, Grace was not certain it would have made any difference. Her aim now was to regain the safety of her friends' company.

But they proved every bit as elusive as Lord Steadwell and Mrs. Cadmore. Grace checked a number of rooms to no avail, her unease growing. Where could they be?

She circled around a clutch of chattering, laughing guests only to find her way blocked by the sultan again.

How could it be so difficult to find either of the two couples she sought, while the man she was determined to avoid appeared around every corner?

"We meet again, my dear." His lips spread in a leering grin. "It seems the Fates are conspiring to bring us together. Will you reconsider my invitation to dance? I assure you, it will be a far pleasanter way to pass the time than hurrying about, getting yourself all flushed and bothered. Though the former is quite becoming."

Why must this odious man besiege her with his attentions? Did he think she was playing coy to rouse his interest?

"The Fates may conspire all they like, sir. I have no intention of dancing with you, so pray do not ask me again." She fled from the sultan in a blind panic, not caring which way she went as long as it was away from him.

What had made her think she could attend an event crammed with wealthy, powerful men who felt entitled to take whatever they wanted from a woman? Worse yet she had been foolish enough to flaunt her looks and figure in such a flattering gown, with only the flimsy disguise of a mask to conceal her identity.

Had the fact that Lord Steadwell behaved with honor toward dowdy Miss Ellerby made her forget the liberties other men were eager to take with an attractive woman? Or had she been willing to run that risk in the hope that her master would see her true appearance and be drawn to her? How could her fancy for him have grown to such self-destructive heights when she had done everything in her power to suppress it? Could those efforts have only intensified her feelings—like putting a stopper in the spout of a boiling kettle?

Those thoughts flitted through Grace's mind like a flock of frightened starlings as she strove to escape the lecher who pursued her. But they only added to her growing alarm, which the predator seemed to scent. The long curled toes of his slippers did not slow him down. At last he cornered her in a distant sitting room where refreshments were being dispensed.

"Let me help you to a cup of punch, dear lady," he insisted. "Then perhaps you will feel more like dancing."

Though Grace told herself her virtue was safe with so many people around, no one seemed to notice or care that she was being harassed by this horrible man. His relentless pursuit revived terrifying memories of the night she'd returned to her quarters and discovered her master's uncle waiting for her.

He had flattered her and offered to make her his mistress. When she declined and tried to flee, he had blocked her way and attempted to take by force what she refused to surrender willingly. Somehow she had fought her way free, escaped from him and hid below the stairs until the next morning when she'd crept out, packed and given immediate notice. She hadn't bothered to tell her mistress what happened—she'd learned the folly of doing that in her previous position. She sensed Mrs. Hesketh suspected something amiss, though the lady did not bother to seek the truth. Perhaps guilt for that had led her to give Grace the good reference.

"Please, sir, let me be!" Grace implored her pursuer. Though only a few inches taller than she, the sultan looked easily capable of overpowering her. "I have told you I do not wish to dance. I am trying to find my friends."

She peered about for any sign of Rebecca and Lord Benedict. Why had she been so daft to stray from the protection of their company?

"They are poor friends if they let you wander off, my beauty." He seized her hand and subjected it to the assault of his demanding lips. The sensation made Grace's gorge rise. The heavy musk of sandalwood that wafted off him sickened her further. "Make me your new friend and I assure you I will be more constant."

"Please, sir, keep your distance! The last thing I want from you is constancy!" She wanted to scream for help, but her fear of drawing attention to herself was even greater than her terror of him. Since she'd left school and the protection of her friends, harsh experience had taught her that no one would come to her rescue.

Had he been there long enough? Rupert peered around one of the less crowded refreshment rooms at the Countess of Maidenhead's Victory Masquerade and wondered if anyone would notice if he went home early.

The evening had not turned out at all the way he'd planned. He had been so certain a masked ball would provide the perfect setting to tender his marriage proposal. In the convivial atmosphere, with their faces partially hidden, he could pretend that he and Mrs. Cadmore were different people entirely. That might provide the spur he needed to overcome his irrational reluctance.

He had been all dressed and ready to set out when he received a message from Dungrove that Mrs. Cadmore would not be able to attend the masquerade after all. Young Henry had fallen ill and she could not bring herself to leave his side. Rupert did not blame her for putting the welfare of her son above all other considerations. After all, it was her motherly devotion he most valued in his prospective bride. Yet he regretted this missed opportunity to propose. When would he find another quite so good?

Part of him wanted to shed this costume and spend the evening at home since his chief purpose in attending had evaporated. Then he caught sight of his reflection in the looking glass and realized that would not be wise. His costume was called a *bauta*. The sweeping cloak and cowl topped with a large black tricorne were the traditional disguise worn in Venice during Carnivale. Its featureless white mask covered the entire face except the mouth and chin. His uncle had brought one back from his Grand Tour. Rupert had worn it a number of times over the years, dismissing Annabelle's claim that it defeated the purpose of a masquerade to always wear the same costume.

If only he were not so well known by his Venetian *bauta,* he might have stayed away from tonight's masquerade and no one would have been the wiser. But he did not want his absence to be noted and commented upon. It would appear unpatriotic and nothing could be further from the truth. He loved this land and its people. He rejoiced that it was safe from conquest at last. He honored the sacrifice of those who had fought to keep it free. Attending an evening's entertainment was little enough he could do to show his gratitude.

Yet he knew better than to suppose he would enjoy the evening for its own sake. He'd never been comfortable in large crowds. The only thing that had made such events bearable in the past was Annabelle's enjoyment of them. He had been content to bask in her pleasure. Left to his own devices he preferred to stay at home, savoring a quiet stroll under the linden trees or watching the sun set and the first stars appear in the evening sky.

The masquerade was well under way when Rupert arrived. It seemed at least half the *ton* had made the trek into Berkshire for the countess's ball. Every room was packed with garishly costumed guests drinking and talking loudly. The warm, still air hung heavy with the conflicting scents of expensive perfume. It made Rupert's stomach roil.

Picking his way through the celebrating throng, he acknowledged the hearty greetings of several people he did not recognize but who clearly knew him. At last he found a less crowded room, drawn there by the whisper of a breeze wafting through a pair of glass doors that opened onto the countess's magnificent gardens. Rupert collected a cup of punch from the refreshment table and retired to a spot near the open doors.

An hour later, as he was debating whether it was too early to head home, he became aware of a disturbance nearby. A man in the garb of an Oriental sultan was making a nuisance of himself with a fair-haired beauty. Something about the lady seemed familiar to Rupert, though he could not guess who she might be. She wore a Stuart-era gown of coral pink with a full skirt and enormous puffed sleeves trimmed with lace. Her golden curls were pulled into two bunches of ringlets, framing her delicate features. She looked soft, feminine and vulnerable to the unwanted attentions of the scoundrel who pursued her so relentlessly.

"Please, sir, let me be." Rupert overheard her beg the sultan, "I have told you I do not wish to dance. I am trying to find my friends."

"They are poor friends if they let you wander off, my beauty. Make me your new friend and I assure you I will be more constant." With that the scoundrel seized her hand and pressed it to his lips again and again as if he meant to devour it.

The lady shrank from his attentions. "Please, sir, keep your distance! The last thing I want from you is constancy!"

Rupert's pulse thundered with outrage that he was hard-pressed to contain. Slamming his punch cup down on the refreshment table, he strode toward the pair and slid between the sultan and his victim. "The lady asked you to leave her alone, sir. I suggest you behave like a gentleman and withdraw."

The sultan's thick lips bowed in a sinister scowl. "And what if I ignore your suggestion?"

"Then I shall phrase it as a demand." Rupert lowered his voice to a menacing rumble. "One you would ignore at your peril."

His adversary's gaze wavered. "Want her for yourself, do you? See how far you get with the icy little prude!"

With that he stormed off, deliberately bumping into a footman and sending a tray of refreshments crashing to the floor.

Rupert spun around, expecting to glimpse nothing more than the lady's pink skirts as she disappeared into the crowd. To his considerable surprise he found her still standing there.

"Thank you for your assistance, sir." She dropped a rather wobbly curtsy. "It was most gallant of you to intervene on my behalf."

Her voice was breathless and high-pitched, yet Rupert fancied he had heard it somewhere before. Could this be one of the debutantes he had met at Almacks? Surely he would not have been so quick to dismiss her. "Pay no heed to that scoundrel's malicious claim that I only chased him away to acquire your company for myself. Nothing could be further from the truth. However, if you would care to linger in my vicinity, it might discourage any other such rogues who would try to force their attentions upon you."

"That is kind of you to offer, sir." She regarded him with a wary air, as if trying to decide whether he was any better than the predator he had frightened off. "But would it not interfere with your enjoyment of the evening to have a strange woman following you about?"

The fierce emotions that had possessed him a few moments earlier now melted away under the influence of the lady's quiet charm. His lips relaxed into a smile. "Quite the contrary. In the first place my enjoyment of such proceedings is not that great. And in the second, being shadowed by a mysterious beauty strikes me as a rather pleasant novelty."

The visible portion of her face took on a cast only a few shades lighter than her gown. "Pardon my curiosity, but what are you doing here if you do not enjoy such events?"

Without mentioning Mrs. Cadmore's name or his intentions, Rupert explained that the person he had planned to accompany had been prevented from attending at the last moment.

"I still believe our victory is an event worth celebrating," he concluded. Suddenly he was glad he had decided to attend the masquerade after all.

Yet something about his explanation seemed to alarm the lady. She drew a sharp breath and her slender frame grew tense. Or perhaps it was something else altogether.

"Forgive me." He made an apologetic bow. "I should have asked if you are quite recovered from the fright that wretched bounder gave you. Would a cup of punch revive you? Or perhaps you would prefer to find a seat in the garden and let the fresh air calm you. I would be happy to stand guard at a distance and make certain you are not disturbed."

She cast a longing glance toward the open doors. "That does sound pleasant. But I really must locate my friends."

So that had not been an excuse to fend off the sultan's advances. Rupert tried to quell an unaccountable sting of disappointment. "If you would like me to accompany you on your search, I am at your service. At least it would provide me with a useful occupation."

After taking a moment to consider his offer, the lady nodded, making her golden curls bounce in the most winsome manner. "I would appreciate your assistance, though I fear it may be difficult to locate my friends in this crowd."

Rupert found himself curiously untroubled by the prospect of a long, fruitless search in the lady's company. In fact, their quest proved even more enjoyable than he'd hoped. From room to room he followed her, always hovering close enough to discourage any other men from approaching her. At the same time, he tried to keep a respectful distance between them so she would not feel threatened by his presence. Each time they exchanged a few words, he racked his memory to recall where he had heard her voice before.

After they had peered into a number of rooms to no avail, Rupert asked, "Can you describe how your friends are dressed? Two pair of eyes may work better to spot them."

"An excellent suggestion." She leaned closer and raised her voice to carry over the loud conversations around them. "The gentleman is dressed as King Arthur and the lady as Helen of Troy."

The most ridiculous quiver of satisfaction ran through Rupert when she failed to mention a third gentleman who might have been her escort. He told himself not to be so daft. It should not matter to him whether the lady was spoken for. He was about to ask another woman to be his wife. Yet he could not suppress a rush of relief that his plans for the evening had gone awry.

Though he kept diligent watch for the lady's friends, Rupert's spirits rose as more and more time passed without a glimpse of them. At last he and his mysterious companion found themselves back in the refreshment room where they'd started.

"I am sorry to have taken up so much of your time, sir—" she let him help her to a cup of punch "—with nothing gained for your efforts but a thirst."

Rupert took a sip of the cool, tart compound of orange and lemon juices sweetened with sugar syrup and spiced with a hint of cinnamon and cloves. The punch was almost as welcome refreshment as her company.

He gave a cheerful shrug. "For your sake, I am sorry we were not able to locate your friends. For myself, I have no such regrets. Our search passed the time much more agreeably than I would have done if left to my own devices."

Rupert doffed his oversize hat and waved it to fan himself. He longed to venture outside for a breath of cooler air but he could not bring himself to abandon the lady.

She seemed to divine his thoughts. "Does your earlier invitation to take a stroll in the garden still hold, sir? After wading through such a crush of humanity, a little peace and coolness would be most welcome."

"To me, as well." The only boon more welcome at that moment was the opportunity to savor more of her company in quiet and privacy.

After her disagreeable encounter with the sultan, Rupert would have understood if the lady shrank from being alone with any man. He was flattered and touched by her demonstration of trust in his honor, especially after so brief an acquaintance in which they had not even exchanged names. This mysterious lady, who he'd known less than an hour, engaged his interest far more than his prospective bride.

Did she also suspect a previous acquaintance between them? Rupert could not escape the sense of familiarity. But the harder he strove to place her, the more her identity eluded him. Besides, part of him resented any thought that distracted him from the enjoyment of her company.

As they wandered out into the moonlit garden together, Rupert fancied his disguise somehow hid him from his old heartache and fear of future hurt. Suddenly he wanted to live again. Not just for the sake of his children and Nethercross, but to experience the divine gifts of life—and perhaps love—to their richest depths. Perhaps he had been wrong to sacrifice all his hope for future happiness upon the altar of safety.

Someone else had tried to tell him that, but he had not been able to understand until tonight.

The gentleman in the black garb and strange white mask was the very one Grace had set out to find. When he first strode to her rescue, she had been too surprised and grateful to notice he was wearing the very costume Charlotte had described. In any case, he appeared to be alone. Only after the gentleman explained how he had come to be at the masquerade by himself did she realize his true identity.

Knowing there was no fear of his lordship proposing to Mrs. Cadmore that evening, Grace had meant to return home at once and share her good news with his daughters. But to do that she must first find her friends while trying to avoid that beastly sultan and others like him. Against her better judgment, she'd accepted Lord Steadwell's offer of assistance.

But as they searched in vain for the Benedicts and his lordship showed no sign of recognizing her, Grace began to wonder if she ought to take advantage of this incognito meeting. Since her previous efforts to suppress her feelings for the gentleman had only intensified them, perhaps indulging those feelings might break the dangerous hold he had gained over her heart. Tonight might be her only opportunity to find out without risking the life she had made for herself at Nethercross.

Plucking up her courage, she asked if he might accompany her on a stroll in the garden.

His swift acceptance made her heart flutter, like a butterfly emerging from its drab, safe cocoon to spread its glorious wings for the very first time. Was she truly seeking to purge her feelings, as prudence demanded, or was she only using that as an excuse to indulge her forbidden fancy? Her rebellious heart refused to consider the question.

Once outside, the frantic clamor of the ball gave way to the whisper of fresh night breezes subtly sweetened with the aroma of country flowers. A welcome sense of ease stole over Grace as she inhaled a deep draft of that cool, flower-scented air. "I am in your debt, sir. First you came to my rescue, then you gave me your protection and assistance. How can I ever repay you?"

He dismissed her suggestion with an airy wave of his hand. "What need is there for repayment of services you never requested? Do they not say virtue is its own reward?"

Before Grace could answer he continued, "Not that I claim my actions were *virtuous*. That sounds insufferably self-righteous. I only mean to say I acted of my own accord. Even if you did owe me a debt, the pleasure of your company would be more than sufficient payment."

The music and raised voices from the party had muted to a pleasant backdrop for the soft rustle of her skirts and their unhurried footsteps on the brickwork path that wound through the flowerbeds and herbaceous borders. The pleasure of *his* company was worth more to Grace than she dared reckon.

"That is high praise, for the assistance you provided was invaluable to me. All the more so because none of the other guests seemed disposed to intervene on my behalf."

"That is to their shame, not to my credit." His tone

took on a sharp edge of scorn. "I do not approve of the way some people cast off their principles when they put on a mask. I doubt that scoundrel in the purple turban would have dared accost you in so reprehensible a manner if you had met at an assembly where his face and name were known."

"Perhaps I share some of the blame," Grace ventured. It was a secret fear that had hounded her ever since Captain Townsend had offered to make her his mistress rather than his wife. "If I had only dressed more modestly, rather than in a manner likely to attract attention…"

"Nonsense!" His retort cut through the night air like a switch, yet it did not alarm Grace, for she knew his vexation was not directed at her. "No woman should be obliged to conceal her beauty to prevent men from taking liberties. Part of the reason I came to your aid was that I wanted to show you we men are not all like him."

"I know that," she murmured without true conviction.

For years she had regarded all men as alike in that respect and she'd treated them accordingly. But since coming to Nethercross, she had begun to realize some men were different. *He* was different. His actions this evening only proved what she'd believed about him for some time. His declaration about women not hiding their beauty helped ease her feeling of responsibility for the harassment she had suffered.

"But let us not dwell on that unpleasantness," he suggested. "I do not wish to oppress your spirits."

"Nor do I," Grace agreed. "Let us enjoy this quiet time together in our unsociable way."

"I would not call myself unsociable." He tempered his protest with a wry chuckle. "I quite like good company in small doses and familiar surroundings."

"How small a dose do you favor?" She teased him in a flirtatious way mousy Miss Ellerby would never dare.

"Usually more than one," he quipped back. Then his voice softened. "But tonight I reckon it is a perfect number."

Did he mean that the way it sounded? He had no idea who she was and must assume she was equally ignorant of his identity. He might think he could say anything to her without fear of consequences. Perhaps he, too, had inconvenient feelings he sought to purge before he embarked on a marriage in which love would play no part.

For this one night, Grace felt free to speak words she had never dared address to him before—words she would be obliged to lock away in her heart beginning tomorrow. Might they place less of a burden on her heart if she gave them their freedom now?

"Tonight it is my favorite number," she murmured in reply, "provided *you* are that one."

His step slowed even more. "You sense it, too?"

"I beg your pardon?"

"This." He gestured from him to her and back again. "Between us a…bond…or connection."

He struggled to explain something he seemed not to understand himself but hoped she might. "I feel as if I know you far better than our brief acquaintance would allow. Is it possible we have met before?"

How could she reply to that threatening question? Those delightful little bubbles in Grace's stomach rushed upward to clog her throat. Must she deny her feelings for him with an outright falsehood? Or did she dare tell him the truth and trust that he might understand?

Chapter Twelve

What had made him blurt out that question? As his mysterious, yet oddly familiar, companion inhaled a sharp little gasp and froze in her tracks, Rupert cursed his blunder.

The whole point of a masquerade was the secrecy in which it shrouded the guests' identities, freeing them from the bonds of strict propriety to behave in ways they might not otherwise. He had railed against it in the case of men like the lecherous sultan. But for others—ladies in particular—the motives and consequences might be far more innocent.

Would his charming companion have dared steal away with him into the moonlit garden if her reputation had not been shielded by that mask? Now his intrusive question threatened to rip away her flimsy protection. Might she consider it almost as brazen a liberty as the sultan had tried to take with her? Might she flee from him, too, and perhaps from the masquerade itself?

If he frightened her away, he might never discover who she was and never learn whether the feelings she stirred in him were genuine.

"Forgive me!" he cried before she could turn and flee. "I do not mean to demand your identity."

"You don't?" Even the deep shadows of a summer night could not conceal her relief.

Rupert shook his head. "I only wanted to explain this unaccountable familiarity I sense between us. But perhaps I am mistaken—deceived by a trick of the moonlight."

"I feel as if I know you, too." She began walking again. "You are Hercules and Galahad and every fairytale hero who ever came to the aid of a damsel in distress."

Could it be as simple as that? Part of him wanted to accept her explanation. Was his head so full of his daughters' Mother Goose stories that the beautiful lady he'd rescued came to represent every fairy-tale princess? Was that why he'd taken such an immediate fancy to her as well—because that was how love blossomed in those stories?

Love? Rupert chided himself for letting that foolish notion even enter his head. This mysterious beauty engaged his interest to the point of fascination, but that was a different thing entirely. Yet he could not deny it was the closest he had felt to that heady, all-consuming emotion since Annabelle. He'd assumed his capacity for that sort of feeling had died with her. Or perhaps it had been channeled into his devotion to their daughters.

Part of him tried to resist his overwhelming attraction to the masked lady with her air of wistful innocence. He feared such feelings might be a betrayal of his late wife's memory. And yet his heart welcomed this unexpected reawakening after a long fallow season of grief. It made him question whether he was wrong to seek a marriage that would be nothing more than a "practical arrangement" unsanctified by love.

"I am no storybook hero," he warned, not wanting her enamored of a false image, "just a simple man who enjoys simple country pleasures."

He longed to tell her all about himself and learn everything about her—her tastes, her beliefs, her past experiences. But would she consider such questions a further effort to discover her identity?

"I see no reason why a simple countryman cannot also be a hero in his own way if he does his duty and treats those around him with honor and kindness." Something in the lady's voice seemed to suggest that she still considered him a hero in spite of his protests to the contrary.

It did not sound as if she were referring to a nebulous ideal but to him in particular, praising qualities she knew he possessed. While her words gratified him, they bolstered his conviction that they had a previous acquaintance. Could it be that she recognized him in his well-known *bauta* but he did not know her? Though that would put him at a disadvantage, Rupert could not resent her for it.

He wondered what subjects they could chat about without revealing too many personal details.

"A very fine night, is it not?" He fairly cringed at his own words. How tiresome of him to talk about the weather. Too much of that and his mystery lady might flee back indoors, prepared to risk the sultan's liberties rather than be bored out of her wits.

"Very fine, indeed." She did not sound bored—not yet at least.

But he must find something more interesting to say

that might make her want to remain in his company. "The moon is bright. I fancy I can see human features on its pale face—the man in the moon, looking down on us from the night sky."

As a topic of conversation that was a little better at least.

"I see the face." She stopped on an ornamental stone bridge, which spanned a narrow stream that wound down the hill. "But I have always thought it looked more like a woman's. See how delicate the features are?"

"Perhaps." He came to stand beside her, close enough to satisfy his compelling inclination to be near her but not so close that it might frighten her away. "But a bald woman seems rather improbable."

His quip coaxed forth a melodic trill of laughter that blended with the trickle of water beneath the bridge. "I suppose it does. But what if the night sky was her black hair adorned with diamond-studded combs?"

Even that could not compare to the beauty of the lady who spoke those words, though Rupert guessed the silver moonlight did not flatter her. He longed to see her golden curls kissed by the first rays of dawn, while the rose-colored horizon echoed the hue of her gown and her lips.

"But what does that beauty signify—" his companion sighed "—when the lady in the moon looks so mournful? I wonder what sorrow afflicts her?"

"Loneliness perhaps," Rupert suggested. "Or grief at being parted from her beloved, the sun."

"Loneliness is a great misery." A poignant note in the lady's voice assured Rupert she had experienced those emotions for herself, perhaps even longer and deeper than he. But how that could be for someone with so many attractive qualities, he could not fathom.

She looked toward the great house all lit up from within and fairly pulsing with the sounds of revelry. "It is possible to be lonely even in the midst of a crowd. Indeed I believe a person can feel more isolated than ever when all around them are making merry."

"That is true." Rupert recalled his miserable forays into London society in search of a wife. "Yet all it takes is the company of one truly congenial person to dispel that feeling."

Her hands rested on the railing of the bridge. Rupert edged his left hand over, not to cover hers, but to lay beside it, barely touching. He held his breath, fearing she might move away and break the tenuous contact between them. To his relief she did not.

A ripple of warmth spread through his hand and up his arm toward his heart. Prudence warned him he had no business engaging in such conduct when he was on the verge of proposing to another woman. No, his freshly stirred heart responded, what he had no business doing was planning to wed a woman he did not love. Perhaps meeting this masked lady tonight was a warning to that effect. Suddenly he pitied anyone who did not feel as alive and alight as he did—even a great cold orb of rock circling the earth.

"Perhaps the fireworks will cheer up our mournful moon maiden," he suggested.

"Fireworks?" his companion echoed, though not in the tone of excitement he expected. In that small strip of flesh where their hands touched, he fancied he could feel her pulse pick up speed.

"Just before midnight." He arched his hand then lowered it again to brush against hers in a subtle caress. "To celebrate our glorious victory and signal the traditional unmasking."

He could scarcely wait for that, to see her entire face in all its beauty and discover if they were already acquainted. Where their acquaintance might go from there, it was far too soon to speculate.

But his heart had its hopes.

The prospect of unmasking at midnight alarmed Grace more than if a Roman candle were aimed directly at her with its fuse lit. Her feet itched to flee as fast as they could carry her. Yet she could not bear to bring this sweet interlude to an end one moment sooner than she must.

This evening walk and chat with Rupert reminded her of the ones they had shared at Nethercross. It was a hundred times better, though, for she was not obliged to constantly guard her tongue to keep from betraying her feelings to him. As the mysterious masked lady, she was able to say things Miss Ellerby would never dare and thrill to words he would never utter to his daughters' governess.

Had his brush with the masked lady given him second thoughts about marrying Mrs. Cadmore? Grace hoped and believed it must have. He was too honorable a gentleman to behave with a woman as he had with her if he still intended to wed another. Even the innocent contact between their hands was a greater intimacy than he would have undertaken if he meant to pledge himself to someone else.

The girls would be delighted to hear that.

But Grace knew better than to let herself believe

Rupert Kendrick truly cared for her. If he had, then surely he would have expressed his feelings to Miss Ellerby, in spite of her plain appearance and humble station. He only imagined himself smitten with a lady of beauty. Such feelings had no more substance than a fairy tale, no more truth than a masquerade.

For all that, she sensed they were coming to know one another on a different, deeper level through tonight's conversation. Seeking to avoid subjects that might reveal too much about their identities, they spoke instead about the feelings common to every person regardless of outward appearance or rank. It was as if their masks and costumes allowed them to shed the facades they wore in daily life to reveal glimpses of their truest selves.

"Tell me," she asked him at last, "what is it you want from life and the future?"

They were still standing beside one another on the ornamental stone bridge, the sides of their hands barely touching. Yet Grace found herself as intensely aware of that glancing contact as if it had been a full embrace.

Rupert gave her question several moments of silent reflection, perhaps searching his heart for a nugget of precious truth to offer her. "I used to think I wanted to be the kind of hero you mentioned—doing my duty to those who relied upon me without seeking anything for myself. At least nothing beyond a bit of relief from the ache that has gnawed at my heart for so long."

"But that has changed?" Grace prompted him in a gentle murmur as she would to one of the daughters who sought to unburden herself. "What is it you want now?"

He shook his head slowly. "It is too soon to tell. I only know that…meeting you here tonight has made me question whether perhaps I am settling for too little. You have made me hope life may have something better in store for me yet."

She had done that for him? Grace's eyes tingled. There was so much she wished she could do for him, so many things she would have liked to give him, but this one favor might satisfy her.

"Am I a fool," he asked, "to raise my hopes on the strength of a chance meeting and a few brief hours with you? Am I intolerably selfish to think of disregarding my duty to those I hold most dear?"

"Never!" She pressed her hand harder against his, wishing she dared offer him greater reassurance. "Even on the strength of a chance meeting and a few hours, I know you are neither foolish nor selfish. You deserve far more from life than you were prepared to seek. I am certain those you care for would not want you to give up any hope of happiness on their account. If it were me I could not bear that."

Her voice caught and she was obliged to pause to gather her composure. "I hope with all my heart you will find a way to do your duty without sacrificing the happiness you deserve."

"Perhaps I will." He lifted his little finger and brought it to rest upon hers. "Perhaps I *have*."

Tonight might be an elusive fancy, with no more substance than moonshine, but the happiness it brought Grace was as genuine as any she'd ever felt in her life.

"What about you?" he asked in a murmur warm with concern yet shaded with doubt. "Do you want the things to which most women aspire—a brilliant marriage, children, a glittering social life?"

What did she want? Grace had never truly considered

that question until now. What had been the use in wanting things her circumstances made impossible? Now she searched her heart and struggled to articulate what she found there. "I would prefer a soft, steady glow to brilliance and glitter. I would rather have tender devotion, or even simple friendship, than the most advantageous marriage without love. As for children, I did not always have a hankering for them, but now I do."

She wanted children and thanks to him she had them—three girls, each so different in her way yet all so dear. They were hers to teach and raise and love.

"There is one more thing I want." She had not meant to speak of it but since she'd relaxed the guard on her tongue the words slipped out.

He had asked and tonight Grace could not deny him.

"I want to be valued for the person I am inside, not just my outward appearance."

Had she given herself away? The moment she spoke those words Grace feared he would recognize the sentiment Miss Ellerby had confessed to him. Did she *want* him to guess her identity, even if it risked the safe, satisfying life she had found at Nethercross?

Rupert hesitated to reply. Instead he tilted his head slightly, as if straining to catch an elusive whisper. When he turned toward her, Grace could not resist the impulse to face him.

"You cannot blame people for being attracted to such a lovely appearance." He raised the hand that had so recently pressed against hers to graze her cheek with a stroke no heavier than the brush of a butterfly's wing. "From what I can tell, you are every bit as beautiful inside as out."

Her lips parted slightly to release a quivering sigh.

Perhaps he could care for her in a way no other man had—merging his respect and sympathy for Miss Ellerby with his attraction to the masked lady.

"There is something I must tell you." Grace wished she could see his eyes, to judge his reaction. But they were obscured by his mask in the moonlight.

"Speak then." His fingers glided over her cheek again. "You have my complete attention."

Grace gathered her breath and her courage.

Then suddenly the night sky erupted in a thunderous explosion of light and color. Grace recoiled as she might from a nearby musket shot—and with just cause. The fireworks aroused all her fears to a shrieking pitch that was impossible to ignore.

In a few moments Rupert would remove his mask to reveal his identity and he would expect her to do the same. Would he recognize her then? Or would the moonlight, the shadows and his refusal to think of his daughters' governess in a romantic way all conspire to keep him blind? Grace could not bear that, for it would make a cruel mockery of his claim to admire her for more than her appearance. And it would destroy her belief that he was different from those other men who'd pursued her.

And what if he did realize that the object of his fancy was the same woman who had lived under his roof and raised his daughters for the past several months? Would the revelation delight him as she'd hoped, or would he react with shock and suspicion? As the fireworks splashed across the night sky in all their violent splendor, Grace pictured Lord Steadwell demanding answers and questioning her motives for coming here tonight.

Might he accuse her of spying on him? And if he did,

could she truthfully deny it? Worse yet, he might suspect she had attended the ball with the deliberate intention of luring him away from the woman he'd planned to marry.

The raging colors overhead bathed his white mask in lurid shades of red and orange. Grace could picture his dark brows hunched over blazing eyes, his upper lip wrinkled in scorn. She recalled such looks all too well from other men when she had denied them what they wanted from her. Their reactions had made her fear for her safety and her virtue, yet they were nothing compared to the damage this man could wreak upon her heart if he chose. Her feelings for Rupert Kendrick armed him with a powerful weapon—one perhaps capable of destroying her.

The sound of the fireworks drew many of the masquerade guests out to the garden. Before long a substantial crowd had gathered around the little bridge. While Rupert's gaze was fixed upward at the spectacle unfolding above them, Grace seized her chance to protect her heart and the happiness she had found in her present position. She slipped between a pair of tall revelers, then ducked behind the shrubbery. Once out of sight of Lord Steadwell, she plucked up the front of her skirts and fled the garden as fast as she could run.

Only when she was quite certain he could not easily track her down did Grace pause to wonder how she would get home. Nethercross was only a few miles away from Winterhill, but it was not a distance to walk in such an elaborate old gown and a pair of borrowed slippers that were beginning to pinch. But neither did she dare accept the offer of a drive from anyone except Rebecca and her husband.

Thinking of her friends gave Grace an idea, though she feared it might be in vain. On the unlikely chance that Lord and Lady Benedict were still at the party, she checked the spot where they had parked their carriage. If it was still there, she could take refuge inside until they were ready to leave.

To her surprise, the carriage stood exactly where they had left it. Not only that, their coachman lingered nearby rather than gathering with the others around a small fire some distance away.

"Miss, it's you!" he cried when she appeared. "I was beginning to worry. Her ladyship felt unwell and they couldn't find any sign of you so they borrowed another carriage to take them back to the inn. His lordship said you'd likely come back here sooner or later and I should fetch you home."

"I looked for them, too," Grace announced in a breathless rush as he helped her into the carriage. "We must have missed one another in the crowd. I only wish I'd thought to check here sooner."

But then she might have missed out on her innocent tryst with Rupert, Grace reflected as the driver climbed onto his perch and the carriage rolled away. Though she dared not risk her future on what had passed between them this evening, she would remember it always.

Bright fire soared across the sky, bursting into a shimmer of falling stars. At the same time, vivid emotions lit up Rupert's heart with forgotten wonder.

It was the sort of night when nursery tales might come true with their promises of *love at first sight* and *happily ever after*. Of course he did not love the woman he had only met that evening and whose name he still did not know. But he had been in love before and knew his feelings already went deeper than a superficial attraction to her looks alone. How much stronger those feelings would grow as he came to know her better, he could only guess.

Breathtaking as the fireworks were, Rupert doubted they would hold a candle to his companion's beauty once her face was unmasked. Then he would know for certain if they had a previous acquaintance.

He glanced back down at her, intending to draw her close in case she felt threatened by the surge of other guests surrounding them. But when his gaze fell to the spot where she had been standing only a moment ago, the lady was no longer there.

His first impulse was to call her name at the top of his lungs, but that was impossible since he did not know it. Instead he peered this way and that, searching desperately for a glimpse of pink skirts or golden curls. In more than one direction his view was blocked by clusters of guests, staring skyward and exclaiming over each new burst of color. Rupert no longer cared about the fireworks. They were nothing but a loud, gaudy distraction from his search.

He pushed his way through one knot of spectators, ignoring their indignant protests. He scarcely thought of them as people—neighbors, political allies, perhaps even relatives. To him they were only animated statues that got in the way of what he was trying to do. Surrounded by people he'd never felt more alone—just as his companion had observed.

He latched onto someone's arm. "Have you seen a lady in a pink gown? She was here just a moment ago."

The owner of the arm pushed him away roughly with a curse he probably deserved.

"Please." Rupert tried someone else, forcing himself to show better manners. He repeated his question.

"She brushed past me," came the reply, shouted to carry over the noise of the fireworks and the crowd. "Headed back toward the house, I think."

Rupert shouted his thanks and plunged off through the press of revelers, craning his neck and hoping for a glimpse of the lady.

With one final ear-splitting flare the fireworks display ended and guests began removing their masks. Rupert threw off his hat, whipped back his cowl and tore the white mask from his face.

Where was the lady in pink and why had she disappeared so abruptly?

He ran through the house, which was now nearly deserted. He peered into every room, but with no more success than he'd had out in the garden.

She must be there somewhere. Rupert plowed his fingers through his hair. He must find her to make certain she was not in any difficulty and to demand an explanation for her sudden disappearance. Did she think he would not notice her absence or not care that she had abandoned him without a word? If so, she was wrong on both counts.

He had noticed and he did care. He cared far more than he had expected—far more than he'd wanted to. Especially in light of the manner in which she'd slipped away. One moment she'd been there by his side with everything ahead of them. The next, she was gone without an explanation or even a proper goodbye.

Was he thinking of his mysterious companion or his

late wife? Rupert wondered as anger and a sense of abandonment warred within him. Though he knew Annabelle had never intended to desert him, he could not deny the effect of her death upon him. Tonight's events echoed it far too closely for his peace of mind.

Determined to get some answers, he stationed himself outside the front entrance of the Maidenhead's country house and kept watch for the lady. By the time the last few stragglers departed in the early hours of the morning, it was clear to him that she had long since gone. If he had not been such a practical man, Rupert might have questioned whether he had imagined his whole encounter with the masked lady.

Now he could only wonder what had made her take flight. The timing suggested she did not want him to discover her identity. What reason could she have for that unless there was something more than her face she wished to hide? Could she have been a married woman dallying with his affections for an evening's amusement?

In the midst of so many unanswered questions, there were two things he knew for certain. The first was that he'd been a fool to throw his accustomed caution to the winds and pursue a deceitful stranger. The other was that he had been right in seeking to choose a wife with his sensible head rather than his foolish heart. This incident renewed his intention to propose to Barbara Cadmore at the earliest opportunity.

Chapter Thirteen

Grace stood in a moon-dappled garden with Rupert Kendrick. He had removed his white mask, allowing her to look into his eyes. There she glimpsed a soft glow of admiration and a tantalizing glimmer of attraction. They echoed the very feelings that swelled in her heart for him. He raised his hand to caress her cheek…or so she expected. Instead his fingers clutched the corner of her mask and tore it from her face. Recognition dawned upon him, extinguishing all the light and warmth with which he had regarded her only a moment before. In their place glittered cold disdain and suspicion.

With a rough jolt, Grace woke from her disturbing dream. Her eyes flew open and she gasped to find a pair of round blue eyes staring at her.

"Good morning, Miss Ella," Sophie chirped. "Did you have a nice time at the ball last night? I hope you didn't lose a slipper."

For a moment Grace was too disoriented to make sense of what was clearly intended as a jest. Then she understood. "Like Cinderella, you mean? I am happy to report I returned home with both of the slippers Lady Benedict was kind enough to loan me."

She *had* fled the ball at midnight, but Grace did not intend to mention that to her imaginative young pupil.

The sound of their conversation drew Charlotte and Phoebe from the nursery.

"What happened last night, Miss Ella?" asked Charlotte. "Did Papa try to propose to Mrs. Cadmore? Were you able to stop him?"

"I was not obliged to." Grace sat up, stretched and yawned. "Mrs. Cadmore was not able to attend the masquerade after all."

The girls gave a cheer and clambered onto her bed. Though Grace knew it might be a mistake to encourage such familiarity, she could not bring herself to order them off. Instead, she wrapped her arms around Sophie's shoulders and cast a smile at the older girls. It was good to see them all looking so relieved and happy.

Grace could not decide how she felt about the events of the previous night. Though she feared she had taken a terrible risk for nothing, she could not bring herself to be sorry she had shared a moonlit evening of chaste intimacy with Rupert. It was an encounter she would remember and treasure always.

"Did Papa go to the masquerade?" Phoebe's nose wrinkled in a doubtful frown. "Perhaps he went to Dungrove instead and proposed to her there."

Grace shook her head emphatically. "Your father was at the masquerade all evening. I spoke with him."

"And he didn't know you?" asked Charlotte. "Or recognize the dress from the painting? I told you men never notice clothes."

"What did the two of you talk about?" Sophie demanded.

"This and that." Not eager to dwell on the subject,

Grace scrambled out of bed. "He said I looked familiar, but he could not think who I might be. Now we all need to get dressed and you must help me put that pink gown back to its trunk before anyone else sees it. We don't want your father to know I was there keeping watch on him."

Her words drove any further questions from the children's minds. They bounded off her bed and away to get dressed.

As Grace donned her ugliest dress and hid her hair beneath her most unflattering cap she recalled how pleasant it had been last evening to wear a becoming gown and to feel the breeze whisper through her curls. But after last night she would have to take special care to look as unattractive as possible so Rupert... Lord Steadwell would have no cause to suspect she might be the lady from the masquerade.

Still all the risk and the need for added caution would be worthwhile if their encounter had persuaded him that his heart was not as dead to romantic feelings as he tried to pretend. Grace hoped their conversation might make him reconsider the wisdom of settling for a marriage of mutual convenience.

She and the girls bolted a quick breakfast then set off to smuggle the pink gown back to its rightful resting place. Charlotte and Sophie went ahead to scout the route and warn their governess if anyone was coming. Phoebe was assigned to bring up the rear in case anyone approached from behind them.

As it turned out their carefully laid plans were not necessary. They reached the State Apartment without meeting a single soul. As Grace wrapped the pink gown back in its swath of linen, she fancied it let out a rustling sigh of satisfaction that it had been brought out one last time to be worn and admired.

"That was exciting," Sophie announced as she skipped down the gallery on their way back to the nursery. "I wish we could do secret things like that more often."

The child's remark smote Grace with a pang of conscience. It was her job to bring up Sophie and her sisters as well-educated, accomplished young ladies of good character. Teaching them to sneak about, keeping secrets from their father hardly qualified as the latter.

Sophie's skipping drowned out the sound of approaching footsteps until suddenly Lord Steadwell's valet rounded the corner moving faster than Grace had ever seen him. He almost collided with the child, who sought refuge in Grace's arms. They all started in a guilty fashion.

"I beg your pardon." The valet seemed very flustered about something more than nearly charging into them. "I did not expect to meet anyone in this part of the house. What are you doing here?"

Tempted as Grace was to resent his accusing tone, she had to admit the man had reason to be suspicious.

Phoebe came to the rescue. "Papa likes us to learn about our family history. All the oldest paintings are in these rooms."

Both statements were perfectly true and the child had not actually claimed that's what they were doing. Still Grace felt she was setting a very poor example for her impressionable young pupils.

"Back to the nursery, girls." She shooed them on their way then fixed the valet with a questioning gaze. "Is something the matter, Mr. Willis? You don't seem quite yourself."

'It's the master who's not himself," muttered the valet, who was ordinarily the soul of discretion. "He's in a foul humor this morning. If he wasn't the most temperate gentleman I ever served, I would swear he was suffering from a bad *morning after.*"

"That doesn't sound like his lordship at all," Grace agreed, trying not to show how much the news troubled her. "Perhaps he did not sleep well after all the excitement last evening."

Mr. Willis did not look as though he gave her explanation much credence. "Lord Steadwell sent me to tell the cook we might have guests for dinner. *Might,* indeed! The cook will give me the sharp edge of her tongue over that, you can be certain."

"Did his lordship say who might be dining with him?" Grace did not like the sound of his plans, tentative though they were.

"Mrs. Cadmore and her son, if the boy has recovered from whatever was ailing him," Mr. Willis replied. "I'm to deliver the invitation to Dungrove as soon as I've spoken to the cook. If you'll excuse me, I had better be on my way or he'll have my head, the black humor he's in."

"Yes, of course." Grace was sorry to have detained the poor man, though she appreciated the information. If only she knew what it meant.

After the attention he'd shown her last night, why was his lordship inviting Mrs. Cadmore to dine? Grace pondered that question as the valet hurried off. Had the baron meant nothing he'd said last night? Had he only been flirting with her from behind the safety of his mask?

No! Rupert Kendrick was not that kind of man—she would stake her life on it. But if he was sincere, how might he have reacted to her abrupt disappearance? Not knowing who she was, he could not begin to guess her motives for running off. Did he assume she had deserted him? Could that be what had put him in a foul mood this morning and perhaps driven him back to Mrs. Cadmore?

Just then Sophie appeared at the end of the gallery, her hands planted on her hips in a perfect imitation of the cook when she was vexed. "Aren't you *ever* coming, Miss Ella?"

"Yes, of course, my dear." Grace followed Sophie back to the nursery, her head spinning with worries and regrets.

"Gather your sketching boxes, girls," she bid them. "Let us go outdoors and find some flowers to draw."

She wanted to be out of the house in case Lord Steadwell decided to visit the nursery. But she did not want the children making a racket that might disturb their father if he were trying to rest.

The air was warm, still and heavy when they ventured outside. A light haze veiled the sky. Though many garden plants were in bloom, Grace suggested they walk down the lane in search of wild flowers. The farther they stayed from the house the better.

Just beyond the rows of linden trees the girls found plenty of scope for their artwork—daisies, betony, red campion and heartsease. They did some fine sketching and were beginning to tire of it when Lord Benedict's carriage turned down the lane and drew to a halt nearby.

Grace flew toward it, casting a guilty glance in the direction of the house. "Rebecca, how are you feeling today? I was sorry to hear you were taken ill last night."

Her friend waved away her concern, ever stoic as their time at the Pendergast School had taught her to be. "It was only a digestive upset, probably from eating richer food than I am used to. I felt so badly for leaving you behind. I was relieved to hear that you had the presence of mind to look for our carriage."

"It was my own fault," Grace assured her friend. "I should not have wandered off while you were dancing."

"But you enjoyed yourself, I hope." Rebecca searched Grace's eyes for the truth. "You were by far the most beautiful lady at the masquerade. I overheard more than one gentleman asking who you might be."

The interest of those *gentlemen* did not flatter Grace—quite the contrary. There had been only one man present whose admiration mattered to her. But at the moment, she could only fear that he might look out a window and spy Lord Benedict's carriage.

As if he had read her thoughts, the viscount spoke. "We are on our way to London and from there to visit Miss Fletcher in Kent. I thought I might pay my compliments to Lord Steadwell before we leave. I have long admired the diligence with which he undertakes his duties in the House of Lords. I only wish there were more peers like him."

Much as Grace would have liked to grant Rebecca's husband his wish, she feared a meeting between the two gentlemen might expose her growing cache of secrets.

She ventured a furtive glance back toward the house. Was it only her guilty imagination or was someone looking out from an upstairs window?

"I'm certain Lord Steadwell would be honored by your praise, sir. But I am afraid this would not be a good time for him to receive visitors." She cast Rebecca a look that pleaded for understanding.

"Very well." The viscount seemed disappointed and

perhaps even a trifle offended. "If he is indisposed, I do not wish to disturb him."

Rebecca and Grace parted with rather strained good-byes. "Please give my best wishes to our other friends. Perhaps one day we may all get together."

To her relief the Benedict's coachman managed to turn their vehicle in close quarters without going all the way to the house and rousing unwelcome questions.

As Grace and the girls waved to her departing friends she could not help thinking what an exhausting and worrisome business it was to maintain her pretense. More and more she wished she could tell the truth and be herself. If only there was not so much at stake....

Who in blazes was Miss Ellerby talking to down at the end of the lane? From his bedchamber window Rupert could only glimpse bits of the distant figures partially shielded from sight by the linden trees. He could see enough of the vehicle to recognize it as a traveling carriage of the kind he used to get back and forth to London.

What was it doing here, lingering so long in the distance rather than coming straight down to the house? Had the people lost their way perhaps and stopped to ask directions? The more time that passed, the less likely that explanation seemed. They could have gotten directions all the way to Dover in the time they spent talking to Miss Ellerby.

When at last the carriage made a tight turn and drove away, Rupert's curiosity and suspicion had been roused to a keen pitch. He donned his coat and strode off in search of answers.

He found his daughters and their governess at the end

of the lane sketching wildflowers. The girls did not call out and run toward him as they usually did, and Miss Ellerby seemed to shrink from his approach. Did he look so formidable?

Perhaps so, he acknowledged ruefully, making a determined effort to relax his severe frown, stiff stride and arms clenched behind his back. It was not easy after the events of last night.

"Sketching again, are you?" He glanced over at Sophie's drawing with an approving nod. "Very good. Perhaps later you could go over it with your watercolors."

"I think I will, Papa."

He wandered past his two older daughters, casting admiring glances at their work. They seemed to concentrate very hard on what they were doing—too hard to make eye contact with him.

Their governess kept her gaze downcast and seemed to brace herself as he approached. Rupert had never seen anyone look so transparently guilty. What she might be guilty of, he had no idea. But he intended to find out.

"Miss Ellerby."

"Sir." She dropped a furtive curtsy and refused to look up at him.

"I thought I saw a carriage stop here and the occupants speak to you."

"Yes, sir." The governess clenched her lips in a thin, stubborn line, as if she feared he might try to pull her teeth out.

"I thought it odd that this carriage did not continue on to the house. Can you offer an explanation?"

She swallowed visibly. "The people only stopped for

a moment, sir. They were on their way to London. I did not want them to disturb you after your late night out."

"How do you know I was out late?" The question came out sharper than he intended.

It made Miss Ellerby start. "I just assumed, sir. Since you were away to a ball…"

"As a matter of fact I *was* out late," Rupert admitted. And he had not slept well once he reached home. Was that what made him so gruff and suspicious this morning? "But I am wide awake now. Tell me, were the people in that carriage acquaintances of mine? Of yours?"

She drew a deep breath. "Of mine—yes. The lady is an old friend from my school days, recently married. She and her husband stopped by on their way to London."

Rupert glanced toward his daughters, who had been staring at them but now returned to their sketching with fierce concentration. "Girls, why don't you take your sketch boxes back to the nursery? Then I will take you for a punt on the river."

"Yes, Papa," they chorused but without the enthusiasm Rupert had expected.

They packed up their drawing materials with lightning speed then headed for the house.

Their governess tried to follow, but he stepped into her path. "A moment if you please, Miss Ellerby. I sent the girls on ahead because I wanted a private word with you."

"What about, sir?"

"About the people in the carriage, of course!" he snapped, vexed with her for pretending she didn't know. "If they were friends of yours, why did you not invite them in for a visit?"

She continued to keep her gaze lowered. "Because it is not my house, sir."

Her answer took him aback. The house might not *belong* to her, but he liked to think it was her home now. "I am dismayed by your assumption that I would not allow you to receive guests at Nethercross."

"I'm sorry, sir. But it is not usually permitted."

"So you sent them on their way just like that—a friend you have not seen in how many years?"

She hesitated. "Nine, sir."

"I'm afraid I don't believe you." Rupert hoped that might shock the truth out of her. "I see no reason for you to be so evasive about an old friend paying a call. Admit it—you are seeking a new position with another family!"

The possibility made him feel betrayed and strangely... jealous? No—that was ridiculous! It must be some residual feeling from last night.

He had come to believe Grace Ellerby was one woman who would never abandon him and his children. At first he'd thought that because she had no other options available to her. But lately he had come to trust in her loyalty and devotion. Her evasive answers to his questions made him feel like a fool for placing his trust in her. The notion that she might be making plans to go elsewhere felt like a personal betrayal.

It took Miss Ellerby a moment to produce an audible reply.

"That is not true!" she burst out at last. "I have no intention of leaving Nethercross unless you wish me to go."

She sounded sincere, but when he tried to seek the truth in her eyes, Miss Ellerby scowled and looked away—the very picture of a guilty conscience. It was bad enough if she meant to leave. That she would lie to him about it grieved Rupert beyond measure.

"Of course I do not wish you to go. But if you cannot trust me with the truth and I cannot trust what you tell me…" His words trailed off with a weary shrug and a sigh.

He did not mean it as a threat. Even if he had, his plea seemed to have no effect on Miss Ellerby. Her lips remained shut, imprisoning any words she might have confided in him.

"Then perhaps it is just as well I wed Mrs. Cadmore as soon as possible." He flung the news at her. "If she and her son can dine with us tonight, I shall propose. Please make certain the girls are prepared and warn them to mind their tongues around the lady who will be their new mother."

With that he spun on his heel and stalked off, his spirits sinking lower with every step.

"But you said everything went well at the ball last night," cried Charlotte, when Grace informed the girls of their father's plans. "What changed his mind? Was it seeing those friends of yours?"

"Don't be silly, Charlotte." Phoebe scowled at no one in particular. "How could that make any difference about Papa and Mrs. Cadmore? We're going to have to get used to the idea of having a stepmother, that's all."

Grace wished what Phoebe said was true but she feared it was not. This was her fault as Charlotte had implied. Her cowardly flight from the ball must have made Rupert want a woman who would remain with him—even if the motive for her constancy was not love.

"I won't ever get used to it!" Sophie wailed. "I don't want a stepmother!"

"Nor do I." Charlotte stooped and wrapped her arms around her little sister. "Especially not Mrs. Cadmore."

"I don't care for her, either." Phoebe flung herself onto one of the nursery chairs. "But if Papa is determined to marry, we could do even worse."

Grace did her best to soothe the girls as she helped dress and groom them for dinner. But how could she hope to persuade them all would be well when she was more certain than ever their father was making a grave mistake—one into which she had pushed him?

"P-please, Miss Ella," Sophie sniffled as Grace brushed her hair. "Isn't there *anything* you can do?"

Was there? Grace's conscience demanded even as she tried to pretend otherwise.

One possibility did suggest itself, though she quailed at the thought. Lord Steadwell had already hinted that he might dismiss her, and the action she contemplated taking would likely remove any doubt.

But if he did marry Mrs. Cadmore, Grace feared he would end up every bit as miserable as his children. She could not bear for that to happen, even if her effort to stop him made it impossible for her to remain at Nethercross.

"Hush now." She wiped Sophie's streaming eyes and pressed a soft kiss upon her forehead. "Perhaps there *is* something I can do to help. But I will need you to be on your best behavior at dinner and act as if nothing is wrong. Can you do that for me?"

The child gave a brave nod and her lips spread into an unsteady smile.

"Did you mean that?" whispered Charlotte as Grace

looked her over. "Or did you only say it to keep Sophie from blubbering all through dinner and making Papa angry?"

"A little of both," Grace admitted. "I don't want her making this evening any worse. But there is one last thing I mean to try. I don't know if it will work, but I cannot stand by and do nothing."

In spite of the doubt she had expressed, a hopeful glimmer kindled in Charlotte's eyes.

"Thank you for trying at least!" She threw her arms around Grace's neck.

A lump rose in Grace's throat as she soaked up the encouraging warmth of Charlotte's embrace and exchanged a fond smile with Phoebe. She had come to feel so much more for these three dear girls than she had for any of her other pupils. Though she did not know how she could bear to be parted from them, she would rather that than stay and see their family become as wretched as hers had been. The anguish of witnessing their unhappiness would be made doubly bitter by the knowledge that she might have been able to prevent it, if only she'd dared try.

"There now, you look lovely, as usual." Grace could not resist bestowing a little touch upon each of the girls—smoothing hair, adjusting a ribbon, plumping a sash. "Bessie, will you kindly escort the girls down to the dining room? And please ask his lordship if I might have a brief word with him before dinner on an urgent matter."

"Yes, Miss," replied the nursery maid with a puzzled look as she ushered the girls off. "Is everythin' all right? You're not ill are you?"

Grace shook her head. Not ill—only sick with fear.

Her instinctive response to that feeling was to run away and hide. It was what she'd been doing all her life. But now she must stand firm and throw off her protective disguise.

Turning toward the looking glass, she removed her father's spectacles and her starched white cap with its unbecoming lappets. Then she picked up the brush and began to dress her hair in a style that complimented her appearance.

A while later, she stood waiting outside the dining room, her hands clasped in front of her in an effort to still their trembling. She tried to draw slow calming breaths, but each one exhaled as a quivering sigh. If Lord Steadwell did not appear soon, she feared she would turn tail and scurry back to the nursery.

So taut were her nerves that the faint rattle of the door opening nearly made her scream. She stifled the sound while it was still only a squeak.

"What is it you wish to tell me, Miss Ellerby?" his lordship demanded in an impatient grumble as he closed the dining room door behind him. "I hope you will keep it brie—"

His sentence halted abruptly as he got a proper look at her. His mouth fell slack and his eyes widened. "Good gracious!"

The first shock was followed by one even greater. Grace feared his eyes might bulge out of their sockets. "Good gracious!" he repeated. "You!"

Chapter Fourteen

What in blazes did Miss Ellerby have to say to him now that she could not have said earlier when he'd confronted her in the lane?

Rupert's daughters and guests were already seated when Bessie relayed the message.

It was on the tip of his tongue to reply that whatever Miss Ellerby wanted could wait until the Cadmores had gone. He had no intention of delaying their dinner so she could flog a dead horse with more pleas that he abandon his plan to wed his comely neighbor. Did she not realize his daughters were becoming resigned to the idea? Once they saw that he had not saddled them with a wicked stepmother from out of a fairy tale they would accept his marriage and all would be well.

But what if the governess meant to go further by threatening to resign her post if he proposed to Mrs. Cadmore? Though Rupert had no intention of allowing her to coerce him, he thought it worth hearing what Miss Ellerby wanted at least.

"If you will pardon me for a moment." He cast Mrs.

Cadmore an apologetic smile. "There is a matter I must attend to, then we can begin."

"Is it that urgent?" The lady made no effort to conceal her impatience. "Surely it can wait until after dinner."

"I'm not certain it can," said Rupert, even though he knew Mrs. Cadmore was probably right. "It will be a very brief postponement, I assure you."

As he strode to the door he refused to admit that part of him welcomed this delay, fleeting though it would be.

"What is it you wish to tell me, Miss Ellerby?" he muttered as he closed the door behind him. His impatience was less with her than with his divided inclinations. "I hope you will keep it brie—"

Then he turned and his gaze swept upward from her familiar dull-green dress to the startlingly attractive woman wearing it. "Good gracious!"

It couldn't be plain Miss Ellerby—yet it was. Rupert would never have credited a cap and spectacles with making such a striking difference in a person's appearance. How beautiful she might look in a pretty gown, he could only imagine.

To his further shock Rupert realized he *could* imagine it all too easily.

"Good gracious!" he gasped again. "You!"

The woman before him was Grace Ellerby—he could tell that, just barely. But she was also the mysterious beauty from the masquerade. Now he understood why she had seemed so familiar. No wonder he had not been able to place her. He had plundered his memory for every beautiful woman he'd ever met, but his daughters' mousy governess had not numbered among them.

"You do know who I am, then?" She looked ready to shrink from a blow that might fall at any moment.

He gave a stiff nod. "Now that I see you without your disguise. Without *either* of your disguises."

To think he had congratulated himself on hiring a governess who would never abandon his family to elope. What a blind dupe he'd been!

The realization that he had been so thoroughly hoodwinked did not improve his temper. "You owe me an explanation, Miss Ellerby, if that is indeed your name."

She flinched as if that were the blow she'd been expecting. "It is. I may not have told you the entire truth about myself but I tried to tell you as much as I could. As for my explanation—you will get it, I promise. But there is not nearly enough time now."

Her words reminded Rupert of the party in the dining room awaiting his return. The sight of her had driven every thought of them from his mind. "What do you want with me then?"

"Just to beg you not to propose to Mrs. Cadmore until I've had the chance to explain my situation. I have reason to know you are not done with love as you claim. It would be a grave misfortune indeed if you undertook a marriage of convenience only to later meet a lady you could care for."

He had been beguiled into fancying he cared for *her*.

"Is that why you stole in to the masquerade?" he demanded. "To seek me out and make up to me so I would abandon my marriage plans?"

The emotions that had possessed his heart in that moonlit garden last night had not entirely released him. But they did have to battle equally potent feelings of betrayal and abandonment.

"I did not steal in." Grace shook her head so hard her golden hair billowed around her face. "My friend Lady Benedict secured me an invitation. It was she and her husband in the carriage you saw earlier. Viscount Benedict wanted to pay his respects to you but I was afraid it might raise awkward questions and you would discover what I'd done."

Lady Benedict? Rupert had heard about the viscount's recent marriage as well as some wild rumor about him proposing to the lady in front of a great crowd at Bath. But that did not mean Grace Ellerby was telling him the truth.

"I did not 'make up' to you to ruin your marriage plans," she continued with vehement sincerity. "You came to *my* rescue, remember? I did not even know who you were at first."

"At first?" Rupert seized on those words to distract himself from the memory of trailing after her like a calf-eyed schoolboy, eager to protect her from the unwelcome attentions of other men. "When did you realize who I was? And why did you keep on pretending we were strangers?"

A wave of shame seemed to quench her spirit. "Because I feared you would suspect the worst of me…as you do. The truth is I accepted my friend's invitation so I could keep watch on you in case you tried to propose to Mrs. Cadmore."

"What would you have done then? Thrown yourself into my arms? Pretended you had a prior claim upon me?" In spite of his outrage, Rupert could not suppress a traitorous wish that she had done those things.

"No!" Grace Ellerby's forceful denial felt like a rejection of the feelings she'd stirred in him. "That is…

I don't know because that is not what happened. Instead you came to my assistance, then we walked in the garden and talked. You told me—"

"I am not responsible for anything I said under the influence of that romantic atmosphere!" Rupert lashed out against the sting of that rejection. "Today I woke up to the practical necessities of life."

She flinched from the intensity of his anger but refused to back down altogether. "Nonetheless, what happened last night convinced me you will never be happy married to a woman you do not love."

Her quiet certainty shook him to the core and threatened to rally his own doubts against him. "There is much more at stake than my happiness!"

"But if you are not happy, your daughters will not be, either." If only she would respond with anger, it would have been easier to dismiss her claims. Her heartfelt pleas were much harder to disregard. "I know you are trying to do what is best for them but this is not it! I do not believe your wife would want that for any of you."

Rupert's temper flared. "Do not presume to tell me what my wife would have wanted! I will be the judge of what is best for my children, Miss Ellerby. Now, I must get back to my guests, but I will expect a full explanation later for why you entered my employ under false pretenses, which you have continued to this day."

Fearing she might say something more to detain him, he turned and fled back into the dining room, shutting the door firmly behind him.

"Is there some difficulty, Lord Steadwell?" Mrs. Cadmore inquired in a tone of concern. "We heard raised voices."

Rupert shook his head and made a determined effort

to regain his composure. "A minor issue with the staff, though the timing was altogether inconvenient."

Despite his best efforts to prevent it, Grace Ellerby's face rose in his mind. Incidents from the past few months flitted through his memory, featuring Miss Ellerby in her true attractive appearance.

As he strode back to his chair and tried to carry on as if nothing had happened, Rupert caught his daughters exchanging furtive looks. Had they put their governess up to attending the masquerade to spy on him? Suddenly he realized why her pink Stuart-era gown had looked so familiar. How long had his children known about the secret beauty hiding in their nursery?

Besides the feeling of betrayal that his daughters had conspired to deceive him so, it also made Rupert realize how desperately opposed they still must be to his marriage plans.

There. She had done it at last—the thing she should have done from the very beginning if only she'd known what kind of man her new employer would turn out to be.

As Grace watched the dining-room door swing shut behind him, her conscience protested. It had not taken her long to discover that Rupert Kendrick was a trustworthy, honorable gentleman who would never have tried to prey upon her like so many other men she'd known. From that moment there had been no excuse to repay his decency with deception—except her lack of courage.

Neither Rebecca nor Marian would have behaved as she had. Heaving a sigh of regret Grace turned and headed back to the nursery with slow, weary steps. Her

friends would have confessed the truth at once and accepted the consequences with fortitude. Perhaps that
was why they had been rewarded with security and happiness while she was about to be cast out from the safety
and serenity of Nethercross—the first place that had felt
like home to her in many years.

Clearly her stepmother and teachers had been right.
Her fair looks were a superficial mask to hide a flawed
character. She had been pulled far too easily into the
sticky web of deceit. But now she was free. No longer
would she have to devise new lies to cover up old ones.
No longer would she have to be less than truthful with
the man she admired and cared for.

Perhaps those blessings alone would be worth the just
punishment she would now suffer for her transgressions.

She might as well begin packing her trunk, Grace
decided when she reached the empty nursery. Lord
Steadwell might be kind enough not to send her away
this very night, but she could not deny the anger with
which he'd reacted to her revelations. He would not want
someone who had demonstrated such a lack of integ-
rity to continue raising his beloved daughters. And she
could not blame him.

If their places had been reversed, she would have
done the same. However, she hoped she might have been
able to find a drop of pity in her heart for the person
who had acted out of fear and desperation rather than
malice.

The time dragged by as Grace gathered her meager
belongings and stowed them away in her trunk. Between inquisitions of her conscience, she wondered
what was happening down in the dining room. Had
Lord Steadwell proposed to Mrs. Cadmore in front of

their children? If he must do it, Grace hoped he would wait until after his daughters had left at least. She feared that Sophie, in particular, would not be able to hide her dismay.

If the child burst into tears or referred to wicked stepmothers from her fairy tales, it might provoke her father's anger and Mrs. Cadmore's resentment. Any small chance of future happiness for their family would be poisoned. Would that be her fault, too? Grace could not deny the possibility.

Perhaps if she hadn't allowed old wounds from childhood to fester within her, she would not have encouraged Charlotte, Phoebe and Sophie in their resistance to their father's remarriage. Then he and Mrs. Cadmore might have stood some hope of blending their families into a reasonably happy one. Though Grace still had her doubts, she could not deny her fault in making a bad situation worse.

At last she heard the approach of footsteps. Swallowing her bitter brew of fears and regrets she composed her features and went to meet the girls. Her first priority now must be to make the changes that were coming as easy as possible for them to bear.

They rushed in, all trying to squeeze through the door at once and all speaking at the same time.

"Girls, please!" Nursery discipline reasserted itself. "I cannot understand a word you're saying. One at a time, then we must get you to bed. Sophie first, for she looks as if she's about to explode."

Charlotte and Phoebe did not look pleased with that, but they allowed their little sister to speak. "What did you say to Papa, Miss Ella? We heard you talking quite loudly outside the dining room. Anyway, it must have worked because he didn't ask Mrs. Cadmore to marry him."

That unexpected good news made Grace's heart bound. If she had succeeded in keeping Lord Steadwell from making a terrible mistake, her exile from Nethercross, no matter how painful, would not be in vain.

Now that Sophie had spoken, Phoebe seemed to feel it should be her turn next. "Why have you not got your cap and spectacles on, Miss Ella? Did you let Papa see you looking pretty? Did you think it might make him want to marry *you* instead of Mrs. Cadmore?"

"Nothing like that!" Grace cried. She could tell by the girls' expressions that such a notion shocked them. They had no desire to trade one stepmother for another. She could not blame them for feeling that way. After all she had encouraged them to resist the prospect of having a stepmother regardless of whether it might be someone capable of loving their father and them.

"I wanted him to know he had spoken to me at the masquerade and some of the things he said made me certain it would be a mistake for him to wed Mrs. Cadmore. Besides, your Papa has treated me with kindness and respect ever since I arrived at Nethercross. I repaid him poorly, by not being truthful with him. I thought I had good reasons for keeping secrets but now I am not sure any excuse would be good enough. I only hope you girls will learn from my mistakes and not follow my example."

"Is that why Papa was angry?" demanded Charlotte, her face suddenly pale. "When I first saw you looking pretty you said Papa would dismiss you if he found out."

Before Grace could reply Phoebe spoke up. "Papa

said we must tell you to come down to his study once we were in bed. Is he going to send you away, Miss Ella?"

"No!" Sophie cried, flinging her arms around Grace's waist. "He mustn't!"

Touched as she was by their dismay at the prospect of losing her, Grace was sorry to be responsible for causing them any unhappiness.

"Hush now." Grace ran her hand over the child's head in a reassuring caress and manufactured a smile for Sophie's sisters. "Let's not borrow trouble—it will only spoil your sleep. Your father told me he wanted an explanation for my actions—that must be why he wants to see me."

If Lord Steadwell did want her gone from Nethercross, tomorrow would be soon enough to talk it over with the girls and make them understand it would be for the best. They would be better able to accept the news after a good night's rest.

"Come now, let's get you ready for bed." Grace strove to sound untroubled so the children would not worry. "I do not want to keep your father waiting."

"What about our bedtime story?" Sophie asked as Grace pulled her nightgown over her head.

"It is too late tonight, I'm afraid. Perhaps tomorrow you can get ready for bed a little earlier and have two stories then." Grace tried to sound as if she had no doubt she would be there tomorrow night to read those stories.

The two younger girls seemed to accept her reassurance, but she sensed Charlotte did not. At least the girl had the kindness not to burden her sisters with her worries. As soon as all three were in bed, Grace took a moment to sit with each of them before she headed off to meet with their father.

When she reached Lord Steadwell's study and tapped on the door he called her to enter. She found him standing beside his writing table with his back to the window and his arms held stiffly behind him. His crisp features were set in a stern frown and his dark brows were drawn together.

For all his well-composed severity, he gave a start when she appeared—as if he had still not managed to reconcile his image of his daughters' plain governess with her true appearance.

"Now, Miss Ellerby, you promised me an explanation for why you have deceived me from the moment we met." It was clear from his harsh tone and stiff stance that none of the excuses she had given herself for her behavior would satisfy him.

He had already made up his mind to dismiss her. Nothing she could say would salvage the respect he'd once had for her. It was equally doubtful that anything she said could make him despise her more. That left her with nothing to lose and no reason to conceal a shred of the truth.

When Grace Ellerby entered his study, Rupert strove to conceal the shock and unease her presence still inspired in him. Ever since she had ambushed him with the revelation of her true appearance, part of his mind had struggled to grasp that his daughters' mousy governess was the mysterious beauty from the masquerade. What troubled him most was that some deeply buried intuition seemed to have grasped this baffling contraction already. Could it be the same part of him that wanted to invite Miss Ellerby for a walk in the garden to discuss the matter? Reason warned that would be the worst of bad ideas.

Of course, reason was still vexed that it had not succeeded in getting him to propose to Mrs. Cadmore this evening. In spite of its urging and the lady's pointed hints, he had remained stubbornly silent on the subject. He could hardly blame the poor woman for wanting to be certain of his intentions after he had shown her such particular interest. Yet Rupert knew he dared not take such an irrevocable step until he had sorted out his complicated feelings for Grace Ellerby.

Even as she gathered her composure to offer an explanation, he wondered how he could have been so blind to the beauty hidden only by an ugly cap and a pair of spectacles. Vexed as he was with her for making such a fool of him, he found it impossible to forget the slow-blossoming admiration and immediate fascination her two very different personalities had inspired in him.

Which of them was the real Grace Ellerby? Or was that a woman he would not recognize at all—a cool, calculated deceiver with motives he could not begin to fathom?

"The truth is," she began, "I disguised my appearance at first because I was not sure if I could trust you."

"Trust *me?*" The words erupted from Rupert's lips edged with bitter irony.

Grace Ellerby flinched—but whether it was from his angry outburst or from the pain of her conscience, he could not tell for certain. "I realize now that you are a gentleman of honor but I had no way of knowing it at first. I have been acquainted with too many of the other kind."

"What do you mean?" Rupert muttered, though he

could guess her answer after what he had witnessed between her and that sultan brute at the ball.

Her hands were clasped in front of her. Now they began to fidget. Her delicate features reflected the struggle within her—not wanting to speak of painful events from the past but knowing she had no choice.

"It began during my very first position when I was only nineteen—fresh out of school and hopelessly naive. The brother of my mistress paid me a great deal of attention, flattered me, claimed he loved me and persuaded me to fancy I was in love with him. I assumed he meant to marry me, only to discover that gentlemen like him do not want a penniless, orphaned governess as a wife. When he offered to buy me a house and set me up as his mistress, I ran away."

"The gall of the brazen whelp!" Rupert cried before he could restrain himself. "I'd have thrashed any brother-in-law of mine who dared to conduct himself in such an infamous manner under my roof!"

It was more than righteous indignation that roused his anger. He envied the young fool who had won Grace Ellerby's heart when it was soft and trusting.

She raised her gaze to meet his, clearly determined to make a full confession. "It was as much my fault as his. I was completely unguarded. I encouraged his attentions."

Hard as he tried, Rupert could not let that go unchallenged. "But you said yourself, you were scarcely more than a child! How were you to know his intentions were so thoroughly dishonorable?"

"I was employed in his sister's home," she insisted. "I should not have permitted any familiarity between us. The experience taught me a painful lesson but a useful one I never intended to forget. At my next post, I tried to be more careful. I concentrated on my duties and went out of my way to discourage any attention from visiting gentlemen.

"That worked well enough for a while. But then a friend of the master's took a fancy to me. For some reason, he seemed to consider my reserved manner a challenge. He set about to win my favors and the more I resisted the more determined he became."

"Why did you not complain to your employers?" Rupert demanded in a sharp tone. His stomach seethed with indignant anger. He wished he had both the cads who had imposed upon Grace Ellerby in front of him so he could knock their vile heads together!

"I tried," she insisted in a defensive tone as if she assumed his anger was directed at her. "I spoke to the mistress about my fears, but she refused to believe me even though the man had tried to flirt with me in her presence. She said it was not my place to criticize a guest in her home. I was left with no choice but to seek a position elsewhere."

Rage rose in Rupert's throat like thick black bile. The number of people he longed to confront and punish kept growing while Grace Ellerby fell lower and lower on the list. "I suppose it was the same at the next place?"

"Worse." Her gaze faltered and her hands moved more restlessly than ever. "Not only did I cultivate a more guarded manner, I also dressed as modestly as possible and wore my hair in a severe style. That kept me safe until last fall when Mr. Hesketh's uncle returned from the Indies to live with the family."

She went on to describe how the lecher had pursued her and her increasingly desperate efforts to avoid him until the night he had entered her bedchamber and lain in wait. By the time she finished her account, Rupert's throat was so constricted he could scarcely speak.

"I knew after that," she concluded, "I could not afford to keep moving from one post to another or I would never be able to save for my old age. I decided I must employ more drastic measures to discourage gentlemen from taking an interest in me."

"But I am not like those other men!" Rupert forced the words out of his constricted throat. "I would never behave toward any woman as they did!"

As strenuously as he insisted it, his conscience could not deny his immediate attraction to Grace at the masquerade. Nor his current urge to take her in his arms and vow to protect her from anyone who might do her harm.

Was he really any better than those other men? And did he frighten her as they had?

The way her gaze skittered from his made him suspect he might.

"I know that now. But how could I at first? Especially when I learned…"

"That I was widowed," Rupert finished her sentence. He recalled her intense reaction to that discovery and how it had puzzled him at the time. Now it became clear.

She nodded. "None of the men who pursued me were married. If I had known you were not, I would never have applied for the position. By the time I realized you were a gentleman of honor, I had guessed you only hired me because you believed I was plain and unmarriageable. I feared if you discovered otherwise, you would send me away from Nethercross and I would never see your daughters again."

Grace Ellerby was the picture of abject remorse, and Rupert found his vexation with her melting away like snow on a mild spring day. How could he blame her for doing whatever she must to remain at Nethercross with his girls? In her place, what might *he* have been willing to do? What rules of proper behavior might he bend? How far would he allow honor to lapse?

"I wanted to tell you the truth." Her words trembled with that longing. "The more time that passed, the more I wanted to, but the harder it became. I was certain you would not understand and now I know I was right."

She wasn't right at all, Rupert yearned to reassure her. There were parts of what she had done that he understood far too well. But other parts still bewildered him.

"My daughters knew, didn't they?"

Their governess gave a brief guilty nod, as if that was one facet of her prolonged deception that troubled her most.

"When did they find out?" It made him feel a greater fool than ever to have been blind to something his children had long since realized.

Was it their innocence, their lack of concern with appearance that had allowed his children to see through her dowdy disguise? He, however, had looked Grace Ellerby over only long enough to decide that she was unattractive and thus no threat to the stability of his household. After that, he had never bothered to observe her more closely.

"Several months ago." She went on to tell him how

Sophie had coaxed her to don the beautiful old gown and how she'd been discovered by Charlotte.

"They kept your secret all this time." Rupert could not decide whether he felt betrayed by his daughters or admired the lengths to which they had gone to protect their governess.

"I should never have asked them to take part in my deception," Grace murmured. "I am not proud of any of my actions, but that is the one I regret most."

Determined to get to the bottom of this whole business, Rupert asked, "Whose idea was it for you to attend the masquerade?"

When Grace Ellerby hesitated to reply, it occurred to him that she was as determined to protect his daughters as they were her. Clearly she had not intended to engage his affections last night for her own sake, as part of him longed to believe. Instead, seeing how much he fancied her, she had led him on in an effort to prevent the marriage she feared would make his daughters miserable.

"The girls made you go, didn't they?"

"They did not *make* me do anything," she protested. "My friend Lady Benedict offered me an invitation. Your daughters only urged me to accept and provided me with a costume. I pretended to let them persuade me, but the truth is I *wanted* to go. What happened last night was not their fault."

In spite of everything, he could not be angry or sorry she had gone, even if their moonlit encounter had brought him to the troublesome realization that his heart was not entirely ready to give up on love.

"I know you have no reason to believe me." Grace's gaze flitted from the floor to his face and back again. "I *was* going to tell you the truth last night. But at the last moment I lost my nerve and ran away. It's what I always do when things go wrong."

She put Rupert in mind of a wild doe, ears alert for the slightest noise, nose sniffing the breeze for any whiff of danger, muscles coiled to sprint away at the first sign of peril. She needed a safe haven and a strong protector. She deserved them.

"You didn't run this time," he reminded her, aware how difficult that must have been. "You could just as easily have slipped away and left me a note explaining all this."

"I almost wish I had," she admitted with a rueful grimace. "But your daughters deserve better than that from me. So do you after what I've done. The result will be the same though, won't it? I shall have to leave. I cannot blame you for not trusting me to raise your daughters after the lack of character I've shown."

Leave? The prospect of losing her from his home jarred Rupert. He had not thought beyond this confrontation to its consequences. Reason warned him that dismissing her was the only prudent course. She had already gained too perilous a foothold in his affections. By her own admission, she was the sort of woman who posed his heart the greatest danger—one who was apt to take flight and abandon him.

But how could he do that to his daughters when it was clear how much they had come to care for their new governess?

"I cannot pretend I approve of your actions." He could scarcely force the words out—so torn was he about what course of action to take. "But I understand why you felt compelled to hide your beauty in the beginning."

His tongue tripped over the word *beauty,* for it reminded him anew how much her looks attracted him.

Rupert cleared his throat and continued, "I acknowledge the part I played in making you feel you must continue the ruse or lose your position. But I am gravely disappointed that once we became better acquainted you continued to doubt I would understand."

For the first time that evening he thought he glimpsed the faint shimmer of tears in her eyes. "I'm sorry, sir."

"I believe you are." He resisted the intense urge to stride toward her and offer her the comfort of his embrace. She would assume he was no better than those other men who had tried to take advantage of her innocence and prey upon her beauty. Recalling how he had ignored his growing fondness for plain Miss Ellerby only to indulge his instant fancy for the masked lady, Rupert could not be altogether certain he *was* any better. "And I hope you will try to make it up to my family by staying on at Nethercross as my daughters' governess."

He held his breath as he waited for her answer. For his daughters' sake he knew he could not dismiss her. But for himself he could not decide if he was more alarmed at the prospect of Grace leaving…or staying?

Chapter Fifteen

"Stay?" Grace could not believe her ears. After all she had told him, she'd been certain his lordship would pack her off to Reading that very night.

He nodded. "Please. It is clear my girls care a great deal about you and you about them. I promise you will never have anything to fear under my roof like you suffered in your past positions. In turn I hope that from now on you will always be truthful with me."

"I will, sir, most gladly." Grace did not need any such inducements from him. She had learned how treacherous the slippery slope of secrecy could be. "Thank you, sir. This is far greater forbearance than I deserve."

Grateful and relieved as she was, Grace could not stifle the feeling that she had escaped the just punishment due her. "If you will excuse me, then, sir, I should return to the nursery in case any of the girls are still awake."

He replied with a wordless nod.

Grace was halfway through the door when curiosity got the better of her. "Please, sir, if the children ask, what should I tell them about you and Mrs. Cadmore?"

Was she already straining the promise she'd just

made to his lordship about being truthful? It was quite as much for her own sake that she needed to know as for her pupils. "I ask, sir, because I fear the lady might not approve of me once she sees my true appearance. I would not want my presence in the house to place a strain on your marriage."

Lord Steadwell turned to gaze out the window.

"Now that I perceive the depth of my daughters' opposition to that match, I believe I must abandon any thought of it." His words trailed off in a sigh.

Had she been wrong about his feelings for Mrs. Cadmore? Did they run deeper than she'd wanted to believe? Or had his lordship acknowledged the likelihood that his daughters would never accept any other woman in their mother's place?

If that were true, it would be a great pity for him, Grace reflected as she closed the study door softly behind her and returned to the nursery. Now that he was beginning to cast off the cruel bonds of grief, must he remain alone until his daughters were all married before he dared take a wife? How many more years must he endure the loneliness of which he had spoken at the masquerade?

The masquerade—Grace thought back upon the event as if it had taken place weeks ago rather than just last night. Recalling the things he had confided in her, the chaste but tender touch of his hand, she had been so certain he felt something for her. But once he discovered the identity of the lady behind the mask, there had been no mention of anything that passed between them. He had been vexed with her for deceiving him and pretending to be the sort of lady he might have cared for as an equal.

For the sake of his children he was willing to let her keep her position. But his promise that she would not be exposed to any romantic attentions while under his roof made it clear he would not permit himself to have feelings for someone in her position.

Lord Benedict had been willing to accept an impoverished bride of noble birth. Captain Radcliffe, though now a wealthy landowner, had once been an ordinary sailor with a blemished reputation. The captain might not have perceived any social gulf between him and Marian Murray that love could not span. But Lord Steadwell clearly shared Captain Townsend's belief that a gentleman should not take a wife so far beneath him.

When Grace slipped back into the nursery, Charlotte stirred and called out in a whisper, "What did Papa say, Miss Ella? Are you to be dismissed? We won't let him do it, you know. We'll go and tell him the masquerade was our idea and you did not want to go."

"Shh." Grace made her way to the child's bed and perched on the edge of it. "We don't want to wake your sisters. I appreciate your willingness to intercede for me with your father, but it will not be necessary. After he listened to my explanation, he was kind enough to say I may remain at Nethercross."

Charlotte shot upright and flung her arms around Grace's neck. "That's wonderful, Miss Ella! The girls will be so happy! Now we can all continue on as we have been. Unless…" She pulled back from her eager embrace. "What about Mrs. Cadmore? Does Papa still plan to marry her?"

Torn between relief and guilt, Grace shook her head. "He understands now that you cannot abide having a stepmother. So he has given up the idea of remarrying for the present."

Charlotte renewed her embrace tighter than ever. "It's all turned out well, then. *Happily ever after* as Sophie would say!"

A fortnight after his interview with Grace Ellerby, Rupert could still recall with perfect clarity her look of rapturous relief when he'd begged her to remain at Nethercross and promised he would not trouble her with his unwelcome attentions. Clearly their encounter at the masquerade had meant something quite different to her than it had to him. Had she only permitted him to draw close to her so he would realize he could not settle for a loveless marriage?

Recalling his former marriage plans reminded Rupert that he owed Mrs. Cadmore an explanation and an apology. Not wanting to put it off any longer, he called for his horse to be saddled and rode at once to Dungrove.

The lady received him with frosty civility. "Lord Steadwell, to what do I owe this unexpected honor? I am surprised you can tear yourself away from home these days—the nursery, in particular."

Rupert refused to inquire what she meant by that remark. "I know I should have come to speak to you sooner. I must beg your pardon for that and for a great deal more. I have imposed upon you of late in a most shameful fashion."

"Indeed you have, sir." She fluttered her fan to stir the sultry August air, though her manner betrayed not the slightest degree of warmth. "I confess I am at a loss to know why. I thought you and I had an understanding that an alliance between our families would be of mutual benefit."

"I used to think so too." Rupert toyed self-consciously with the brim of his hat. "I assure you it was never my intention to lead you on. I planned to make you an offer of marriage, but when the time came I found I could not."

Mrs. Cadmore arched one raven eyebrow and fixed him with an icy glare. "And why was that, pray?"

"For the same reason you should have refused me if I had proposed." Much as he regretted aspects of his conduct, Rupert no longer doubted he had done the right thing. "Because I do not love you, nor do I believe you have any tender feelings for me. I persuaded myself that did not matter to me only to discover...it does."

The lady's fan snapped shut. "Sentimental nonsense! I took you for a rational, practical man of property, not some calf-eyed schoolboy. I find you most attractive and excellent company. I have no doubt we could have grown quite fond of one another in time."

Rupert gave a decisive shake of his head. "You may always rely upon me as a friend and neighbor, but I now realize it would have been a grave mistake for us to marry without love."

Mrs. Cadmore sniffed. "It's that governess, isn't it? I saw her in church last week and scarcely recognized her without that hideous cap and spectacles. I suppose she made herself look plain and respectable to gain a footing in your household, then threw off the disguise to catch your fancy."

"That is not true!" Rupert protested, shaken to discover the intensity of outrage an insult to Grace provoked in him. "Miss Ellerby is an excellent governess to my daughters, whatever her appearance. But she is nothing more to me than that."

He wanted to assure Mrs. Cadmore that Grace had nothing to do with the change in his intentions toward her, but that would not be true.

But was it true that Grace Ellerby meant nothing more to him than any other valued employee? Rupert's conscience demanded an honest answer as he took his leave of Mrs. Cadmore and rode back home.

Certainly he *wanted* it to be true, especially after their discussion about Grace remaining at Nethercross. The last thing he needed was to lose his heart to a woman he had promised not to subject to any romantic attentions, when she would now surely attract the interest of *other* men. His only hope of keeping Grace in his household lay in stifling whatever tender feelings sought to take root in his heart. As for other men who might try to steal her away, he must hope her past experiences would make her too wary to encourage them, even if their intentions were honorable.

Somehow it troubled Rupert to think of keeping her at Nethercross, bound by the force of her fears. Much as she obviously cared for his daughters, was it fair to deny her the opportunity to enjoy a home and family of her own?

Those worries continued to nag at him as the weeks passed and Parliament recessed. Like his fellow peers he headed to the country, though not to devote all his time to hunting, as many of them would. Instead he looked forward to supervising the harvest and spending more time with his daughters... which meant more time in the company of Grace Ellerby.

He tried to persuade himself it was no different than

when she'd first come to Nethercross but soon realized that was not true. Every time she appeared, he had to stifle a gasp of wonder at her delicate, golden beauty and ask himself how he could have been blind to it for so long.

Perhaps because she felt safe and able to be herself her face had taken on a luminous quality, as if a devoted ray of sunshine followed her everywhere. With her eyes no longer hidden behind those hideous pinched spectacles, Rupert could see they were a soft, winsome blue, like the sky in those first moments after daybreak. When she smiled, as she now did so often, he could not help but admire the generous shape and the ripe color of her lips. How hard she must have worked to hide those attractive features from his notice.

Her looks were not all that had transformed. Her manner took on a sparkle of animation and her voice a sweet lilt. Her laughter set something alight inside Rupert, beckoning him to join in. Yet beneath those superficial changes remained all the fine qualities he had valued in plain, severe Miss Ellerby—a gentleness of spirit, a quick mind and a nurturing heart.

He began to suspect he had been half in love with her long before that fateful masquerade. Had he willfully ignored any fleeting glimpses of her beauty out of a secret fear that it might force him to acknowledge his feelings for what they were?

Now he struggled to fight those feelings, knowing what they could cost him if he allowed them to overwhelm his stubborn will. But every day he lost a bit more ground and some traitorous part of him cheered those small defeats.

Spending time with her in the company of his daughters was a joy that made his heart swell with new life, but it no longer satisfied his thirst for her companionship. He wanted to spend time alone with Grace Ellerby, learning more about her. He wanted to confide in her and seek her advice. He wanted to learn how she felt and offer his support.

Even as he tumbled down that slippery slope, wondering when he would strike bottom, Rupert knew he did not dare act upon those feelings or he might frighten Grace away. He also knew from bitter experience what that loss would do to him.

Was this how *happily ever after* was supposed to feel? Grace pondered that question as she and the girls joined their father at the traditional feast he hosted for his tenants to celebrate the harvest. In most ways, the past several weeks had been among the happiest she'd ever experienced. Life at Nethercross had returned to the way it should be—the way it had been before Rupert took the notion to remarry.

For Grace, life was far better because she no longer needed to hide behind that horrid old cap and her father's spectacles. Rather than stifling her pleasure for fear it would spoil her disguise of plain severity, she could now smile when she felt like smiling, which was a great deal of the time.

The opportunity to be herself without fear of criticism or unwelcome attention was a blessing she had not known since childhood and one for which she would always be grateful. She owed so much to Lord Steadwell—far more than she could ever repay. But she was trying to repay him by approaching her duties in a new way. She had always been diligent in carrying them out, but now she threw herself into her work with zest. More and more she found that teaching was not simply a respectable means to support herself, but a true vocation that brought her enormous fulfillment.

The more enthusiasm she brought to her duties, the more her pupils rewarded her efforts with their excellent progress. Charlotte no longer protested that too much learning would hurt her chances of a good marriage, but applied herself to her studies, especially geography and history. Phoebe discovered an interest in subjects other than horses, while little Sophie proved something of a prodigy in reading and composition.

Delighted as she was by their progress, Grace sought plenty of opportunities for them to enjoy a carefree childhood. Once their father returned home from London, she was willing to drop lessons at a moment's notice for them to go riding with him or play a game. As the harvest feast approached, the four of them had thrown themselves into preparing one of the cavernous old outbuildings for the festivities.

"Can I open my eyes yet?" asked Rupert as Sophie and Phoebe led him in to view their handiwork before welcoming the neighbors and tenants.

"Not quite yet," called Charlotte, who led the way arm-in-arm with Grace. "Just another minute. My, but you are impatient."

The child was in particularly high spirits that evening because Grace had allowed her to wear her hair up. Nearing her fourteenth birthday, she looked quite the young lady.

They were all growing up, Grace acknowledged, stifling a sigh. Even little Sophie had sprouted a full inch since last winter. The time was slipping by happily but all too quickly. That was a bitter dram in her overflowing cup of happiness. One by one the girls would grow up and leave for homes of their own.

Then she would have to depart Nethercross, too. And Rupert would be left all alone.

Would he take the opportunity to remarry then? Grace wondered as she and Charlotte threw open the doors. That thought brought her a pang, though she told herself it was selfish to wish him lonely. Even in the company of his daughters and her of late she sensed an air of loneliness that he took care to hide from the girls. Had he mistaken his feelings for Mrs. Cadmore? Were they deeper than he had realized…until it was too late?

"Now you can open your eyes, Papa!" Sophie fairly vibrated with excitement, her red-gold curls bouncing around her glowing face.

"What do you think, Papa?" asked Phoebe, in a voice that betrayed her pride in their efforts.

His lordship's gaze swept the interior of the old building, taking in the bright swaths of bunting, the sheaves of corn and barrels of apples tied up with vibrant lengths of ribbon. Baskets of colorful vegetables studded the trestle tables, trimmed with golden autumn leaves and fat brown acorns. Candles and torches cast a warm, welcoming glow over the scene of rustic plenty.

"Think?" Rupert beamed. "Why, I think it puts Almack's fussy assembly rooms to shame! It will be the talk of the county to be sure!"

He wrapped his arms around his younger daughters in a proud embrace, then Charlotte.

Caught up in the joyful moment, he turned toward Grace and seemed about to embrace her too. At the last instant he caught himself and only clapped her on the shoulder. "Well done, Miss Ellerby! You quite amaze me."

"Thank you, sir." Grace felt as if tiny torches had begun to burn in her cheeks. Her shoulder tingled at his touch, so different from the tentative brush of their fingers at the masquerade. "The girls all worked very hard. Charlotte has a fine eye for decorating."

She would have liked to remain there basking in his admiration, but they were quickly overwhelmed by a flood of guests eager to take advantage of his lordship's hospitality. While the girls and their father gathered at the entryway to greet their guests, Grace retreated into the shadows, the better to go unnoticed by any men. It also provided an ideal vantage for her to gaze at Rupert all she liked.

Her scrutiny intensified when Mrs. Cadmore arrived in the company of a ruddy, robust gentleman who she introduced as Admiral DeLancey, newly retired from the Royal Navy. Rupert shook hands with the admiral and professed himself delighted to welcome any particular friend of his good neighbor. Yet Grace thought she glimpsed a hint of wistful longing beneath his cordial greeting. She could not be certain, however, for at that moment he cast a glance in her direction. Hurriedly she looked away, not wanting to be caught staring at him.

When the feast commenced, the girls insisted Grace must join them and their father at the head table with the vicar and his sister and the local magistrate's family. Cook and her helpers had outdone themselves with a fine feast—great joints of beef and lamb, game pies, succulent sausages and roast potatoes, all washed down with cider from the Nethercross orchards. But Grace's appetite could not do any of it justice. The more she dwelled upon Rupert's recent demeanor, the more she feared he might be pining for his lost chance at happiness with Mrs. Cadmore.

If so, she was responsible for his unhappiness. Had she truly tried to keep them apart for the sake of the children—or as Phoebe had suggested, because she wanted him all to herself, if only as governess of his motherless daughters? Had Rupert been right in believing the girls would have accepted his remarriage if she had encouraged them rather than poisoning their minds against *wicked stepmothers?*

After everyone had eaten and drunk their fill, the floor was cleared and a group of local musicians struck up their pipes and fiddles for a lively evening of country dancing. The girls were excited to have their father's permission to stay up long past their bedtime. Unlike the night of Lady Maidenhead's elegant masquerade, Rupert took an active part in the dancing, drawing partners from among his tenants' wives, the vicar's sister and Mrs. Cadmore.

When the vicar invited Grace to dance, she was about to decline out of habit, then realized she had nothing to fear from a man of the cloth on such an occasion. She enjoyed the opportunity to dance more than she ever expected. It diverted her thoughts from regrets about her actions and the growing conviction that she did not deserve any of the blessings she now enjoyed. Once the ice was broken, she accepted an invitation from Rupert's valet, then the admiral.

She was about to sit out the next set when a familiar voice from behind made her heart beat wildly. "Would you do me the honor of a dance, Miss Ellerby?"

"L-Lord Steadwell," her voice emerged in a nervous squeak. "I did not think you cared for dancing."

Immediately she chided herself for referring to their encounter on the night of the masquerade. That was best forgotten…if only she could. She also hoped Rupert would not take her reply as a refusal to dance with him. The prospect of being his partner, even for one brief dance, delighted her.

To her relief, Rupert gave a low chuckle. "As I believe I mentioned, I have no objection to socializing in small numbers and more familiar surroundings. I also enjoy less formality."

Perhaps he was only asking her because he felt it was his duty as host to dance with as many of the ladies as possible. Yet a flicker of eagerness in his dark eyes suggested something more.

She acknowledged his invitation with a curtsy. "In that case, I should be pleased to accept, sir."

"Capital." He offered her his hand and they hurried to take their places as the music commenced.

Until now the musicians had played lively tunes with quick tempo, well suited to the high spirits of the guests and the rustic setting. But the melody for this dance was slower with a faintly wistful air. The steps were an easy succession of siding, back to back and turning, with the head couple gradually moving down the line of dancers. Grace particularly enjoyed the turn, when she and Rupert joined both hands and circled with a skipping step. Every time they came to that figure, her heart seemed to skip along with her feet. When the music faded at last, she made her final curtsy with a pang of regret that it could not have gone on longer.

At that moment Mrs. Cadmore and the admiral

passed by conversing in a flirtatious tone. Rupert's smile faltered and he excused himself abruptly to seek out the next partner on his duty list. Grace was soon besieged with invitations but declined them all with the excuse that she must keep watch on the girls, all three of whom were enjoying the festivities immensely.

Sophie raced around the edge of the dance floor in some sort of game with a few of the tenants' children. Meanwhile Charlotte was dancing with Henry Cadmore and Phoebe with her old nemesis, Peter the stable boy. As she watched them, Grace sipped cider and tapped her toes to the music, often scanning the crowd for a glimpse of their father. All evening the baron kept up a convivial facade. But every now and then his crisp features would settle into an expression of restless sadness. Whenever she glimpsed that look, it brought Grace a sharp pang.

As the evening wore on, Sophie came and snuggled on Grace's lap. Later Phoebe sat down beside them.

"I believe Sophie has gone to sleep, Miss Ella." The child yawned and rested her head against Grace's arm.

"So she has," Grace murmured. "And so will you soon, I expect. I wish I'd thought to take her back to the nursery while she was capable of walking on her own. She is too heavy for me to carry all that way but I fear she will put up a fuss if I wake her now."

"Give her to me, then."

Grace gave a start when the children's father appeared, as if summoned by her need for assistance. A sleepy-looking Charlotte followed him.

"I know it is far past their bedtime," he continued in an apologetic tone, holding out his arms to receive his youngest daughter. "But they all seemed to be enjoying themselves so much."

"An occasional late night should not do the girls any harm." Grace hoisted Sophie into her father's arms with a faint pang of envy. How pleasant it must be to rest safe in his strong arms, head lolling against his broad shoulder. "I shall let them sleep in tomorrow morning."

"Come then, girls." Rupert glanced at Charlotte and Phoebe and nodded toward the door. "Before you two fall asleep, as well."

To Grace's surprise neither of them protested but followed along on either side of her, yawning now and then. Once they reached the nursery, all three were tucked up and asleep in no time.

"I should get back to the party—" Rupert made a vague gesture in that direction "—to bid my guests good-night."

The guard on Grace's tongue seemed to have fallen asleep along with the children. "Before you go, sir, there is just one thing, if I may."

She must speak now, while they had a bit of privacy, a rare occurrence of late. Besides, if she waited any longer, Grace feared her feelings for him would grow too deep to let her say what she must.

"I should not linger." He seemed uncomfortable in her presence and eager to escape, yet he responded to her beseeching look. "Go on, then. What is it?"

Grace steeled herself and plunged ahead. "Sir, I could not help noticing that you seem...unhappy of late. I know it is not my place but I beg you to tell me what is wrong. Perhaps I can help."

"You are mistaken, Miss Ellerby." He backed away from her shaking his head. "I assure you I am quite... content."

Before he could make his escape, Grace tried again.

"So you say, but your tone contradicts you. Sir, I promised I would be honest with you. Pray do me that same courtesy."

He froze as if pulled in two different directions at once by equally strong forces. His tongue seemed paralyzed, too.

"Is it Mrs. Cadmore?" Grace prompted him. "Was I mistaken about your feelings for her? Do you care for her more than you realized? Do you pine for her company and wish I had not forced you to give up your marriage plans?"

Rupert seemed to be trying to muster a reply but could not yet manage. Perhaps he needed to know her thoughts in the matter.

"If that is the case, I am very sorry to have come between you." She struggled to keep her voice low so as not to disturb the children while still infusing it with sincere conviction and concern for him. "Perhaps it is not yet too late. If you want to ask Mrs. Cadmore for her hand, I will do everything in my power to persuade the girls to accept her. It was wrong of me to do otherwise!"

The tension within Rupert seemed to break under pressure like a bow string suddenly released.

"I don't care for *her!*" The words erupted from his lips as if propelled by a force much greater than his will—a force that his will had perhaps struggled to contain. "I care for *you,* Grace Ellerby!"

His abrupt, unexpected declaration made Grace's heart bound in a mixture of elation and disbelief. At the same time, past experience made her shrink from his fierce tone.

Chapter Sixteen

He should have held his tongue and kept his feelings to himself as he'd promised Grace he would.

Rupert's spirits plummeted as he watched the woman he cared for cower from him. He had tried so hard these past weeks to resist his growing feelings for her. When that became impossible he had hidden them instead, which proved equally difficult.

This evening had been worse than ever, for it reminded him of the one they had shared at Lady Maidenhead's masquerade. In so many ways his harvest feast was better. At the masquerade ranks and titles had been concealed but taken for granted. Tonight they were acknowledged but set aside as everyone celebrated the harvest that crowned a year of common endeavor. On such an evening, the master of Nethercross might dance with a farmer's wife or his daughters' governess and no one would think it amiss.

No doubt he should have resisted the temptation to dance with Grace Ellerby. But seeing Mrs. Cadmore and her new beau so happy together had eroded his resolve. Their dance had brought so many buried emotions closer to the surface. Later, when they'd brought his daughters back to the nursery and put them to bed, Rupert could not escape the overwhelming sense that they were a family...or should be.

Grace's tender show of concern for his happiness had strained his composure to the breaking point. It had made him do and say the very things he'd sworn he would not. But now that he had, the only possible way to undo the damage was to press forward and hope for the best.

He snatched a deep breath and summoned his voice, trying to keep it low and calm. If Grace felt threatened, he knew he might lose her and so might his daughters. "Forgive me for startling you. I know I promised not to subject you to attentions of this sort and I swear I will not speak of my feelings again if they distress you. But I cannot permit you to assume I care for Mrs. Cadmore when I do not and never could. I repent ever thinking I could wed a woman I do not love. You were right about that and I only wish I had heeded your excellent advice sooner."

"It was not good advice," she replied with a stricken look. "It was selfish advice masked as concern for your daughters. I never should have meddled in your life as I did."

Why? Because if she hadn't he might be safely married to another woman and not pestering her with his unwelcome attentions? Rupert shuddered to think of the terrible longing and guilt he might have suffered if he'd finally awoken to his feelings for Grace after he had wed Barbara Cadmore.

"Please hear me out, I beg you." Fighting his deepest inclinations, Rupert took a step backward so she would not feel cornered. "I have tried to root out my feelings so as not to distress you with them, but they have proved even more stubborn than my will. Is there any hope I can persuade you to trust and care for me in return?"

Her gentle blue eyes widened. In them, Rupert glimpsed far too many emotions he did not want to see...fear, sadness, regret.

"I *do* trust you," she admitted in a furtive whisper as if it were something shameful. "More than I have any other man. And I have come to care for you far more than I ought to."

"Why more than you ought to?" Rupert asked, not certain whether he should be encouraged.

"Because you are my employer, of course." Her voice took on a sharp edge as if she were vexed with him...or herself. "Besides, you only think you fancy me on account of my looks. I have encountered that enough over the years to know it is not love."

There was a tiny grain of truth in what she said. How could he convince her of the depth of his feelings when he had given no sign of caring for plain Miss Ellerby?

"Our positions should not affect how we feel about one another," he argued. "If I ever thought otherwise, I was a fool. As for the other, even before I became aware of your outer beauty, I had grown to admire the beauty of your heart and character. I became closer to you, Miss Ellerby, than to any other woman since my wife, though I could not acknowledge it. Not even to myself."

Would she believe any of that? Or would she assume he was only the latest in a disreputable line of men who would say or do anything in order to possess her?

"When I met you at the masquerade," he continued, "I cannot deny the immediate attraction I felt. But I truly believe that owed less to your beauty than to the ease I felt in your company. I am certain my heart recognized you that night even though my stubborn mind refused to."

"It did?" Her voice trembled. "But you told me you could never care for another woman as you did your wife. Even if you could, you swore you did not want to risk your heart again."

"I said a great many foolish things," Rupert admitted with a rueful shrug. "I will gladly recant them all if only you will give me hope. Before I met you, I thought grief was the penalty I must pay for having loved. The cost was so dear I feared it would bankrupt my heart."

His voice grew husky with emotion. "But you have made me see that love is not like gold, to be hoarded and doled out a miserly piece at a time. Love is a bottomless well that will never go dry as long as we keep drawing from it. The more we give away, the faster it refills, so we will never run out."

She looked as though she desperately wanted to believe him, yet something held her back.

"As for my being your employer," he continued, "I would never abuse that power to impose upon you. I want to make you an offer of marriage. If you truly care for me as I do for you, please agree to be my wife."

"Wife?" One trembling hand rose to her throat as if she could not catch her breath. "I…I…"

Her frightened gaze swept around to his sleeping daughters. Was she afraid that only by accepting his proposal would she be able to remain with the children she loved?

Marriage to Rupert Kendrick? Even the possibility of it made Grace fairly swoon for joy. To think that all this time his restless dejection had grown out of his repressed feelings for *her*. It seemed too good to be true. And perhaps it was—too good for her compared with what she deserved.

She glanced around at her sleeping pupils. If she had feared the opportunity to stay on at Nethercross was a blessing she did not deserve, the prospect of wedding their father was a hundredfold more so.

And yet, deserved or not, she ached to accept his proposal. She felt pulled so hard in opposite directions she could not frame a coherent reply. "But…the girls."

Rupert clearly did not understand what she was trying to say—and who could blame him? "I am certain you would make a wonderful mother to my daughters. But if you feel you must refuse me, I want the next best thing for them—to keep you as their governess. I swear to you, I would never speak of my feelings again. We could continue on as we have been. But please do not refuse me for the wrong reasons. Reject my offer only if you are perfectly certain you do not and cannot love me as I have come to love you."

Grace's legs threatened to give way beneath her. She stumbled to the nursery settee and sank down on it. Sophie's storybook lay within arm's reach, full of impossible tales of talking cats, fairy godmothers and scullery maids who captured the hearts of princes. Those stories also told of something Grace had encouraged the children to believe in—cruel, uncaring stepmothers.

"There is more to marriage than love." She sighed. "You said so yourself, and you were right about that at least."

Her collapse upon the settee brought Rupert flying to her side. Grace was reminded of their very first interview at the inn in Reading and the unwarranted kindness he'd shown to a fearful, dowdy governess. Looking back she wondered if she had begun to fall in love with him that very day.

"Have we exchanged outlooks, you and I?" His gaze searched her face in a fond caress as he eased himself down beside her. "Tell me, then, if there is more to marriage than love, what else can possibly compare in importance?"

"The happiness of your children, of course." Grace lowered her gaze, afraid she would falter and give in to her selfish desires if she stared into his compelling dark eyes for too long. "You know how bitterly opposed they are to your remarrying. And I have done more than anyone to foster that uncharitable attitude. This is my just punishment. Much as I want to, I cannot marry you and risk having the children I love so much grow to resent me."

Perhaps she should not have confessed her desire to accept Rupert's proposal for it seemed to encourage him in a way she could ill afford.

Gently he took both her hands in his, as they had clasped during the dance that evening. "Dearest Grace, you know my daughters care for you quite as much as you do for them. Whether you are their governess or their mama, I cannot believe that will change."

Perhaps he could not, but she could all too easily. She shook her head and tried to pull her hands from his grasp. "You did not hear what they said when I told them what happened at the masquerade. Sophie was aghast at the thought that I might become their stepmother. They will never accept me—I am certain of it. And there will be gossip in the neighborhood about such an unsuitable match, which will only make things worse."

Her fears were running away with her, whipped up by the potent consciousness of all the wrong she had done since coming to Nethercross. She could not bear to do more simply to get what she wanted.

"Hush now, hush," Rupert clung to her hands with tender but steadfast resolve. "I will talk to the girls and persuade them they have nothing to fear. All will be well, I promise you."

How could she resist her feelings for such a man, whose presence promised her security, protection, understanding—everything she craved? But how could she give in to them when the result might be the kind of strife that had blighted her family? She cared too much for Rupert and his daughters to let that happen.

"Don't you see? They may *pretend* to be resigned to a marriage between us for fear of losing your regard. If they cannot truly accept me, it could poison your feelings for them and theirs for you. That is too great a risk. I cannot take it. Please do not ask me to!"

Hard as she tried to maintain her composure, hot tears rose in her eyes.

"So much fear." Rupert's whisper enfolded her with its fond sympathy. "After all you have suffered over the years I reckon it is no wonder you always expect the worst. I have no right to talk, for I was every bit as fearful of giving my heart away again at the risk of losing it forever. But even if I were to lose you, I could never be sorry to have loved you. You brought me to life again and gave me back my heart. Having you here at Nethercross has been a blessing for which I shall always be grateful."

He disengaged one of his hands from hers and wiped away a tear that slid down her cheek. Much as his words touched her and his gesture brought comfort, Rupert's reference to a blessing reminded her why they could not be together. "You and your daughters have been a blessing to me as well but one I do not deserve. I kept secrets from you and spoiled your plans. Even worse, I made the girls a party to my actions. I encouraged them in believing that all stepmothers must be horrid. Now I must reap what I have sown. It is a judgment upon me."

"Is that why you will not accept my proposal?" he asked. "Because you feel you do not deserve to be happy?"

Blinking back the rest of her tears she gave a slow nod.

"We all make mistakes," Rupert replied. "I hired you for the wrong reasons. I refused to acknowledge my feelings for you and planned to marry a woman I did not love in spite of my daughters' objections. Does that mean I should never know happiness?"

"Of course not! It isn't the same thing at all."

"Are you certain?" Rupert nodded toward his peacefully sleeping children. "You cannot deny the girls have their faults, yet you care for them just the same and would do everything in your power to make them happy."

"You know I would." That's what she was trying to do, if only he would not let her.

"Even Charlotte who made things so difficult when you first came here?" he persisted.

"She didn't mean to," Grace protested. "She didn't understand in the beginning and once she did she was so remorseful."

"And you forgave her, just like that?" Rupert sounded skeptical. "Even though she might not have deserved it?"

"I…" At last Grace understood what he was trying to say. "That is…"

"Then why do you find it so hard to believe God would forgive you as you forgave Charlotte?" Rupert took her left hand and lifted it to his lips. "Please trust your heart to my love and to the Lord's grace."

Could it truly be as simple as that? Simple, perhaps, but not easy.

From dark closets of Grace's memory the voices of her stepmother and her teachers emerged to recite a long litany of her faults that justified their hostility and harsh treatment. The men who had pursued her joined in, claiming she had invited their dishonorable attentions.

But then the voices of Rebecca and her other friends rose in protest, saying she was worthy of their support and affection. Charlotte, Phoebe and Sophie joined in her defense. So did their father.

Grace lifted her eyes to meet his. "Perhaps…"

That seemed to be all the encouragement he needed. Every shadow of the frustration and sorrow she'd glimpsed in him of late vanished. More than any words it assured her that the feelings he professed were entirely sincere and that her love could help him find the happiness she so wanted for him.

"We will talk to the girls in the morning." Rupert lifted her hand to his lips. "If after that you still believe our marriage would destroy the affection they now have for you, I suppose we could carry on as we have been and wait to wed until they are grown and married. It would not be easy for me but for their sake and yours, I could wait."

His offer soothed the worst of her fears. Gingerly, she raised a hand to stroke his cheek. Rupert leaned into that delicate caress with a murmur of supreme contentment.

Now that she was certain of his feelings and hers, it would not be easy to wait so long. She must trust in the girls' understanding, in Rupert's love and most of all in the power of grace.

Rupert rose early the next morning, propelled by a volatile mixture of eagerness and anxiety. He could not blame Grace for her difficulty in accepting good fortune when he could scarcely believe his.

For the sake of his daughters he had resigned himself to pining in secret for their beautiful governess. But when she had seen through his disguised feelings and offered to help unite him with the woman she thought he loved, he could not tell whether that meant she cared nothing for him…or everything. He only knew he must be as truthful with her as he'd urged her to be with him. His reward had been to discover how much she cared for him and his daughters.

Thinking of the girls provoked his unease. Last night, seeking to persuade Grace, he had been certain his beloved daughters would be no stumbling block to his happiness. In the cool light of an autumn morning he was not so sure.

Another worry also nagged at him. Would he find Grace in the nursery this morning, or might she have fled during the night as she had from difficult situations in the past?

Unable to bear the uncertainty he hastened to the

nursery where he paced back and forth in the corridor until he heard the sound of voices, assuring him the girls were awake.

"Is something wrong, Papa?" cried Phoebe when he strode in with his mounting worry etched upon his features.

The moment he caught sight of Grace, pale and anxious-looking but very much present, his lips relaxed in a broad smile of relief. "No, indeed, my dear. Everything is as right as can be. I hope you all slept well."

They nodded.

"We just woke up," announced Sophie, though it was evident from the fact that they still wore their nightgowns.

"What are you doing here so early," asked Charlotte in a wary tone, "if nothing is wrong?"

He beckoned them over to the settee, which held sweet memories of last night's conversation with Grace. "There is something I wanted to talk to you about."

"Can't it wait until after breakfast?" asked Phoebe.

Gathering Sophie onto his lap while the older two snuggled on either side, Rupert shook his head. "This is very important and the sooner it is settled the better for us all."

"Come sit with us, Miss Ella," Sophie called out to Grace.

Rupert added a smile of encouragement to his daughter's invitation but Grace hung back. "I will join you a little later perhaps."

She busied herself around the room. Did she think the girls would be less apt to give a sincere response with her sitting there? All the more reason to get the matter sorted as soon as possible.

"Now girls," he began, "you know I loved your dear mama very much, as I know you did."

They all replied with grave nods, including Sophie, whom he doubted had any clear memory of Annabelle.

"After she died, we were all sad for a long while and I was afraid to love anyone but you three in case I might lose them as I lost her. That was why I wanted to marry Mrs. Cadmore because I knew I would never care for her that deeply. But you and Miss Ellerby helped me see that was wrong and rather cowardly."

"You're not a coward, Papa!" Phoebe's voice rang with indignation.

He gave a rueful grin. "When it comes to risking my heart I fear I have been. Now I am trying to be more courageous but I need your help."

"You haven't changed your mind about Mrs. Cadmore, have you?" demanded Charlotte.

Before Rupert could respond Sophie piped up, "I hope not because we don't want a wicked stepmother!"

He cast a glance at Grace who had turned away, her shoulders slumped.

"I have not changed my mind about Mrs. Cadmore but I have altered my opinion of marriage. I hope you also will keep your minds and hearts open to change. Not all stepmothers are alike any more than the three of you are. Some may not be as kind as they should but others are good and loving. I hope you will not let the loss of your mama make you close your hearts to new love as I tried to. It has been a hard lesson for me to learn but I believe you are wiser than me."

His daughters seemed to wrestle with what he was trying to tell them. He only wished he'd had this talk with them a long time ago.

"I don't understand, Papa," said Phoebe at last. "If you aren't going to marry Mrs. Cadmore, what does any of that matter?"

"Because," said Charlotte, "I think he wants to marry…Miss Ella."

"Is that true?" Sophie cast her father an accusing glare. "Do you want to turn Miss Ella into a wicked stepmother?"

Rupert shook his head. "I want to make her a stepmother who will love you almost as much as your own mama. But she is afraid to marry me if it might make you unhappy and not care for her anymore. What do you think of that?"

"Is that true, Miss Ella?" asked Phoebe.

Grace turned toward them again and nodded.

Rupert held his breath as he waited for his daughter's reply.

Charlotte rose from her place beside him.

"That's just ridiculous," she announced in a tart tone, walking toward Grace. "Miss Ella could never be wicked and no one could make her that way, especially not Papa."

She took Grace's hand and drew her toward the settee.

"Of course not," Phoebe agreed. "Will you please marry Papa, Miss Ella?"

Wiping away a tear, Grace sank onto the settee with the rest of the family. "What do you say, Sophie?"

The child thought for a moment.

"This isn't a story, you know." She spoke with innocent wisdom. "We can make the ending come out any way we please."

With that she slid off Rupert's lap onto Grace's.

"I know how I would like our story to come out." Grace wrapped her arms around the child and rested her head against Rupert's shoulder in a gesture of reliance and tender trust.

"How?" asked Phoebe as Rupert opened his arms wide enough to embrace all four of his ladies.

Grace's smile seemed to light up the whole nursery. "…and they all lived happily ever after—in Berkshire."

Epilogue

One month later

As she glanced in the looking glass on the morning of her wedding, Grace forced herself to breathe slowly and deeply to maintain her composure. Every time she contemplated the approaching ceremony that would make her a wife and mother, she feared she would burst into tears of gratitude and joy.

The woman who looked back at her from the glass was as different as could be from the one who had come to Nethercross the previous winter. Instead of an unflattering starched cap, a circlet of ivy and myrtle studded with white roses from the conservatory at Winter Hill set off her golden curls to perfection. Her unflattering dress of sickly green had been replaced by a simple but elegant white gown and a spencer of coral pink velvet. Her eyes were no longer obscured by spectacles but shone with happiness.

Grace beheld her reflection with a warm glow of contentment. Though she wanted to look nice for Rupert and the girls, she trusted they would love her every bit as much if she were still plain and dowdy.

In the distance she heard church bells toll the half hour, followed by a knock on her door.

"Are you ready, Miss Ella?" Charlotte called in an anxious tone. "Lord and Lady Benedict are here to take us to the church."

"I am quite ready." Grace opened the door and savored the child's gasp of admiration. "Are you and your sisters? We do not want to keep your papa waiting."

"We've been ready for ages, at Charlotte's insistence," said Phoebe, who stood nearby holding Sophie's hand. "I hope that she won't go back to bossing us so much just because you aren't in the nursery to keep her in line."

"Now, now." Grace's nerves calmed as she fell back in to her familiar role with the children. "Let's not spoil such a happy day with quarreling. You all look lovely. We will make a splendid wedding party, don't you think?"

Before they went downstairs to meet the Benedicts, she gathered each of the girls into her arms for a kiss. "One of the sweetest blessings this day will bring me is three such delightful daughters."

"*Step*daughters," Sophie reminded her.

"Call it what you will." Grace gave the child's hand a reassuring squeeze. "I shall love you just as much."

When they descended the stairs a few moments later, Rebecca blinked back tears as she caught sight of Grace. "I always knew you would make the most beautiful bride."

The two friends embraced.

"I am so happy you could come to my wedding," said Grace. "I only wish Marian and the others could have been here, too."

Rebecca nodded. "Marian wished she could come but with her confinement drawing near, Captain Radcliffe would not hear of her risking a long carriage journey. But he said you and your family must come to Knightley Park for a visit once the baby is born. Their two girls are anxious to meet yours. As for Hannah, she has her hands full. I shall tell you her news on our way."

They all bundled into Lord Benedict's fine carriage and drove to the church. Rebecca kept up a constant flow of news about their friends, no doubt hoping to divert the bride from any wedding jitters.

But Grace found herself surprisingly calm.

Once they reached the church, Sophie, Phoebe and Charlotte marched down the aisle ahead of her while Grace followed on the arm of Lord Benedict. As they approached the altar, Rupert turned for a first glimpse of his governess bride. His eyes widened and he appeared to catch his breath at the sight of her. His lips spread into a wide, doting smile that made Grace's heart bound.

"Dearly beloved," began the vicar and the marriage ceremony proceeded according to its age-old form.

When it came time to recite their vows, Grace and Rupert stared into each other's eyes and spoke as if there was no one else present. Though she knew her bridegroom had made those same sacred promises to his first wife, Grace did not feel it diminished his commitment to her in any way. Indeed, knowing what a devoted husband he had been to Annabelle, she believed with all her heart that he would show her the same love, fidelity and kindness.

Later, when Sophie read the lesson without making a single mistake her parents exchanged proud, fond smiles.

At last the service concluded, the parish register was signed and the happy couple left the church hand-in-hand to return to Nethercross for the wedding breakfast.

Once they were settled in the carriage, Rupert leaned back in the seat and gave a warm chuckle mingled with a sigh of supreme contentment. "I must confess, dear wife, that I had an anxious moment or two while I stood at the altar awaiting your arrival."

"Indeed?" Grace cast him a flirtatious smile, delighted that as a married couple they no longer had to mind so much about propriety. "And what did you have to be anxious about, pray? Did you entertain second thoughts about marrying me?"

She felt secure enough in his affections to jest about a matter she might once have feared in earnest.

"Quite the contrary." He slipped his arm around her and drew her even closer. "I had an unreasonable fear that you might change your mind or some misfortune might prevent you from keeping our appointment with the vicar. But when I saw you come up the aisle looking so serene and happy, I knew all would be well."

By now they had driven out of sight of the small crowd of wedding guests gathered in the churchyard. Rupert took advantage of their privacy to seal their union with a slow, sweet, tender kiss.

Grace returned it with all the feeling she cherished in her heart for him. Not long ago, she would have been plagued by fears of what might go wrong, unable to trust in her good fortune. But now she looked forward to their future with faith, hope and love.

* * * * *

Dear Reader,

Ever since I started writing romance novels, I have enjoyed retelling favorite story types such as *My Fair Lady* and *Beauty and the Beast*. But one popular story I had never retold was *Cinderella*…until now. Though all the stories in my Glass Slipper Brides series have the theme of a poor, servant heroine capturing the heart of a successful gentleman, *The Baron's Governess Bride* goes even further.

Governess Grace Ellerby, is a beauty in disguise. Harsh experience has taught her that attractive looks can be a burden and single gentlemen cannot be trusted. At first she is wary of her new employer, Rupert, Baron Steadwell. Deeply grieved by his wife's death, Rupert refuses to risk his heart again. But for the sake of his daughters and his estate, he needs to remarry. When the girls send their governess to a masked ball, Grace and Rupert see one another in a whole new light! But can they overcome old fears to live *happily ever after?*

Deborah Hale

Questions for Discussion

1. Grace discovers that a seemingly harmless deception can turn into a slippery slope as she must work harder and harder to protect her guilty secret. At what point in the story do you think Grace should have told Rupert the truth? How do you think that might have affected the course of their relationship?

2. Rupert tells his daughter not to judge her new governess by appearance. Do you think he follows his own advice? What judgments does he make about Grace based on her appearance at various points in the story? Have you ever felt you were judged by your appearance? How did that make you feel?

3. Rupert's daughters don't all welcome their new governess with open arms. Why do you think Sophie and Charlotte are resistant to Grace? Have you ever won over someone who didn't welcome you in the beginning? How?

4. Grace and the girls all think Rupert's desire to marry Mrs. Cadmore is a mistake and try to stop him. Have you ever been in that situation with someone you care about? Did you try to stop them or support their decision even though you disagreed? Looking back, do you wish you'd acted differently?

5. Rupert's heart is finally beginning to heal after his wife's death and he doesn't want to risk it again.

Have you ever felt the pain of loss was too high a price to pay for love? Did anything happen to change your mind?

6. Grace is pleasantly surprised when Rupert supports her authority and decisions as his daughters' governess. What effect does this have on her self-esteem? What could you do to boost the self-esteem of someone you know?

7. How does Rupert's favourite hymn, "I Sing the Almighty Power of God," reflect his character and faith? How does your favourite piece of sacred music reflect yours?

8. Grace has received many negative messages about herself over the years that make her feel she doesn't deserve to be happy. How do you deal with negative messages from your past?

9. Certain qualities we possess can have both a positive and a negative side. What are the positive and negative aspects of Rupert's stubbornness? Do you have any qualities that can be negative or positive? How might you channel them in the more positive direction?

10. Many verses in the Bible speak of people who have eyes but do not see. How does this relate to the characters in this story? Have you ever been "blind" to someone or something then suddenly you saw them more clearly or in a different way? How did that happen and how did it make you feel?

INSPIRATIONAL

Love Inspired

celebrating **15** YEARS

HISTORICAL

COMING NEXT MONTH
AVAILABLE JULY 2, 2012

WOOING THE SCHOOLMARM
Pinewood Weddings
Dorothy Clark

Schoolteacher Willa Wright has given up on romance—
until Reverend Matthew Calvert sneaks his way into
her heart.

THE CAPTAIN'S COURTSHIP
The Everard Legacy
Regina Scott

London's whirlwind season would seem manageable to
Captain Richard Everard...if it hadn't reunited him with the
lady he'd once loved.

THE RUNAWAY BRIDE
Noelle Marchand

Childhood rejection closed Lorelei Wilkins's heart to Sean
O'Brien. Is a forced engagement love's chance to finally
conquer them both?

HEARTS IN HIDING
Patty Smith Hall

Beau Daniels is captivated by Edie Michaels, but can love
withstand the ultimate test of loyalty when he discovers
her family ties to Nazi Germany?

Look for these and other Love Inspired books wherever books
are sold, including most bookstores, supermarkets, discount
stores and drugstores.

LIHCNM0612

REQUEST YOUR FREE BOOKS!

2 FREE INSPIRATIONAL NOVELS
PLUS 2
FREE
MYSTERY GIFTS

Love Inspired
HISTORICAL
INSPIRATIONAL HISTORICAL ROMANCE

YES! Please send me 2 FREE Love Inspired® Historical novels and my 2 FREE mystery gifts (gifts are worth about $10). After receiving them, if I don't wish to receive any more books, I can return the shipping statement marked "cancel". If I don't cancel, I will receive 4 brand-new novels every month and be billed just $4.49 per book in the U.S. or $4.99 per book in Canada. That's a saving of at least 22% off the cover price. It's quite a bargain! Shipping and handling is just 50¢ per book in the U.S. and 75¢ per book in Canada.* I understand that accepting the 2 free books and gifts places me under no obligation to buy anything. I can always return a shipment and cancel at any time. Even if I never buy another book, the two free books and gifts are mine to keep forever.

102/302 IDN FEHF

Name	(PLEASE PRINT)	
Address		Apt. #
City	State/Prov.	Zip/Postal Code

Signature (if under 18, a parent or guardian must sign)

Mail to the **Reader Service:**
IN U.S.A.: P.O. Box 1867, Buffalo, NY 14240-1867
IN CANADA: P.O. Box 609, Fort Erie, Ontario L2A 5X3
Not valid for current subscribers to Love Inspired Historical books.

Want to try two free books from another series?
Call 1-800-873-8635 or visit www.ReaderService.com.

* Terms and prices subject to change without notice. Prices do not include applicable taxes. Sales tax applicable in N.Y. Canadian residents will be charged applicable taxes. Offer not valid in Quebec. This offer is limited to one order per household. All orders subject to credit approval. Credit or debit balances in a customer's account(s) may be offset by any other outstanding balance owed by or to the customer. Please allow 4 to 6 weeks for delivery. Offer available while quantities last.

Your Privacy—The Reader Service is committed to protecting your privacy. Our Privacy Policy is available online at www.ReaderService.com or upon request from the Reader Service.

We make a portion of our mailing list available to reputable third parties that offer products we believe may interest you. If you prefer that we not exchange your name with third parties, or if you wish to clarify or modify your communication preferences, please visit us at www.ReaderService.com/consumerchoice or write to us at Reader Service Preference Service, P.O. Box 9062, Buffalo, NY 14269. Include your complete name and address.

LIH11B

Love Inspired HISTORICAL

celebrating
15
YEARS

DOROTHY CLARK

brings you another story from

PINEWOOD
WEDDINGS

When Willa Wright's fiancé abandoned her three days before the wedding, he ended all her hopes for romance. Now she dedicates herself to teaching Pinewood's children, including the new pastor's young wards. If she didn't know better, Reverend Calvert's kindness could almost fool Willa into caring again. Almost.

Wooing the Schoolmarm

Available July wherever books are sold.

www.LoveInspiredBooks.com

LIH82923

Violet Colby's life is about to get turned upside down by a twin sister she's never met.

Read on for a preview of HER SURPRISE SISTER by Marta Perry from Love Inspired Books.

Violet Colby looked around the Fort Worth coffee shop. She didn't belong here, any more than the sophisticated-looking guy in the corner would belong on the ranch. Expensive suit and tie, a Stetson with not a smudge to mar its perfection—he was big city Texas.

That man's head turned, as if he felt her stare, and she caught the full impact of a pair of icy green eyes before she could look away. She stared down at her coffee.

She heard approaching footsteps.

"What are you doing here?"

Violet looked up, surprised. "What?"

"I said what are you doing here?" He pulled out the chair opposite her and sat down. "I told you I'd be at your apartment in five minutes. So why are you in the coffee shop instead?"

Okay, he was crazy. She started to rise.

"The least you can do is talk to me about it. I still want to marry you." He sounded impatient. "Maddie, why are you acting this way?"

Relief made her limp for an instant. He wasn't crazy.

"I think you've mistaken me for someone else."

He studied her, letting his gaze move from her hair to a face that was bare of makeup, to her Western shirt and well-worn jeans.

Finally he shook his head. "You're not Maddie Wallace, are you?"

"No. Now that we have that straight, I'll be going."

"Wait. It's uncanny." A line formed between his eyebrows. "Look, my name is Landon Derringer. If you'll be patient for a few minutes, I think you'll find it worthwhile." He flipped open his cell phone.

"Maddie? This is Landon. I'm over at the Coffee Stop, and there's someone here you have to meet.

"Okay," he said finally. "Right. We'll be here."

Violet glanced at her watch. "I'll give you five minutes, no more."

"Good." He rose. "I'll get you a refill."

"That's not—"

But he'd already gone to the counter. She glanced at her watch again as he came back with the coffee.

He glanced at the door. "You won't have long to wait. She's here."

The door swung open, and a woman stepped inside. Slim, chic, sophisticated. And other than that, Violet's exact double.

To unravel the mystery, pick up HER SURPRISE SISTER, the first of the TEXAS TWINS series from Love Inspired Books.

Available July 2012

SHLIEXP0712